THE FAR SIDE OF PROMISE

AN ANTHOLOGY

MATTHEW S COX

DIVISION ZERO PRESS

An Anthology of Short Stories by
Matthew S. Cox
© 2018 – All Rights Reserved
Second edition © 2020

ISBN (ebook): 978-1-949174-64-9

ISBN (print): 978-1-949174-65-6

CONTENTS

INTRODUCTION

Some years ago, the small press that published my first books put out a call for short stories because they wanted to assemble an anthology. Up until that point, I hadn't written too many short stories having been mostly a novelist. I sat down and tried to think of an idea to write a short story... and came up with a whole bunch at once. I couldn't decide which one to write... so wrote them all.

Three short stories I wrote during this process (Emma and the Banderwigh, One More Run, and Innocent Deception) received such a positive response from early readers, I ended up developing them into full novels. (Innocent Deception became Heir Ascendant). It didn't seem purposeful at the time, so I did not keep the short story versions of them around.

The Far Side of Promise anthology is a collection of my short stories for your enjoyment.

Happy reading!

-Matt

THE STORIES

— Into the Beneath —

A spirit warned young Kirsten Wren that her mother would take her life. While cruel, the woman's zealous hatred of her daughter's psionic gift seemed unlikely to prove fatal. When one desperate ghost refuses to let the child ignore her, the eerie warning takes on a new, terrifying truth.

— Evergreen —

Seventeen-year-old Harper Cody is all that stands between her little sister and a world broken in the aftermath of nuclear war. Only months after everything fell apart, it's clear they can't go on living in the streets. Her Dad thought Evergreen, Colorado would be a safe place... if she can survive long enough to get there.

— Ouroboros —

Eric lives in two worlds, one real and one virtual. In one, he obeys all the rules; in the other, he makes his own. Every man has his breaking point, and when a risky gambit offers him the chance to cast off the shackles of the nine-to-five, he takes it.

A privateer in deep space dreams of a destroyed world. Her visions grow in intensity with each passing week, beckoning her. No longer able to resist the lure of the strange luminous creatures that fall like snow, she heeds the irresistible call pulling her into deep space.

I

INTO THE BENEATH

ABOUT INTO THE BENEATH

The nice thing about having readers who find me on Facebook is hearing comments and suggestions from them. One reader who is a fan of my Division Zero series asked me on a few occasions for a peek into Kirsten's early life. If you haven't read any of that series, the books start when she's twenty-two and already an active agent with Division Zero. There is a flashback scene where Kirsten revisits a night from her childhood when she was eight years old. (That moment is alluded to in this story).

Please note this story deals with the subject matter of child abuse and may be upsetting to some readers. Kirsten's mother believed her psionic powers were a sign of the Devil and beat her mercilessly for it. The woman is legit insane and using her religion as a feeble excuse to be a miserable horror to her child. In the Division Zero series, Kirsten starts the story with a serious hatred for all religion, but she does eventually meet someone who is both religious and not a bad person, and he ultimately softens her perceptions.

This story goes back to the night when Kirsten ran away from home as a ten-year-old. It is set twelve years before the first novel, Division Zero.

1

INTO THE BENEATH

Desperate to keep her food down, Kirsten cradled her stomach. She sat sideways in her father's lap, resting her head on his shoulder, feet on his leg. He traced his fingers over dark spots on her shin before resting his hand atop her foot. Warmth eased the numbness in her toes, and she snuggled into him. Terrified her mother would notice her trembling, she forced herself to sit still and kept her head down. He seemed afraid; a hesitant finger hovered at the corner of her eye before he tried to move a strand of blonde hair away from her face. Strawberry shampoo tinted the air with the scent of fruit. She looked away so he couldn't see her crying, watching a shiny, silver bot gliding back and forth across the carpet. Azure laser light shone through drab green fibers as the disc-bot carried on its endless pursuit of dirt.

It started when she was six years old. The first time she called on her ability, she did so by accident. For days, she felt something watching her at night. A feeling of not being alone while alone unsettled her. The unusual mood seemed concentrated on the corner of her bedroom as if someone invisible stood there. When she wanted to know who watched her—a man appeared, a man who'd been shot. A ghost. It took her a while, but she eventually learned she could turn her power on at will. She could see ghosts whenever she wanted to, it only made her a little bit tired and her eyes glow white. The dead man in her room that night knew she looked at him. He told others. They all came to ask her for help. Worst of all, Mother had seen her eyes glow.

Kirsten didn't remember much from the night Mother saw the glow in her eyes. She did remember a priest, and her mother shaking her by the shoulders demanding she reject something called "The Devil."

From then on, Kirsten tried to ignore the ghosts. The apartment suffered patches of cold, strange noises at all hours, doors slamming, and fog on the windows, but the worst was never feeling alone. Always, someone watched, always *something* wanted. Even if she refused to use her power to look at them, she often heard them whispering.

Mother hadn't taken the aggressive haunting well.

Four years ago, Kirsten 'destroyed' her family—at least, according to her mother. The woman blamed everything on her, not on the throng of tortured souls who came in search of help. It didn't take long for her once loving mother to descend into righteous madness. Kirsten dreaded the litanies of how someone named Jesus would punish her. It didn't matter what Kirsten did. If she ignored the ghosts, they became restless and Mother punished her for it. If Kirsten tried to use her power to make the ghosts be quiet and go away, Mother punished her for it. The woman no longer considered her a daughter or even a child—she had become a spawn of evil.

"Don't cry, sweetie." Her father rubbed her back, making her whimper by touching bruises he didn't see. "I'm not angry with you for breaking the cabinet. I'm happy you didn't hurt yourself. Promise me you won't try to climb them again?"

Kirsten shivered. *Don't throw up.* A ghost had opened three drawers, demanding attention. Mother had been there to see it. Kirsten closed her eyes, reliving Mother flinging her against the cabinets. The door cracked the third time Mother slammed her into it. The woman lied, one of those things the scary book Mother made her read said people shouldn't do. Her father believing she'd broken the cabinet because she tried to climb the door made her feel sick. She convulsed, cradling her belly full of precious food. *Don't throw up; he's leaving again.*

"What's gotten into you, sweetie?"

She dug her fingers into his shirt, clenching two fistfuls of cloth. *Don't let me go. Don't go away again. Please…*

Her father tensed. He was afraid of the ghosts, just like Mother. However, he didn't hit. He ran. This proximity came from a moment of guilt overpowering his fear. She looked up at him, shaking, hot tears on her cheeks. As always, he couldn't bear to look her in the eye. Tightness gripped her chest and heat flooded her face. She wanted to tell him what Mother did to her whenever he went away on long business trips, running from the spirits who came calling.

Mother appeared out of nowhere, rounding the seat with a large glass of iced tea for her father. Kirsten flinched as the woman's hand came toward her. Her body went limp with relief when the woman only rubbed her hair, acting as if she cared, all a show for Daddy.

"She's exhausted, dear." The sound of kissing made her dinner try to leap into her throat. "She's worked up that you only got home this morning and you're leaving already. Those idiots at TMC are asking too much of you."

Who is she pretending to be? Kirsten sniffled, forcing herself to smile. "Please don't go, Daddy. Please stay home."

Mother met her fearful expression with a hard smile. As soon as he wasn't watching, she glowered. Her father patted her on the head and felt around her shoulder before reaching under her arm and squeezing her ribs. Kirsten sucked air through her teeth. He'd found a bruise too painful for her to hold back. Mother's eyes darkened. A command to keep quiet.

He ran his fingers over the top of her foot, then gripped her heel and held her leg up. "Look at how bony she is. She's wasting away. We should take her to the med center. She ate enough for a grown man and look at her. She shouldn't be this thin."

Kirsten kept her gaze down. *She doesn't let me eat much when you're gone.*

"I was worried about that too," said Mother. "I had her there Friday. They couldn't find anything wrong."

Isn't lying a sin, Mother? Kirsten gripped his shirt tighter. "Can you stay home, please?"

An automatic door somewhere in the back of the apartment opened despite no one being near it. Something rattled in the kitchen, perhaps a glass sliding across the counter. Mother turned as pale as Kirsten. Father heard it too. He slid his hands under her arms and eased her off his lap, setting her standing. Shivering and sobbing, she clung to him as he got out of the chair.

"Please, Daddy, please stay!"

Mother grasped her shoulder. "Look at you, missy! Acting like a four-year-old."

"She's only nine, Jean. Don't be so demanding."

Her father had been away on 'business' when her tenth birthday came and went a few weeks ago. Mother didn't bother to correct him. A faint thud came from a distant room. Mother dug her fingers in deeper, peeling her away from her lifeline—Daddy.

"You'll miss your flight to the east," said Mother, her smile plastic.

Kirsten's pleas fell to wordless sniveling and begging eyes. Her father avoided looking at her and scurried to the closet. All these years, and he'd never noticed the doorknob was backward, to lock someone *inside*. He gathered his coat and put on his ViewPane glasses. Tiny flickering cyan lights danced in front of his eyes as it synced up to the NetMini in his pocket. His travel case, already packed, waited by the door with a week's worth of clothes.

She dared not shiver with Mother right there. *Tell him.* She looked up, mouth opening. *What if he doesn't believe me? What will Mother do after he leaves?* Kirsten surrendered to fear, staring past silent tears as her father drew close and kissed Mother on the cheek before pausing to ruffle her hair.

How can he not know? Daddy…

"I'll be back on the twentieth, unless the intercoastal gets delayed again."

Eight days alone with Mother. Kirsten gripped the carpet with her toes. She tried to make herself tell him what Mother did to her, but no words came.

"Have a safe trip," said Mother, still impersonating a human.

"I'll vid when I land. No, that'll be too late." He wandered back over and poked Kirsten in the stomach. "You should be sleeping by then. Be a good girl and listen to your mother. I'll vid in the morning."

Tears splattered on her feet as he walked away. Her eyes crept shut; her body tensed. Hell would come as soon as the door closed. *Tell him.* Kirsten trembled, unable to force a voice out of her mouth.

Pssht. The apartment door sealed behind him.

Mother's hand slid up Kirsten's neck, gathering loose hair into a ponytail fist. She stumbled down the corridor, walking on the balls of her feet, head at an angle as her mother pulled her along. The encouragement was firm but, for Mother, mild. Kirsten offered no protest as the unforgiving hold on her hair led to her bedroom. A weak shove at the back of her skull sent her forward. Mother stopped at the doorway.

As soon as she entered the room, an uneasy feeling in the air revealed the presence of a spirit. The ghost wanted to make itself known, but she didn't dare look. Mother's face announced she didn't approve of the way the mood shifted in there.

Four pink walls festooned in two dozen crucifixes of varying sizes surrounded her Comforgel pad. Her father set the electronics in the bed for his idea of a little girl's room: the dense liquid inside the gel mattress glowed pink regardless of whether it heated or cooled. Kirsten didn't have an opinion about pink things either way. Didn't matter. She rarely got to sleep in the bed. It served more as a place to store an innumerable collection of dolls and stuffed animals.

Every time Father went away, he'd bring her one as if apologizing.

Kirsten moved to the edge and lifted one knee to climb in.

Mother cleared her throat. "One of your demons is here, isn't it?"

"Jesus does not want me talking to demons."

"Don't!" screamed the monster impersonating a woman. The sudden noise sent Kirsten to a ball on the floor, shaking. "How dare you speak the Lord's name while you turn your back on him!"

She clung tight to the side of the bed, expecting Mother to stomp over and drag her to the closet. A minute passed with only the sound of raspy, angry breathing. Kirsten whimpered at the shift of weight in the floor.

"Pray." Mother stood right behind her.

She scrambled to her knees, hands clasped at her chin. *Jesus, who art in Heaven, Hallow—*

"I said pray!"

Mother's shadow on the wall raised a fist. Kirsten wailed between sobs. "Jesus, who art—"

"Those aren't the words. Are you corrupting the Lord's Prayer on purpose, or are you just stupid?"

Kirsten cringed, but no strike landed. "I-I'm just s-stupid."

Mother grabbed her; rough hands forced her back into the proper posture for prayer. "Do it right!"

"O-our f-father..." Kirsten sniveled her way through the entire recitation, stuttering over half the words.

"Get in bed, and be quiet. Think about why you turned away from God."

Kirsten crawled among the dolls and bears, curled on her side. The soft *pssht* of the door opening made her jump.

"Lights," grumbled Mother, making it dark.

Sniffling to herself, she rubbed her overstuffed belly with one hand while cradling a soft bear to her chest in the other arm. Mother thought

Kirsten was afraid of the dark. The woman believed programming the house electronics to ignore the Devil's child asking for lights would scare her. The closet had long since cured her of any fear of the dark. She'd even learned how to make her eyes see in the dark. Kirsten didn't need electronic lights to see. Mother's book said lying was bad, but she did it anyway. Mother had to be wrong about other things, too. Like Kirsten's powers. They couldn't be bad. They definitely didn't come from any Mr. Devil.

She'd given up trying to be 'good' because no matter what she did, Mother never changed. Kirsten no longer hoped her mother would love her again, and merely hoped to survive. Hot tears streamed down her cheeks. She buried her face in a stuffed rabbit taller than her. When Daddy came home, she'd tell him. Maybe if she behaved herself, Mother wouldn't kill her before he got back.

Cold at her back woke Kirsten.

The soft whirr of hovercars went by outside, in time with misshapen squares of light sliding over the far wall. Walls of metal crosses glinted. Kirsten brought her knees to her chest, shying away from the suffocating glare of tiny dying messiahs.

The two dozen faces of the little man watched her from every surface, ready to send her to Hell if she disobeyed. What Mother said made no sense at all. How could this Mr. Jesus guy love her so much but be willing to burn her forever if she did any mistakes? Mother had to be lying. Sometimes, the closet didn't seem so bad. In there, Mother couldn't sneak up on her. She snuggled into the mound of dolls and toys. They made her think of Daddy—even if he was a coward.

A watched feeling returned. She hugged the enormous rabbit to her chest, determined to ignore whatever wayward spirit had come here. Mother would hear the smallest sound and fall upon her with fury. The mere thought of it gave her chills. She imagined the unforgiving hand around her ankle dragging her down the hall. Mother had almost beaten her to death when she was eight. Nightmares of lying on the kitchen floor all night, one leg broken, still haunted her two years later. The close call scared Mother into backing off, but only a little. Less beating meant more burning. Mother discovered the little red stimpak for sale. They could grow back skin and mend bones.

Kirsten loved and hated stimpaks. They made the pain go away, but they also allowed Mother to hurt her worse before giving her one.

"Help," whispered an ephemeral woman.

Heavy, cold air fell over the bed. A faint electric hum came from the Comforgel unit as it worked to heat up.

Kirsten huddled around her rabbit, too afraid to even whisper *go away*.

"…isten, plea…"

A presence moved through her, the feeling of sentience passing from behind to in front. Mother remained oblivious to the ghosts unless they broke things. They only broke things when they got angry. They got angry when Kirsten ignored them. Every time a spirit showed up, she played a gamble: risk a beating for talking to them or risk worse if they vented. She sat up, wiping crumbs from her eyes and yawning.

"Help." The phantom words came from her right.

Kirsten glanced at the door, biting her lip, then whispered, "I can't. I'll get in trouble. Jesus will hate me."

"The woman lies," hissed the spirit. "You are no devil."

Chills rode down her spine from the disembodied voice. The apartment hung deathly quiet. She dreaded even her tiny whisper would rouse Mother. No electronics were allowed in her room: no clock, no datapads, no NetMinis and certainly nothing considered entertainment. The Devil's spawn didn't deserve such things.

Dread made her shiver as she clutched the edge of the bed. Kirsten sensed an unusual desperation in this spirit. She'd cause a lot of trouble if ignored. Disobeying one of Mother's most severe commands, Kirsten desired to see the ghost. Darkness weakened to monochromatic sepia as the astral realm permeated her reality. The crosses shimmered; the walls swayed in a constant undulating waver. Everything took on a fuzzy, indistinct quality. Soft white glow from Kirsten's eyes shimmered on her pale arms.

Beside the bed stood the nearly-solid figure of a woman around Mother's age, but thinner and with far kinder eyes. Kirsten rubbed her legs out of nerves, frightened at what Mother would do if she got caught letting her power off its short leash. In seconds, the dead woman took on color and a false sense of solidity, appearing no different from a living person.

"Thank you, sweetie. I need your help. My son is going to die tonight if I don't warn him. Your mother is lying to you. You're not using devil magic. You are a psionic."

Kirsten cast an uneasy glance at her door. "I... I'm not s'posed to talk to you. Mother thinks all spirits are evil."

The woman's hand passed through Kirsten's head as she tried to pat it. "Oh, child... Your mother is very sick, and an idiot. You have such a big heart and don't deserve this."

"I don't think you're bad." Kirsten folded her arms, looking down. "If I get caught talking to you, I'll get in trouble. She burns me and hits me and locks me in the closet. Please, I can't help you."

"You must!" The woman's image blurred for a second and reformed. "My son, Ryan, is only fourteen. His friends got tainted Flowerbasket. They don't know it's tainted. It's going to kill him."

"What's Flowerbasket?"

"It's a drug."

Kirsten scrunched up her nose. "Like a stimpak?"

"No. It's reckless and stupid. Please, you have to warn him not to take it or he is going to die."

"How do you know?"

"The dead know things... I can't really explain it. It's like having a dream of things and then they happen."

"Oh."

The woman pointed at the door. "I will make your Vidphone call him. Please, you must warn him."

"No," Kirsten whimpered. "Mother will wake up. I'm too scared." She ground her toes into the bedding. "Your son won't believe me anyway. No one does."

The ghost shimmered between normal and looking as though she'd been shot in the head and chest. Kirsten recoiled from the gore, covering her eyes. She'd seen worse before. The gore didn't scare her at all, but the energy in the room changing from desperation to rage did.

Thump... thump, thump, thump. Footsteps in the hallway.

Kirsten dove to the side, playing possum as the door slid open with a hiss.

"God sees your lies, girl."

She didn't move.

"The fires of hell burn through your eyelids. Your sin shines!"

"I told her to go away!" Kirsten sat up and burst into tears. "I love Jesus! The ghost won't listen."

Mother clutched her chest, staring aghast at Kirsten's luminescent eyes.

"Jesus wants us to be kind to strangers. She says her son is gonna die and is asking me to warn him. It's not the Dev—"

Kirsten screamed as Mother rushed in and slapped her flat to the bed. "Satan deceives! You let him in this house."

She clutched her burning cheek, curling into a ball and wailing. Some of the sounds coming out of her turned into "Sorry." Mother didn't hit her again until she made the mistake of blurting, "Don't hurt me, Mommy, I love you."

"Get out of her!" Mother howled and pounded her fist into Kirsten's back. "Get out of her!"

A loud crack, metal striking wood, caused silence. Mother shrieked in terror, backing away. Kirsten lowered her arms from shielding her face. She couldn't see the spirit anymore. The pain in her back destroyed her concentration on the power. However, the sight in front of her froze the blood in her veins.

Every cross from her walls had flown together and stacked in an impossible twisting sculpture at the center of the room, reaching inches short of touching the ceiling. Crucifixes balanced on end, arm to arm, without order or reason. No law of gravity known to man should have allowed the assembly to stand.

"I thought you were trying, Kirsten. I really did. I let you sleep in your bed tonight, and this is what you do? You invite the Devil into our home?"

Mother's low voice scared her more than when she shouted.

"I didn't! The ghost just came here." She trembled. "Please, Mommy. I wanted to do what you said."

"Go and think about what you have done."

Kirsten leapt from the bed and ran down the corridor to the living room. Mother walked after her, slow and plodding. Kirsten ducked into the closet and pulled the door closed. Floorboards creaked at Mother's approach. Kirsten backed into the inner wall and slid down to sit under the coats, hugging her knees to her chest. Mother's heavy footfalls stopped right outside.

Click.

Kristen shied away from the locked door, wincing from the pain in her back as she moved to lie sideways on the hard floor. Without blankets or stuffed animals, the cold numbed her feet and set her teeth chattering. The stink of carpet cleaner assaulted her nose. She tucked an arm under her head for a pillow and listened to Mother pacing about in the living room, muttering to God, Jesus, and various saints, asking them why she had been cursed with such an awful, evil creature for a daughter.

Sleep stayed away, helped by the hard floor and terror. Kirsten cried, wishing her father had stayed home. She used to pray he would find the courage to protect her from Mother, but Mr. Jesus didn't listen to her. A few spirits told her he didn't really exist and only crazy people thought he did. If God was real like Mother said, and loved people, he'd never allow Mother to treat her like this. He had to know how *twisted* Mother was. The e-bible she'd been forced to study spoke of love and forgiveness. Mother didn't seem to be reading the same book. The woman showed only hatred and cruelty.

"This is our fault!" *Thud, thud, thud.* "Humanity has brought this on itself!"

Mother ranted and paced outside, complaining. Kirsten cringed with every footfall.

"We have abandoned Him. So few in this evil nation believe anymore. They call us insane for believing the True Word. These so-called *psionics* are everywhere! They grow in number, spreading their sinful ways and devilish powers. You punish us for our transgressions, Lord. Why!" Mother wailed. A heavy slam rumbled the floor. Kirsten imagined Mother kneeling in the middle of the parlor, staring up at her giant stone and brass crucifix. "I am not one of the atheists who have disavowed you. Why do you punish *me* with such a demon for a child?"

Something broke in the distance. Mother gasped. Rattling echoed over silence. A long scraping noise ended with a massive crash. Mother howled. Kirsten shot upright and pressed her back against the wall.

The spirit had to be livid. Her son would take the Flowerbasket stuff and die, and Kirsten couldn't help. A cascade of bangs and clattering came from the left. Mother thundered off in the direction of the main bedroom. After the sound of a door opening, the woman roared. Kirsten didn't need to see the room to understand what happened. The sounds told the story. All the crosses in Mother's room had fallen to the floor. Something glass shattered against the wall.

The ghost lashed out at Mother's religion.

Kirsten gazed down at her feet, shaking in fear. Despite knowing it futile, she tried the knob. It refused to move. Had it been open, she'd have run out into the night. Weeks ago, a kindly old spirit warned her she would die by her Mother's hand if she didn't save herself. She didn't believe him then, but after this desperate spirit's rampage, Mother would come for her… and her wrath would be spectacular.

Tonight was the night the spirit warned her about.

Mother would kill her.

Even the carpet bot ran for cover, zooming under the door and vanishing into its little hole in the back of the closet. Seconds later, the door whipped open with enough force to pull Kirsten's hair over her shoulders. Something shattered in the kitchen, no doubt one of the porcelain Virgins on the stove—the ones that frowned at her whenever Mother burned her for purification.

At eight, the sight of her mother standing in the closet door would have paralyzed her with dread. Perhaps it came from being a little older, perhaps it came from expecting this to be her last night on Earth, but somehow, desperation pushed Kirsten to take a chance. The woman always accused Kirsten of lying anyway. She may as well try telling a lie.

She flung herself into a hug. "I love you, Mommy!"

The woman remained still. Kirsten's fingers scraped the back of her mother's nightdress; she balled her hands into fists, holding on as though her life depended on it, even though she feared and hated the creature her mother had become.

"I tried to tell the ghost to go away. She's mad because her son is in danger. Mothers are supposed to protect their kids."

Kirsten cringed as soon as she'd said it.

Mother threw her to the floor. The act of being thrown away hurt more than the landing.

"You're not my mother anymore. You keep saying I'm bad, but *you're* the Devil."

The woman growled and ran over to grab her. Kirsten scrambled to get away, flailing and kicking at the hands trying to grab and slap her. In seconds, Mother seized her by the forearms and hauled her across the apartment to the kitchen. Kirsten locked her legs, feet sliding over carpet, but her slight weight didn't slow Mother down. As they approached kitchen, Kirsten shrieked and kicked. Mother gathered both of her wrists in one hand and turned on the stove.

Kirsten struggled, putting her foot on the oven door, trying to shove herself away from the source of so much pain. A disc of glowing orange appeared in the glossy black surface. Heat washed over Kirsten's face as Mother forced her hands closer to the element. Skin bunched at her wrists as she struggled to keep her fingers away from the horror that awaited them. She grunted, twisted, and screamed. Mother intended to burn *both* hands tonight.

Desperation flared in her heart. Kirsten lunged forward and sank her teeth into Mother's forearm, but the ogrish woman didn't let go of her. The unexpected attack did make her stumble, buying a few seconds before her fingers melted off.

"Hey!" shouted a man, his voice echoing in the kitchen, far away as if on the other end of a tube.

Mother jumped, and her grip tightened. She always fought to get away from the stove, but never succeeded. Stimpaks fixed everything. Daddy never knew why the stove sometimes smelled funny when he used it to make tea. Tonight, however, Mother would go too far. Terrified, Kirsten let all her weight hang from Mother's grip, braced both feet against the oven door, and pushed, screaming for help.

"Get off that child, bitch!" The air vibrated from the energy in the spectral shout.

Shimmering white light danced over the wall. Mother stood statue still, frozen in schock. Kirsten wrenched herself free, falling on her butt. By the time she scampered backward into the cabinet, Mother babbled nonsense, gawking at the ghostly apparition of a man in an olive-drab jacket standing by the hallway. Scraggly hair the color of wet hay wavered in a nonexistent breeze. He looked filthy, his eyes wild, eyebrows wilder. The stink of body odor, piss, and vomit saturated everything about him. Kirsten gathered her nightgown over her face as a mask and gagged on the stench.

"Devil!" Mother pointed.

The spirit pulled an old gun, so ancient it had no electronics, from his jacket pocket and pointed it at Mother. "Nah, I ain't no devil. But I'm gonna arrange a meeting with him for ya."

Bang, bang, bang!

The gunshots sounded far off and muted as if fired under water. Tiny smears of spectral light zoomed through Mother and vanished into the wall behind her. No visible wounds appeared, but the woman clutched her chest, gasped, and collapsed, either dead or unconscious.

"Hey, kid. Time ta go." The man pointed over his shoulder with a thumb.

She focused on the desire to see spirits, dreading she would see her Mother's wraith. The vagrant ceased glowing. The solid appearance of a living person swam over his formerly vaporous body. Her heels skidded on the tiles as she forced herself upright, back pressed to the cabinet.

"She saw you?"

"Aye." He started to leave but stopped to sigh at her. "Ye be a right bit o' pathetic, you know? Best git on out before she wakes up. She's gonna go too far this time. If'n ya stay here tonight, you're gonna end up a ghost like me."

Kirsten sniffled, shivering, staring at Mother. How long had she been terrified of the monster laying helpless on the ground? Unconscious, the woman didn't look scary at all. Kirsten took a few quick steps after the spirit when he walked out.

"Wait! Where are you going? Who are you?"

The man didn't slow. His coat billowed out behind him as he strolled into the wall and disappeared. Kirsten edged toward the exit, nauseous from panic. A woman in the back of the apartment screamed seconds before another statuette smashed into floor. Kirsten glanced back at her mother, bit her lip, and faced forward again.

"I'll talk to him," shouted Kirsten. "Please hurry."

The thin thirty-something brunette blurred out of the wall of Mother's room. Pure rage had distorted her into a black-eyed horror, but she rapidly calmed, returning to her normal appearance. The spirit moved in a smear of light, closing the distance to the kitchen in an instant.

Kirsten jumped, startled. "I wanted to help, but—"

"I know, child. Please. There isn't much time." The woman stuck her right hand into the Vidphone terminal on the kitchen wall. The device came online. A CTI logo appeared in mirror-covered letters rotating on an otherwise black screen.

"Thank you for using ComTec Internationa," said a pleasant male voice.

The face of a boy in his early teens appeared on the screen, seeming half-asleep, as if the call woke him up. "Huh? You got the wrong number, kid."

"Don't eat the Flowerbasket," said Kirsten. "It's gonna make you sick and die."

He shook his head and hung up.

The spirit stuck her hand into the machine again, making the system call back. "Tell him my name is Jennifer, and his first dog was Nibbles."

"Knock it off, kid. If you call—"

"Your mother's here! Her name is Jennifer. Your dog was Nibbles."

"Whoa… What the hell is up with your eyes? You some kinda crazy doll?" The kid sighed. "Oh, hah. Duh. I get it. One of the idiots is pranking me with a vid hack."

"Don't use Flowerbasket tomorrow. It'll kill you," said Kirsten.

"You're freaking me out, kid."

"Your mom is here." Kirsten jumped at a moan from Mother, gradually waking up. "She says the drugs will kill you."

The boy scowled, reaching to hang up. "She always said that."

"Tell him Z-Bone is trying to impress Warden by poisoning the Chapel Street Gang," said the ghost.

Mother wheezed and twitched. Kirsten blurted the message as fast as she could, leaving the boy dumbfounded.

"Z-Bone? He's a little punk twelve-year-old. The hell does—?"

"If you take the Flowerbasket, you're gonna die!" shouted Kirsten. "Sorry. I gotta go or I'm gonna die, too."

She ran into the hallway. Something scraped behind her. Kirsten stopped in the middle of the apartment, whirling in place. Walls slid by, feeling as false as a holovid: her room, the closet, the front door, the kitchen—all certain death. She clutched her hands to her mouth, shaking.

The vagrant ghost walked in out of the wall. "What the hell ye still doin' here? You wanna get kilt? When she wakes up…"

"But…" Kirsten looked at her room. "Where am I supposed to go? I've never been outside."

"Damn. Well, first time fer everything. Ye wanna grab a doll or what'nae?"

She stared down at her shaking body. *Daddy left me here. He never stops her, just brings me dolls.* A crash came from the kitchen, followed by a roar. Kirsten ran into the living room and slapped the button by the front door. It buzzed, rejecting her. She poked it again. Kirsten whined at the 'parental override' showing on the screen. Mother made sure she couldn't get out. She feverishly looked back and forth from the panel to the arch where Mother would appear at any second. Sudden inspiration made her rush over and hide behind father's recliner.

"Dammit, kid. Ya only got one chance. Run." The ghost pointed at the door, tattered bits of green army coat trailed his swinging arm.

"I can't!" whispered Kirsten. "She's locked it."

"Satan has come to this house!" *Slam.* "You send your dark minions to destroy me, but I have the Lord to protect me!" *Slam.* "You are no child of mine; you are the Beast."

Kirsten cringed at every crash.

The ill-smelling vagrant ghost stuck his hand into the wall by the front door's control panel. A shower of sparks burst out of the sides; the panel went dark. The door snapped open with a faint squeak. Mother's shadow stretched in from the archway between the hall and the living room, crucifix in one hand, steak knife in the other. One arm raised the knife toward the chair.

"I see the false light of your sin on the wall. You cannot hide."

"Mommy, please!" wailed Kirsten. She stood and clutched the side of the chair.

Mother raised the crucifix higher.

Freezing cold swept over her as the spirit took a step into the room. He shimmered with a glimmering, radiant aura. A second later, his body became transparent. As soon as he resembled a ghost to her, Mother shifted the 'aim' of her crucifix to him, mouth agape. The spirit gave off such brilliant white light, it danced on the walls. The room chilled to arctic cold. Shadows distorted Mother's features into a horrible creature of nightmare. She thrust the cross at him, invoking God, Jesus, Mary, and a dozen other names.

The vagrant strode toward her.

Kirsten shivered, clinging to the green fabric of the chair arm. The fabric still smelled like her father—the man too frightened to help her. She gazed into Mother's eyes, awestruck at the sight of that horrible woman seeming scared. The spirit snarled and raised his hands. He pointed his gun at her.

In a panic, Kirsten pushed off the chair and sprinted out of the apartment. She raced down a hallway lined with apartment doors on both sides. At the end, she skidded to a halt in a small lobby area surrounded by fake plants. A long sofa faced six elevators, two of which stood open. She ran to the nearer one, entering a featureless chamber of silvery walls. Three reflections turned with her as she gazed around. She'd never seen an elevator before in person, but knew about them from holo-vids she'd been able to watch while her father was home. A thin black rectangle to the right of the door hinted at where a control panel might be, but it had no buttons. She leaned her face up to the black rectangle.

"Go down."

The silver square ignored her. Kirsten sobbed, tears and snot running down her face as she slapped at it.

As soon as her hand hit the black panel, a chime sounded and the doors closed. She backed against the wall and sank to the floor. Aside from being bright and metal, the elevator reminded her of a bigger closet. Blue light appeared by the rectangle, a holographic rendition of a skyscraper with a little glowing box about halfway up. Kirsten stood and padded closer to it. The position of the light had to represent the elevator's location. She poked her finger into the drawing at the bottom of the building. Another *beep* sounded. The elevator whirred. Kirsten sat on the floor, hugging her legs and rocking, gaze focused on the tiny sinking square.

After another *ding*, the mirrored doors slid apart, revealing a bank of three elevators facing her across a wide corridor of dingy beige tiles. The vagrant ghost stood to the right of a plastic tree in a flowerpot big enough for her to use as a bathtub. Kirsten stuck her head out. To the left, a pair of doors labeled 'Emergency Exit' dominated a wall fifteen feet away. To the right, a huge room waited beyond the elevator hallway, where a legless female doll—a torso and arms on a post—perched behind a reception desk. The front wall, all glass, looked out over a darkened street lit by the neon-shaded light of an uncountable number of advert bots. Spots of glow adorned pedestrians from personal electronics as well as implanted cybernetics.

Kirsten shivered. Going outside scared her, but Mother *terrified* her. It had to be stupid for a ten-year-old to run off into the city alone, especially at night. Going back upstairs would be dumber.

She crept out onto cold faux-marble, shivering as much from the temperature as from adrenaline. The reception doll whirled about with the whine of an electric motor as she entered the lobby. Kirsten froze, feeling tiny in the enormous room. Her entire apartment would almost fit in here. The weight of the artificial woman's stare pinned her. Outside, a cluster of advert bots chased a man in a loose, black coat. Four more hounded a woman sporting glowing green hair. At that hour, the machines outnumbered pedestrians three to one.

"Female child, you do not match any known resident. Your biometrics indicate a panic response condition. Do you require emergency services?" The doll tilted forward. The look on its molded plastic face made it seem as though it would walk over if it had the ability to move.

"C'mon kid," said the spirit. "Don't trust them cops. They'll send ya right back to her."

A couple waiting for the next elevator glanced down at her, noticing the girl only due to the doll's words. Her glowing white eyes made them both recoil and hurry away. The elevator she took beeped. Its doors slid closed.

Mother's coming after me.

Kirsten scrambled up to a run, bare feet squeaking on the polished tiles. She dashed across the lobby and went out into the night. The plastisteel walkway in front of the building warmed her feet, and a nice summer breeze made her thin nightgown tolerable. In seconds, a trio of orb bots pounced, surrounding her with flashing hologram ads for shoes, clothes, video games, and toy dolls. Automated voices chirped at her, telling her she could ask her parents for anything she wanted. Fear of Mother emerging from the building at any moment pushed to keep running down the street, choosing alley after alley without thought, until she collapsed from exhaustion. Trash bags looked soft enough to sit on, so she curled up on them. Kirsten expected to cry, but ended up staring mutely at a silver of traffic a half-block away, framed by grimy buildings. Soon, the reeking bed became comfortable and her eyelids heavy.

Unnatural cold brushed over her shoulder.

Kirsten looked up, seeing nothing. Still dark. Kirsten covered her mouth to conceal a gasp; she had fallen asleep right out in the open on top of garbage bags. It had to be pure luck Mother hadn't found her. She leapt from her resting place, stumbling over some plastic stuck to her legs. She needed to hide, to find some place where Mother would never get her.

"Hey, kid?" called a man.

She whipped around to face the voice, trembling. A man much younger than her father, with canary yellow hair swept over the side of his head, stood at the corner where alley met street. He had a gun on his belt and a few friends who looked scary. One of the men carried a purse with a broken strap and blood on it, clutched in bladed metal fingers. He flashed an overdone grin, hiding his artificial appendage—and the stolen item— behind his back.

Kirsten backed up, almost falling as her foot shot off sideways when she stepped on something slippery. Her father sometimes spoke of 'gangs' who hurt people and stole stuff. Tears streamed down her cheeks. Out of the house for one night and she'd found bad guys.

"Hey... relax, kid. We're not gonna hurt you," said the yellow-haired man.

"Yeah, this one's too young even for Bill."

"Eat a dick," said a guy with green hair. "Amma is nineteen. She's just short."

"Look, you guys get outta here." Yellow Hair waved them off. "I'll deal with the cops. Come on, girl. They'll take you home." He removed small objects from his pockets and tossed them to one of the others. "Hold my meds, Benny. Bastards are gonna search me."

The other gangers wandered out of sight onto the street as Yellow Hair took a NetMini out of his pocket. He held his hands up in a reassuring way. "It's okay, kid. I'm just calling the police. I'm not gonna hurt you or anything. You're too little to be out here alone. They'll get you home."

Kirsten's heart stopped. "No. I don't wanna go home!" She walked backward faster. "Mother is going to kill me."

"Aww. Your Mother doesn't want to hurt you. Whatever you did to make her angry isn't bad enough to make her kill you."

Ice tickled Kirsten's left shoulder. She sensed a ghost behind her and wanted to see into the spirit world. No sooner did her surroundings turn sepia than Yellow Hair froze like a statue, staring at her glowing eyes. The alley looked less dark, less scary despite the walls rippling and blurring.

"Uhh... you one of them whacked out kid dolls?" Yellow Hair took a step back.

"No. Why are you afraid of me?" She tilted her head.

"Shit. Psionic..." He almost tripped over himself to run and vanished around the corner.

The vagrant ghost, now visible, shook his head. "Idiot."

Kirsten looked up at him. He offered his hand. Hers passed right through it, and she frowned.

"Guess you nae' figger'd that trick out yet." He wheezed a chuckle.

"What trick?"

He scrunched his nose.

"Please tell me."

"Some o' you lot can do somethin' and *touch* ghosts. Donnae know how it works."

Kirsten wanted to hold his hand and concentrated on doing so... but only felt a slight gumminess to his body when she attempted to grasp his hand.

"Felt somethin'." He smiled. "Keep practicing."

She followed him deeper into the city for several blocks. Homeless people shied away from her as soon as they saw the light in her eyes. Whispering voices wondered if she was a malfunctioning android or a psionic. The way they said *psionic* sounded like a bad thing. Mother hurled the same word at her. Kirsten hung her head, following the spirit until he came to a halt by a pile of debris in the middle of the alley surface.

"Clear tha' crap away, kiddo." The ghost rubbed his nose with the back of his hand and sneezed a cloud of white powder that faded in a few seconds. "Feelin a bit drained."

Kirsten dug among sheets of plasfilm and crushed shipping cartons, throwing the junk aside handful by handful. Eventually, she discovered a large hatch with a rubberized handle set into the ground. Blue light glowed from a code panel in the center, next to a police symbol and the words 'unauthorized entry prohibited.'

She squatted, tracing her fingers over the writing. "Un… auto-rizz-ed. Author. Rized. Unauthorized entry prohibited? What's that mean?"

"Means momma won't go here." He wheezed into a laugh. When Kirsten didn't challenge him, he shook his head. "You can hide down there." He stuck his hand into the mechanism, causing the panel to sputter and flicker. The hatch emitted a loud hiss and clank. "G'won, lif' it up. Down there, she won't bug yas, and the damn cops won't grab ya either."

Kirsten tugged at the handle, unable to move it. She planted a foot on either side, clutched the squishy grip in both hands, and hauled. At first, it seemed too heavy to move, but it abruptly came unstuck and rose up from the ground on motorized struts. She yelped and leapt away, watching it open.

The ghost wandered off down the alley.

"Hey!" she yelled. "Are you coming with me?"

"Got some wanderin' ta do. There's plenty o' spirits down there what kin watch over ya."

"What's your name?" Kirsten slipped into the shaft, finding the rungs of a ladder sticky underfoot and the air foul. She climbed down until her chin reached the level of the road. "Please?"

"You dinnae wanna know me, kiddo. Imma bad soul."

"But…" Kirsten cringed away from the beeping hatch. "I think you're nice."

He paused, chuckled, and spat. "Heh. Nice. Sure, kid. I'm Ritchie."

Ritchie vanished.

Kirsten descended the ladder. After a moment, the automatic cover closed over her. She stopped going down and clung to the ladder, unsure if she felt locked in or safe from Mother. Eventually deciding it felt safe, she peered down past her wavering nightdress at a narrow shaft leading deeper. The underside of the cover glowed green from a code panel. Even if she wanted out, she couldn't open it. She smiled at the thought Mother couldn't open it either. Kirsten resumed going down, grimacing as her bare feet peeled off rung after rung, wondering if everything down here would feel so *nasty*.

At the bottom, she found herself in a narrow metal corridor, lit here and there by weak maintenance lights. Having no idea where to go, she followed the trail of glowing rectangles past several branching hallways until she reached a second ladder going further down. She squatted at the hole in the floor, feet and hands covered in sticky, black slime. Warm, sickly sweet wind blew up from below, tossing her pale blonde hair at her face. Fifty meters down, the wreckage of the prewar city sprawled over the natural ground. Houses, streets, and cars, all left in place when people built the modern city over them.

Without Mother to punish her for it, Kirsten left her powers on, gazing into the spirit world. She leaned closer to the hole, squinting from the breeze blowing up in her face. The ancient city teemed with the shimmering light of dozens of specters. It had taken a dead person to care enough to save her life. She would no longer be afraid to help them. A ghost saved her life. Helping them was the least she could do.

She grinned with hope, disregarding her fear of the unknown.

The ladder ran down along an immense column, plunging into a hole in the top of a once-fancy house. She felt like a doll with a dollhouse all to herself. Free from the fear of Mother's wrath, Kirsten lowered herself step by step until she reached the roof. As far as she could see, a metal sky laced with struts, wires, and tubes spanned over a dead civilization buried under the modern world built upon the elevated city plates. Grinning, she squeezed past the hole in the roof and scrambled down the ladder to a huge room, decorated with giant paintings depicting people centuries dead, dusty furniture, and random bits of trash accumulated over the years.

Awestruck, she approached a large bay window and peered out at a life-sized glass swan in the front yard. Various ghosts wandered around everywhere. To her, they looked like ordinary people except when they passed through solid objects. She could help them. Maybe they would help her. She'd have to find food and a place to sleep, but didn't worry. No matter what these ghosts offered her, it would be many times better than Mother.

Kirsten had no idea where Ritchie went, but she wanted to find him.

She had to thank him.

II

EVERGREEN

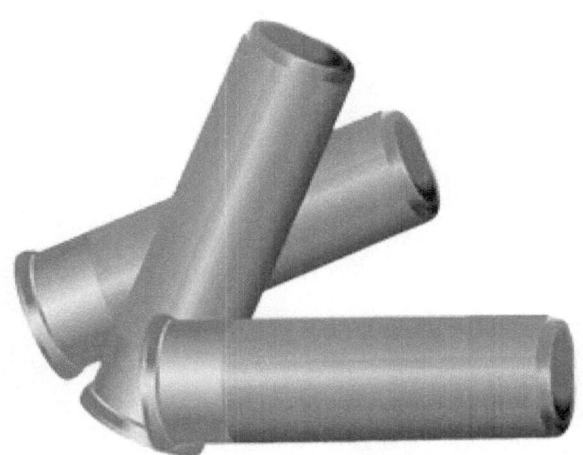

ABOUT EVERGREEN

In mid-2018, I was approached and asked to contribute a story to a post-apocalyptic-themed anthology. Most of the other stories were zombie stuff, and I'm not the biggest fan of zombies but they were open to nuke apoc, too.

I thought for a bit about ideas and it occurred to me I hadn't run into many nuke apoc stories set right around or after the nuclear war. The ones I've seen have all mostly been decades or centuries after the old society died. So, I set my thoughts on doing a story that starts two months after the nukes fell. Initially, I didn't really have specific plans to write an adult or YA story. Harper and Madison sorta came out of the woodwork subconsciously. This ultimately turned Evergreen into a post-apocalyptic YA coming-of-age type story driven by the idea this terribly sheltered, naïve, meek teenage girl is thrust into a situation where she's the only person left who can protect her severely traumatized younger sister.

Evergreen is one of the few times I've had an actor in mind for a character. While writing this story (and the subsequent novels) I pictured David Harbour playing the role of Cliff. This is the original short story version of Evergreen. After I started getting feedback about it and hearing how much people liked Harper and Madison—and wanted to know more of their story, I decided to turn it into a novel. The response was more than I imagined… and the Evergreen series has (at the time of me writing this) made it out to five books.

2

EVERGREEN

U neasy dreams gave way to a bleary vision of a slender girl huddled asleep against the corner of a cinder block wall, snuggled in a nest of trash. Harper Cody sat up, plenty done with lying on unforgiving pavement, and raked both hands up through her wild red hair. Her younger sister Madison had passed out clutching her iPhone to her chest, still expecting to get a text or call from one of her friends.

Harper hadn't the heart to tell her the truth.

A ten-year-old's hope shouldn't be shattered so cruelly, especially not after she'd watched their parents die. Harper frowned at her sister's pink flip-flops. The only reason she even had them is because they'd been forgotten in the front yard, an easy grab while fleeing the only home they'd ever known. Madison had been wearing the same denim shorts and white T-shirt for days. Dad's bloody handprint marked the left shoulder, half concealed by her sister's long, black hair. The girl used her wadded-up jacket as a pillow.

They'd holed up in an alley behind the Colorado Mills Mall, with stone walls on one side and a row of dumpsters on the other. It stank like hell, but the sour smell of months-old garbage beat getting shot—or worse. Harper long ago gave up sleeping with a teddy bear, but she had a new security blanket to cling to: Dad's Mossberg shotgun, currently resting across her lap. Even looking at it frightened her, and wracked her with guilt. If she hadn't hesitated, maybe one or both of her parents would still be alive. The gang thug stood only a few feet away from her after barging in their front door. But, she couldn't do it. Couldn't pull the trigger on another human being. Dad swiveled around and shot him to save her, but the distraction proved fatal.

She'd grabbed her sister and ran like hell.

For about two months, her family tried to remain at home after the world fell apart. But the gang found them eventually. It seemed as though all the decent people fled Lakewood, leaving only thugs behind. She shuddered, remembering what her parents warned her about, what the gang members would do to her—and even Madison—if they got captured. She hated thinking about her little sister screaming as some wild man assaulted her, but forced herself to keep that mental image in her head to overpower her squeamishness about killing. She clutched the shotgun's pistol grip and closed her eyes.

Next time, I won't hesitate.

Harper absentmindedly picked at her fat denim purse full of extra shells, Band-Aids, and a couple plastic bottles of water. To make room, she'd dumped out the useless stuff: her car keys, cosmetics, phone, mp3 player… and all the other random junk she'd been carrying around for four years, ever since her Mom gave her the bag for her thirteenth birthday. It had only been two months since the world went insane, but it felt like forever ago.

"At least I don't have to cram for the SATs anymore."

She forced herself upright, stretched, then crept to the end of the narrow channel between the dumpsters and the wall, peering out at the second-level parking deck full of abandoned cars, not one of them as helpful as a rock. Word said Colorado Springs suffered a direct hit and the EMP reached as far north as Greeley, possibly well past it. That meant every bit of electronic tech here in Lakewood had become about as useful as a lawyer. Not like anyone cared about court anymore.

Seeing no one around, she ducked into a shadowy alcove between dumpsters and dropped her jeans to relieve herself, then hurried back to wake her sister.

"I don't wanna go to school," muttered Madison. "I don't feel good."

Harper nudged her again. "Come on, termite. We have to keep going."

Madison opened her eyes, peering over the top of her dead iPhone. Harper averted her gaze from the red handprint on her sister's otherwise white T-shirt. She couldn't exactly toss it and make the girl run around topless, but that didn't mean she had to look at the morbid reminder of Dad's death.

"We gotta get to Evergreen," said Harper. "It's morning."

After a yawn, Madison glanced down at her phone and pushed the button. Nothing happened. A few minutes passed. When she spoke again, her voice had a far off quality that matched her stare. "Dance class is at five. I can't go to Evergreen. Mom's taking me to Starbucks after."

Harper squatted in front of her, eyes watering from the fumes surrounding the dumpsters. "It stinks here. Let's get some air."

"I guess." Madison sat for a moment more staring off into space, occasionally flexing her toes. "It smells bad."

"Yeah." Harper grasped her sister's wrist and pulled her upright. "Get your jacket on."

Madison picked it up and wriggled into it with all the energy of an android. She looked a bit silly wearing a jacket longer than her shorts, but Harper figured they should keep everything useful. Going home again to grab any of their things would be too dangerous. They'd barely escaped the gang a few days ago. Being chased away from the only home she'd ever known—plus the thought that her parents' bodies would still be there—got her crying and clinging to Madison. The girl didn't appear to mind playing the role of stuffed animal.

She couldn't let Madison see her cry, or understand how much of a chicken she'd been. Even before everything went to hell, she'd been afraid of leaving home to go to school. Weeks before the war, she'd argued with Dad about college. She hadn't really wanted to go at all, especially far away, but she relented on the condition she could stay at home and go to some place close.

I'm a living oxymoron… a shy ginger.

"You forgot your books. You're gonna fail the SAT test," said Madison in a toneless voice.

"The T in SAT means test."

"Brainy," muttered Madison.

Harper gave her a squeeze and released the embrace. "Come on. We should keep going."

"I wanna go home," said Madison.

Yeah. Me too. Harper grabbed her sister's hand and led her out from the space behind the dumpsters. "We can't right now. It's too dangerous."

"I gotta pee."

"There's a drain over there. Use that."

Madison scrunched up her face. "Not outside! I need a bathroom."

It doesn't matter anymore. Nothing does… except for surviving. "It's fine. You won't get in trouble."

"Don't look," said Madison.

Harper pulled the Mossberg off her shoulder and held it sideways, her back turned, standing guard while her sister used the storm drain. Once the soft *pop* of flip-flops approached behind her, she got moving, skirting the outside of the mall.

"You wanna play Xbox tonight?" asked Madison.

"Maybe. We'll see." Their game system, like every other piece of tech in this city, had died. They'd lived for two months on candles and whatever canned food Dad could find searching neighbors' empty houses.

"Mom was gonna get me a new game after the recital."

The monotone voice coming out of her little sister raked like a claw over her heart. Madison also inherited the 'shy' gene, but not to the same degree as Harper—hence why Mom often treated her to stuff as an encouragement to dance recitals or other activities she might've tried to avoid doing otherwise. Up until a few weeks ago, she'd been full of life, even bubbly. More than what had happened to the world, Harper hated the people who started the war because they'd killed her kid sister *inside*.

"Can we go to McDonalds?" asked Madison. "I'm hungry."

Harper rooted around her purse and pulled out an energy bar. One bit of good luck they'd had so far, finding a convenience store that still had some food in it.

"I'm sick of these. I want a burger." Still, Madison took the bar and peeled it.

They continued for a few minutes, Madison munching away. Harper approached a corner where the mall building extended outward, but hesitated when a couple of men's voices echoed from the other side. She edged up to the wall and leaned one eye out to peer around the bricks.

Six men walked toward her. Two, she recognized from school, both a year ahead of her. Jeff and Louis had been part of the 'bad' crowd: drugs, drinking, even getting in trouble with the law. She figured they would've only become worse with the collapse of order. The others looked older, the eldest well into his thirties. All carried weapons ranging from a baseball bat to handguns. Not that the gang had a uniform, per se, but the way these men carried themselves left no doubt in her mind they'd be trouble.

Harper ducked back before they saw her, shifted the Mossberg to one hand, and grabbed Madison's wrist before taking off at a sprint for the mall entrance. Madison's flip-flops clapped on the concrete deck a few times before the pat of bare feet took over.

"Harp!" said Madison.

"Carry them," whisper-shouted Harper as she skidded to a stop and swiveled to point the shotgun at the corner.

Madison scurried back a few steps to collect her flops, then scampered over to Harper.

They dashed for the entrance, ducking inside before any of the gang members noticed them. At least, Harper hoped. No shouts or gunshots happened outside, so she assumed they'd gotten away.

A vast, dimly lit expanse of abandoned stores stretched out before her, heavy with hot, humid air and a stink like the locker room at school, only much worse. Distant dripping echoed, making the place feel even emptier.

"Eww," said Madison, deadpan. "The floor is slimy."

Harper ignored the squish of her sneakers on the tiles. Condensation covered most of the store windows, turning them into opaque panels like frozen smoke.

"Are we going shopping?"

"No." Harper looked around, focusing after a few seconds on a skylight overhead. Water gathered in droplets, falling every few seconds to a silent landing on the floor a few paces forward of where she stood. "We're just walking through to the other side, to stay away from some bad people."

Madison pulled her phone out from her jacket pocket and fiddled with it. The blank, black screen still didn't respond.

We're going to be okay. Harper clutched the shotgun, trying to hold it in a posture like all the video game characters did. Playing *Call of Duty* had been pretty cool. *Living* it, not so much. She advanced down the concourse, shifting to aim at any shadow that moved. Madison dallied a moment to put her flip-flops back on before catching up.

Dad's voice drifted out from Harper's memory. A bit of a geek, he'd built a radio of some kind in the garage. Two months after nuclear war, he made contact with someone surprisingly close by, in the city of Evergreen, west, up in the mountains. According to her father, a lot of people had taken refuge there and started rebuilding it into a proper town. Of course, they wouldn't have electrical power, cars, or anything like that. Total *Little House on the Prairie* stuff... but it sounded a whole lot better than getting kidnapped by the gang.

That could go wrong in any number of ways, from being forced to help thugs murder and loot to being raped, or maybe even cooked and eaten. Dad thought the lack of organized society brought out the worst in everyone, as if the only thing holding humanity back from tearing each other apart had been the law and expectation of civilization. Mom hadn't been so nihilistic. She'd clung to the belief every person had some amount of good inside them—right up until a man trying to drag her out a window shot her dead for stabbing him.

Harper flinched at the memory of her mother crumpling to the ground in their living room. At least Madison hadn't witnessed it. No, she'd been hiding under the kitchen table as Dad tried to shoot it out with a bunch of punks on the deck while Harper stood paralyzed with dread, staring at a man forcing the front door open. The way the gang punk smiled at her made her skin crawl. It could've been sexual or cannibalistic; either way, the *hunger* in his eyes freaked her out so much she couldn't move. As soon as he'd noticed the Mossberg in her hands, he went for a gun, but she couldn't bring herself to kill a man.

"There's a Starbucks," said Madison, dragging Harper out of her daymare. "Can we get something?"

"It's not open." Harper kept on walking, trying to ignore all her memories of this mall. The abandoned brokenness of everything looked *so* wrong, made worse by the near-total silence. As often as she used to come here, every storefront triggered one memory or another—but seeing it like this felt like the world mocked her dead parents, missing friends, and the life she would no longer have.

"That's stupid. It's the morning."

"Look for a way downstairs. We'll go out the other side and go west to the mountains."

Madison followed for a while in silence before asking, "Why are we hiding?"

"Those people are dangerous. They'll hurt us."

"Like they hurt Mom and Dad?"

Harper's throat closed off with a lump she couldn't speak past. She gazed down at the floor, listening to the soft snapping of her sister's flip-flops until she composed herself. "No, worse."

"What's worse than being dead?" asked Madison, no life at all in her voice.

"Don't worry about it," said Harper. Her thoughts again showed her little sister fighting a faceless gang thug carrying her off to do unspeakable things. "I won't let it happen."

At the junction where the concourse widened to a courtyard, Harper paused and crouched behind a large planter box of greenery, aiming the shotgun out over the dead mall. She *should* be sitting on the nearby bench sipping coffee with her friends, *not* running around with a gun. Crappy Christmas music haunted her memories. The same track this place always put on during the holidays, music that would never play here again.

A short distance ahead, an escalator offered a way downstairs. Nothing moved save for unseen dripping.

"My phone won't turn on," said Madison.

"Got the charger?"

"Yeah."

Harper crossed her fingers. White lies. "Well, we'll have to find a plug. Maybe there'll be one in Evergreen you can use."

"Not here?" Madison squatted beside her, half her pale face hidden behind a wall of straight, black hair.

"All the stuff here broke, remember?" asked Harper. "I don't see anything dangerous. Come on."

She got up and walked around the planter box, heading for the escalator. At the top, she paused with an annoyed sigh. The ground floor had flooded several feet deep. Harper spent a moment debating if she'd rather deal with water or hope the gang thugs on the upper level parking deck had moved on.

They're probably going to come inside.

"Damn."

"Why is there a swimming pool inside the mall?" asked Madison.

"I dunno." Harper sat at the top of the escalator. "Pipe probably broke or something."

She pulled her sneakers and socks off, stuffing them in her giant purse. Wet jeans would be bad enough, but soggy sneakers—ugh. Barefoot, she crept down the escalator, shotgun poised to deal with anyone who looked dangerous. Since they likely had gang members entering the mall behind her, Harper figured she had no choice but to keep going forward, even if that meant a confrontation with whoever might be down there.

At the bottom, she stepped into water a little deeper than her knees. The lower floor sat in darkness, except for the open atrium over the central courtyard lit by the skylights in the roof. Each hallway leading off held plenty of shadows. Plastic cups, trash, and a handful of volleyballs floated by.

"It's cold," said Madison as she entered the water, which came up to her thighs. "I left my swimsuit at home."

Harper looked over at her kid sister, who clutched her flip-flops to her iPhone, holding it protectively away from getting wet. "We're not swimming, termite. Just going through as fast as we can."

She sloshed forward with Madison grabbing at her arm. As much as she wanted to offer the comfort of holding hands, she didn't want to let go of the shotgun. If she needed it, every second would matter. Eventually, Madison settled on clutching her belt.

Most of the stores on the lower floor looked as though riots had stormed through already. Much of the inventory had been looted, and an alarming amount of blood spatter painted the walls in places. Harper had spent enough time in the mall over the past few years to know her way around, and headed for the secondary exit to the ground level, opposite from where the gang had been outside. She usually avoided that door due to the legion of smokers who always hung out there—not so much an issue anymore.

Crash.

At the *whump* of metal slamming against metal, Madison leapt into her, clinging, but didn't make a sound.

Harper spun to the left, pointing the shotgun at an Auntie Anne's shop. Something moved inside. Shivering from the icy water lapping at her legs, Harper stood her ground, waiting, watching—and listening to the upstairs for any sign of the gang.

Seven breaths later, a shirtless, shoeless boy with a spherical mop of black hair perched like little Tarzan atop the counter in the pretzel shop. He appeared to be about Madison's age, skinny, and possibly Chinese. As soon as he spotted her—specifically the shotgun she had pointed in his direction—he let off a yowl of alarm and jumped from the counter into the water.

"Hey!" shouted Harper. "Wait!"

The boy didn't bother trying to run. He dove under the surface and swam so fast his shorts almost came off as he raced out from the Auntie Anne's and veered left into one of the dark passages.

"Kid, stop!" yelled Harper. "I'm not gonna hurt you."

She ran after him as best she could move in knee-deep water. The boy swam around a corner some fifty feet from the pretzel shop. Harper rushed after him and rounded the bend—straight into the tip of an enormous silver handgun pressed to her forehead.

A tiny whine escaped her nostrils. It took her a second to collect herself enough to realize a man held the gun. He looked past forty, with a scruffy brown beard and shaggy hair. Somewhere between muscular and mildly overweight, he filled out the uniform of a mall security officer with little room to spare. After six seconds of having a pistol touching her, she recognized him.

"Officer Cliff?" asked Harper.

The glower on his face relaxed. "Oh... I remember you—and your attitude."

"Please don't shoot me," said Harper. "And by the way, there's been a war. There's no such thing as shoplifting anymore. Besides, I don't think there's even anything left to steal."

The boy peered out from behind Cliff, eyeing her warily.

"What were you doin' chasin' the kid?"

Sloshing behind and left reminded her of Madison, but she dared not look away from a man holding a gun to her face. "I wasn't going to hurt him. He looked lonely."

Cliff rested his free hand on the boy's head, patting him. "People haven't exactly been nice to him."

"Why?" asked Harper, chancing a peek left at Madison, who crept into a Hot Topic on the other side of the hallway.

"As you so astutely pointed out, we had a war. Numbnuts out there assume he's Korean and 'his people' nuked us, or started the whole shitstorm."

"My great grandparents are from China," said the boy, barely over a whisper. "I'm not a Korean."

Harper sighed at the kid. "People are stupid. You're an American like everyone else here. I swear I wasn't going to hurt you." She looked up at Cliff. "I just saw him alone and figured he was too little to be on his own."

Cliff lowered his gun. "All right. You're still a kid, too. S'pose you may as well stick around if you want. At least until the supplies run out."

"I'm seventeen. I'm—"

"Still a kid." Cliff smiled.

Harper glanced to the left, watching her sister rooting around the store. "Surprised there aren't more people here. It's like abandoned."

"Yeah. Most people hauled ass away from big cities once they figured out the war started. We got real damn lucky nothing landed on our heads."

"We're leaving," said Harper. "My dad..." She choked up, hearing him scream *Harper! Shoot!* "Uhh"–her voice quivered–"my, umm, dad, had a radio and he heard about a settlement or something up in Evergreen. It's supposed to be safe."

"Sorry," said the boy. "My parents are dead too. People thought they started the war."

Her heart sank. "People suck."

"Ain't that the truth," muttered Cliff. As if realizing he still had a gun out, he glanced at it, then stuffed it in a hip holster.

"We're not safe here. The gang's getting bigger and scarier. It's just me and my kid sister."

Cliff cringed. "Yeah... I can see why you'd wanna get outta here. Especially with her along. Those boys would, umm, yeah."

The former mall guard hadn't meant anything inappropriate, but he'd called attention to her looks all the same. Dad always joked that he bought the shotgun because he had a pretty, blue-eyed, redhead daughter. She didn't need the reminder of why letting the gang find her—or Madison— would be a *bad* idea.

"You want a hand getting to Evergreen?" asked Cliff. "S'pose me and Jon could help make sure you two make it there in one piece."

Harper narrowed her eyes. "And what do you want in return?"

"Nothin', kid." Cliff shook his head. "You're a kid and I'm a trained professional. That's just how stuff is supposed to work."

Something clattered to the floor in the Hot Topic, but Madison didn't yell in alarm, so Harper resisted the urge to dash over there.

"Trained professional?" She raised one eyebrow. "You're a mall cop."

Cliff laughed. "Wasn't always. I *thought* this job would come with fewer bullets flying my way. Seems I was wrong. 'Course, they're flying everywhere these days."

She looked down at her feet, well under water. It would be nice not having to do *all* the protecting. "Okay. That would be really cool of you. Be right back."

Harper sloshed across the mall concourse into the Hot Topic. Thousands of little plastic baubles floated like a layer of pond scum, clinging to shelves and a glass counter. She found her kid sister kneeling atop said glass counter, rummaging in a bin. The girl clutched an armload of cheap jewelry, everything from skulls to pixies.

"Can we get these?" asked Madison, holding up a pair of plastic unicorn earrings. "I left my allowance at home."

"Yeah, it's fine. There's no more money. Just take them."

For the first time in two weeks, Madison's face finally showed a hint of emotion: worry. "But, Harp!" She lowered her voice to a whisper. "He's a mall cop. I can't like steal right in front of him. I'll get in *so* much trouble."

"It's fine." Harper grabbed a small purple-and-black backpack from a shelf, took the bundle from her sister's arms, and stuffed it inside before handing her the pack. "Take whatever you want, but you have to carry it."

After a long, worried stare, Madison accepted the backpack and added a couple more things, including a few adult-sized T-shirts. She followed Harper out of the store, wading over to where Cliff and Jon waited.

The former guard led them back upstairs to a TGI Fridays at the corner of the mall center. Both front windows had been packed with tables, a makeshift barricade. Harper followed him inside to a section of the room they'd made something of a home out of, using sheets hung up as walls around sleeping bags.

"Figure we'll leave first thing in the morning so we have the most daylight, plus some time to pack provisions." Cliff gestured around. "Get comfortable, I'll whip up some food."

"I'm Jonathan," said the boy as he disappeared around behind one of the hanging sheets.

A second later, his soaking wet shorts hit the floor. Madison strolled over and sat in a padded booth seat as though they'd simply went out for lunch and nothing at all had gone terribly wrong with the world. Swinging her feet back and forth, she pulled out her iPhone.

Harper stood there frowning at her wet jean legs for a little while before sitting on the end of the bench and resting the shotgun across her lap. A moment later, she second-guessed herself and checked the safety. *I can't believe this is real.* Two months ago, her biggest fear had been Renee and Christina dragging her to a Taylor Swift concert. Not that she had anything against the music, but crowds bugged her. Harper hated being out among *so many* people.

I am the anti-redhead. Introvert Prime.

Jonathan emerged from his 'room' a short while later, having changed into a dry Nike T-shirt and cargo shorts. He still didn't have any shoes, but seemed much less skittish than he'd been out in the mall. The boy climbed up into the seat across the table from Madison.

"Hey," said Johnathan. "It's cool to have another kid around. What's your name?"

For the most part, Madison ignored him as he kept trying to start a conversation, but after about five minutes, she finally said, "I'm Madison. My phone's not working. I'm worried about my friends."

"I miss my friends, too," said Jonathan. "Glad I found Mr. Barton."

Her kid sister spoke in that same, toneless, far-away voice that stabbed Harper like an ice dagger. "I've gotta go to dance class at five. Mom's gonna pick me up. I can't call her 'cause my stupid phone won't turn on."

"Oh, that's cool," said Jonathan. "I took dance too. It was kinda weird being the only boy there, but I liked it."

Madison looked up from the dead screen. "You didn't go to Taekwondo?"

Jonathan rolled his eyes. "Why, 'cause I'm Chinese?"

"No. Because you're a *boy*. My dance class didn't have any boys. We had one for a couple days, but his father came in and got mad, made him go home." She resumed staring at the blank iPhone. An awkward silence hung between them for a moment. "I think it's pretty cool you took dance."

Harper exhaled with relief. She watched the restaurant entrance while the kids talked shop about dance class for a few minutes. Her mind filled in the ghosts of shoppers wandering back and forth. Cliff returned after a while carrying a tray and handed everyone a plate with a burger and fries.

"How'd you cook this?" asked Harper. "There's no power anywhere in Lakewood. We've been eating out of cans."

"That's true." He scooted in to sit beside Jonathan. "But there's still wood."

"This is a veggie burger," said Madison.

"Meat's gone bad by now." Jonathan shook his head. "This stuff lasts forever."

"It's all chemicals," mumbled Madison.

"Tasty, delicious, still-edible chemicals." Cliff winked and took a big bite.

Harper dug in. The veggie-patty had a definite twang of wood smoke, and the fries had obviously been heated in a pan. However, compared to the 7-Eleven granola bar-and-Hostess fare she'd been surviving on the past few days, it amounted to a feast.

"Well, cars are pretty much toast after the EMP blast," said Cliff. "We're gonna have to hoof it to Evergreen."

Mouth full, Harper nodded.

"Dad just got a new Expedition," said Madison, her unfocused stare boring through her burger like a seer gazing into the depths of a crystal ball. "It's nice. We can all fit in it and it still smells new. It's got a sun roof. Do you think Mom will drive it to take me to dance, or will she use the old car?"

Cliff shot a glance over the table at Harper. His eyes seemed to say 'that poor kid ain't handling it well.'

Jonathan mouthed 'wow' without giving it voice.

Harper looked down.

After they finished eating, Harper spent a while following Cliff around inside the restaurant searching for food items they could pack up and bring with.

Madison approached, holding her iPhone and its charger. "None of the plugs are working. Can we go home?"

Overcome by grief, Harper sank to her knees and wrapped her little sister in a hug.

"I miss Mom and Dad," whispered Madison. "They're not gonna pick me up, are they? They died. Please don't die, too. I don't want to be alone."

The dam broke. Harper burst into tears, clutching Madison tight and rocking her back and forth.

HARPER SNAPPED AWAKE, STRETCHED OUT ON A BOOTH SEAT BENCH. MADISON had curled up on top of her for the night, but she'd disappeared. An inch from panic, Harper grabbed the Mossberg and sat up, but calmed at the sight of her little sister a short distance away listening to Cliff telling a story about a clumsy friend of his when he'd been deployed in Iraq for Desert Storm. Madison almost even smiled, wide-eyed and intent on the story like a kid half her age.

The lump lodged itself once again in Harper's throat. Watching the two of them reminded her of Dad. Reminded her of how Dad died because she chickened out and couldn't shoot a man trying to hurt her. If Dad hadn't turned to save her, he would've been able to shoot the other ganger coming in the patio door. A toxic mood came over her, making her want to lash out at Madison for forgetting their father so fast. That man wasn't their father. How dare she smile at him and let him pretend to be someone he would never be. Her lip curled in guilt disguised as jealousy, and she narrowed her eyes at the impostor.

The last time she'd seen Cliff, she'd been fourteen and spent two hours handcuffed to a metal chair in some back room here at the mall. It didn't matter that she *had* shoplifted and probably deserved to be arrested. However, Cliff had called her parents instead of the cops, something about not wanting to ruin her future over a crappy pair of overpriced pants.

Okay, so he's not a douche. Harper sighed out her nose, letting her anger evaporate. *I messed up once and got Dad killed. Maddie seems to like this guy. I shouldn't mess up again.* She wept in silence for a little while, mourning her parents. With a deep breath, she pushed her sadness back down into a little box. *I can cry later. Right now, I gotta get her outta this place.*

For breakfast, they ate pre-wrapped brownies, likely a smaller component of some 10,000 calorie 'diabetes-on-a-plate' dessert the restaurant had once served. Still, the things would probably last twenty years. None of the toilets in the bathroom worked, since all the water appeared to be loose downstairs. Still, using them felt a lot more normal than going outside.

On the way out of the mall, they stopped at two shoe stores, but the first only had adult-sized sneakers and the other one had been stripped clean. Cliff took an extra pair of hiking shoes in his size, plus a set for Harper, and stuffed them in his giant backpack. Madison didn't seem to care at all about being stuck with flip-flops, and kept trying to get her iPhone to turn on.

They decided to give up on scavenging and made their way to the escalator again.

"Any idea where all this water came from?" asked Harper. She rolled her jeans up as much as she could before wading into the ground floor.

"Main gave out in the boiler room. The water tower down the road emptied into the mall." Cliff picked Jonathan up, carrying the boy on his shoulders to keep his clothes dry.

Cliff avoided the front entrance, opting instead to take a maintenance hallway in back that led out to a loading ramp for trucks. Once they climbed out of the water, he put Jonathan down on his feet. Harper wiped her legs off with her hands, then took her socks and sneakers out of her purse and put them on.

"If you ever run out of ammo for that Mossberg, you can use that bag as a club," said Cliff.

Harper smirked, but couldn't resist a slight chuckle.

They crossed the parking lot, staying as low as possible between rows of cars. Soon, they reached the edge of the mall property and headed into Lakewood proper. Though the area had been spared a direct hit, the city ᵢlooked like a nuke had gone off close enough to shatter every window in sight. Harper thought back to hiding in the basement of her home with her parents and Madison for several days after the news announced war. No official warning ever came from the government; not until detonations started happening along the East Coast did media outlets have a clue the proverbial shit had hit the fan. She'd been convinced a nuclear wave would tear the house away above them, but once a few days passed, she accepted it wouldn't happen. While cowering in their basement, she'd heard terrifying rumbles that could've been distant explosions, and wind like tornadoes ripping by overhead. The instant the power went out, the world became a scary dream. When the gang first showed up a month or so later, the scary dream had become a terrible reality.

For the better part of an hour, they walked in silence, save for the constant *thwap-thwap-thwap* of Madison's flip-flops. Harper gazed around at smashed cars, bent traffic signs, patches of dried blood here and there, and even a few bodies strewn about. She couldn't keep both hands on her shotgun *and* make sure Madison didn't look at any of the gore, so she hoped her kid sister remained preoccupied with her iPhone. Like everything else electronic, it had blown out the first day. Still, the kid thought the battery had run out. Dad's horrible joke about the EMP wave frying the banks made her tear up again.

Well, the house is paid off!

Men popped out of doorways and windows a half-block ahead, whooping and pointing at them.

Harper's tears retreated back into her eyes. Her heart raced.

"C'mere, Red," shouted one. "That one's mine! I call dibs!"

"The hell you say, Spider," roared another, before laughing.

"Get 'em!" yelled another. "You all come wif us an don' fight none, we promise not ta hurt 'cha."

Madison looked up from the dead screen, her face noticeably paler than usual—which said a lot. "I think he's lying."

"Down," said Cliff. He grabbed Jonathan by a fistful of T-shirt and rushed forward, pushing the boy to the ground behind a car.

In Harper's mind, a pack of thugs grabbed Madison and dragged her, screaming, into a dark place. *No!* She ran to cover behind a car that had jumped the sidewalk on the left side of the street and fired at the pack closer to her. The Mossberg hammered her shoulder a lot harder than she expected, but she held her balance.

Madison, who'd followed her, fell to her knees and screamed at the *boom* of the shotgun going off.

Three of the gang thugs hit the ground; the one in the middle didn't move again, but the two on either side of him rolled around, wailing in pain, covered in blood trails. Harper ducked down as the other guys in that group all opened up on her with handguns. *Clanks* and *cracks* surrounded her from the barrage striking the big car. Hunkered against the wheel, she glanced over at Cliff, who popped up, fired his hand cannon twice, and ducked a split second before a spray of fragments exploded from the wall near him.

Jonathan curled up in a ball next to Cliff, both hands over his head. Madison, sitting on the road beside Harper, kept poking the button of her iPhone, making angry faces at it for not turning on.

"What are you doing?" rasped Harper. "Get down!"

"I'm trying to call 911," whispered Madison.

"You goddamned bitch!" shrieked a man, sounding frighteningly close. "I'm gonna—"

Harper popped up over the hood and locked eyes with a twenty-something guy in a black leather jacket. His face warped with rage, and he ran toward her as if intending to jump clear over the car. Madison's imagined scream destroyed hesitation. The Mossberg bucked into the tender spot it made on her shoulder as she fired; most of the man's face disintegrated in a spray of red schlock and flying teeth. The body twisted into a fatal pirouette and collapsed.

On the right side of the street, a gang punk lay dead atop a rifle, bleeding from the chest, Cliff's first target. The others, all armed with a mixture of handguns, bats, and axes, had scattered to cover behind cars, a dumpster, and a small stonemasonry stairwell.

The remaining three guys on Harper's side of the street threw a few more bullets her way, but nothing came closer than gouging the roof of the car. She fired, pumped, and fired again. Her second shot blew out the windshield of a Camry and sent the man hiding behind it running.

Guess Dad was right. Shotguns scare people away.

A high-pitched scream came from Madison.

Harper spun to her right. A scrawny man with a shaved head had come out of nowhere behind them and grabbed Madison. She whirled, aiming the Mossberg at them, but couldn't bring herself to pull the trigger for fear of hitting her sister. The man grinned evilly at Harper while shielding his chest with the thrashing child. Madison screamed and flailed, pounding and kicking at him, but the man largely ignored her and held a handgun to the side of her head. At the touch of metal to her temple, Madison went still.

"Drop the cannon," said the guy.

"Not happening." Harper aimed for his face. "I drop this, we're both as good as dead. How stupid do you think I am? Put her down *now*."

He ducked his head behind Madison's. "Go on, girlie. Shoot us both. You ain't got the nerve. Scatter shot gonna kill your precious little kiddie, too."

Madison squirmed, both hands clutching the arm around her chest.

Jonathan darted out from cover and sprinted across the street, leaping onto the gang punk's back. The boy's impact staggered the man into a spin. Madison fought like a shrieking wildcat the instant the gun broke contact with her skin, wriggling loose from his grip and dropping to all fours. Jonathan bit the man's wrist, drawing blood and making him lose his hold of the handgun, which clattered to the pavement.

Cliff fired a few times rapidly, but he had his hands full from the rest of the gang peppering his cover with a steady hail of bullets.

"Jonathan, get back!" yelled Harper, angling for a clear shot.

The gang thug wrestled with the boy, trying to cling to the only reason he hadn't eaten a face full of buckshot. Harper considered lunging in and walloping him with the gun, but didn't want him to grab it and take it away from her. He looked stronger than her by a good margin.

Growling, Jonathan tried to kick the guy in the balls, but the ganger saw it coming and twisted away, redirecting the boy's bare foot into his hip. He backpedaled, seeming content to run off with Jonathan instead of the girl.

Bang.

A spurt of blood sprayed from the ganger's side. He let off a wheeze and collapsed to one knee. The instant Jonathan wormed free of his grip, Harper blasted him near point blank. Buckshot slapped into his chest, flinging him into the pavement atop a spatter of crimson.

Stunned, Harper glanced toward the source of the single shot.

Madison stood in a wide stance, both hands clutching the thug's dropped Glock. A wisp of smoke curled up from the barrel. She shifted her gaze to Harper. "Ow. This thing hurt my hand. And it's too loud, not like the Xbox gun."

Cliff lunged to his feet and fired another shot. A groaning "Oof" replied from down the street, along with the *thump* of a body hitting the ground. "Kid, you okay?"

Madison stared at the gun. "What do I do with this? I don't wanna shoot myself."

"Get down!" Harper whirled to cover the street, but the only gangers in sight lay dead where they'd fallen. The rest had run off, either scared or wounded.

Cliff jogged over and took the Glock from Madison. She smiled, happy to be rid of it.

"We gotta move. More will have heard that," said Cliff, tucking the Glock in a side pocket of his backpack.

"Yeah." Harper hefted her shotgun in one hand and grabbed Madison by the wrist.

Barely ten steps later, a man leapt out from behind a flipped truck and charged at Harper with a hatchet. Cliff zoomed to his left, intercepting the guy. Before Harper could even blink, Cliff had flipped him over onto the ground and broken his arm. He yanked a knife from the thug's belt and jammed it into his back with two precise thrusts that killed the man in seconds.

Harper gawked. "Holy shit... are you like a Navy SEAL or something?"

Cliff stood, waving them to keep going. "Nah. Army."

She trotted along after him, dragging Madison who struggled to keep up. "Seriously? Army? Which part?"

Cliff checked over the rifle he'd grabbed from the gang thug as he ran. "My last tour was with the Seventy-Fifth Ranger Battalion."

"Oh," said Harper, shrugging. That sounded pretty impressive, whatever it meant. "Cool. Kinda overkill for mall security, isn't it?"

"Hah." He laughed. "Like I said, I saw enough crap to last a lifetime over there. Wanted something quiet."

"Sorry for shoplifting," said Harper. "Thanks for letting me just go home."

"It's okay, kid. Geez, you were scared shitless. I couldn't do it to ya." He chuckled. "Now those little punks with the bad attitudes, they needed the object lesson."

Warmth spread over Harper's cheeks. Yeah, maybe she had been terrified. Probably why she never shoplifted again—or spoke to Denise after that. The girl dared her to steal as a 'coolness test.'

A faint clatter came from behind, but Harper ignored it.

"Harp! My phone!" wailed Madison. "I dropped it."

"It's dead," said Cliff. "Junk."

Madison burst into tears, wailing, "But my friends are gonna call me! I don't wanna miss it if Becca, Melissa, or Eva text me!"

Harper kept going, grimacing at the heart-rending sobs coming from her little sister. The phone *was* junk. It would never work again. Even if it somehow came back to life, the whole cellular network had been fried.

"Harp! Please!" Madison set her heels, her flip-flops becoming tiny surfboards sliding over the blacktop. "My phone."

It was pointless, but… it did make her feel better. Harper slowed to a stop. "Okay. Hurry up."

Cliff spun, raising the rifle to cover the rear as Madison sprinted back for the gleaming patch of black glass on the road. Harper ran with her, refusing to let her sister get more than an arm's length away.

A handful of gangers popped out of a doorway nearby on the left. One charged straight at what he must've thought an easy grab of a child, and about shit himself when Harper shoved Madison aside and raised the Mossberg. The other two fired down the street toward Cliff.

Harper squeezed the trigger. Madison clamped her hands over her ears and fell on top of her phone, cringing from the noise. The ganger who'd come running at her lurched to a halt as his chest erupted in a ripple of red spots. Harper pumped and fired again, reducing his face to a ruin of flesh. In her blurry awareness of the world behind him, the other two thugs collapsed dead on the steps of the building they'd come from.

She glanced back at Cliff, who must've taken them out with the rifle.

Harper grabbed for Madison's arm. The girl swiped her phone from the road, still sobbing, and darted away from her toward Cliff so fast she ran straight out of her flip-flops. Harper picked them up and raced after her.

"I'm sorry!" wailed Madison. She flew into a hug, wrapping her arms around Cliff and bawling, her face buried against his chest.

Harper slowed to a nervous jog when she noticed the blood running down his arm.

"Just a through-and-through," said Cliff. "Keep going."

She looked down.

"It's fine." Cliff patted Harper's shoulder and muttered, "Kid needed it."

Madison let go of Cliff and pounce-hugged Harper, sniffling.

"C'mon, termite. We gotta get out of here before more bad guys show up." Harper dropped her sister's flip-flops.

"'Kay." Madison stepped into her shoes and took Harper's hand.

They walked for hours, mercifully free of contact with any more members of the gang. For much of their journey, they passed by lines of abandoned cars left in place when the EMP washed over everything. By early evening, they reached a clearing of scrub brush in a swath of land between Lakewood and the beginnings of mountainous terrain.

Cliff guided them to a spot where they could rest and shrugged off his backpack. While Jonathan and Madison wandered off in different directions to pee, he dug a small box out of the backpack and handed it to Harper. Next, he unpacked a glass bottle of clear liquid.

She looked down at it. "Sewing kit?"

"Yeah. There's tweezers in there too." Cliff pulled his sleeve up, exposing a bullet wound on his bicep. "Gonna need you to dig the slug out and sew the sucker closed. Toss a splash of this in the hole after the slug's gone."

"What is it?"

"Everclear."

"Booze?"

He nodded. "Almost pure alcohol."

She squirmed. "You want me to like sew *you*?"

Cliff leaned closer, giving her a flat look. "Cellular plans are getting expensive these days."

"Sorry." Harper bit her lip. "I know it's broken, but I couldn't make her—"

"Yeah, I get it. No harm, no foul. Just do the thing."

Jonathan, evidently aware of what went on with the needle-and-thread, occupied Madison a safe distance away so she wouldn't see the amateur surgery. The two of them practiced a few dance moves, which appeared to pull Madison out of her shell, at least for a little while.

Cringing every step of the way, Harper knelt beside him and picked at the wound with the tweezers until she unearthed a deformed pistol slug. Though he grimaced plenty and turned bright red, Cliff barely made a sound the whole time, even as she splashed Everclear into the hole and stitched it up.

Watching him withstand pain like that got her hands shaking. "You're like the terminator of mall security."

He forced a chuckle. "Is that my cue to say something cheesy like *I'll be back*?"

"I don't wanna go back there." Harper squinted into the wind, staring over her shoulder in the direction of Lakewood. "It's not my home anymore. There's nothing there but bad memories." She let out a long breath. "So, umm. Now what?"

"Now," said Cliff, snagging the bottle of Everclear. Much to Harper's surprise, he capped it rather than drank. "We head on up to Evergreen and hope what you heard was right."

She nodded, then leaned in to rest her head on his un-shot shoulder. "Okay. Thank you. Are you gonna stay with us?"

"Hmm." He patted her back. "Yeah. Maybe I can do that. You don't seem like the 'alone type.'"

Harper smiled, watching her sister and Jonathan dancing about and grinning at each other. The two of them became fast friends. Madison had always been slow to make friends, hence only having three—but she made *close* friends. Despite him being the only other kid her age around, she warmed to him abnormally fast. *Guess I'm not the only one who's changed.* She took a couple shells from her purse and stuffed them into the Mossberg. "I used to be so shy and timid."

"Used to?" asked Cliff. "Got over it?"

She racked the pump, chambering a round. "Yeah. Stupid nuclear war."

Cliff laughed. "Ready to get going?"

"Yeah. You?"

He rolled his left arm around at the shoulder. "Hurts like hell, but I'll deal with it."

"Cool. I guess we should keep walking. Evergreen or bust."

Cliff groaned as he stood. "Never say that. The 'or bust' part. Don't taunt luck."

"Sorry." She waved for the kids to come back over. "After you."

Cliff led the way down the road. Harper followed a step behind and a little to the right, scanning their surroundings for any sign of danger. She couldn't figure out exactly at what point she had gone from being afraid to leave home for college to patrolling the highways with a loaded shotgun. The world had plunged into utter chaos, but she'd do whatever it took to protect the family she had left.

Her lips curled in a furtive smile at Cliff's back.

Maybe even the new family she'd found.

"Can we stop at Starbucks?" asked Madison.

"I'll think about it," said Cliff. "All that sugar's no good for ya."

The kids laughed.

As did Harper.

III

OUROBOROS

ABOUT OUROBOROS

Of the stories I wrote for the anthology submission from my former publisher, this one came both from my fondness for cyberpunk stories as well as a book I'd read that followed a certain unique structure. It gave me the idea to write something with a similar structure to the story.

Ouroboros is set in a unique world, though I did end up using the MU (monetary units) terminology in the setting for the Progenitor novels later on. One note of trivia. A few years before I wrote this story, I worked at a place in center city Philadelphia, and took the train in each morning. The train had a stop essentially in the basement of the building where I worked and every day I walked past a Cinnabon store. For the most part, I resisted the temptation but surrendered once or twice a month.

3

OUROBOROS

S hock.

A splintering of electrical impulses spread over Eric's brain, prickling needles marching in endless waves. Blue lightning arced across a world of glossy silicon black, shimmering into a brilliant oblivion at the distant horizon. The ground shattered into a thousand onyx shards.

Silence.

Eric shot upright in his well-worn chair. The presence of reality crashed into his sensorium, a paralytic cascade of sound, as oppressive as if he'd surfaced out from a silent lake into an unruly crowd. Painfully loud squeaking came from the ceiling fan overhead. The whirring of distant electronics hurt like a wood chipper gnawing on his skull. Even the wind outside seemed loud enough to strip the skin off his body. The holographic panel in front of his face offered no information, merely a devouring black void.

He pressed a hand to his head behind his left ear, squinting at the excruciating brightness in the window. The pine trees wavering on the far side of the street shifted to silver before the radiant glow engulfed them. It hurt too much to continue looking. He tentatively probed around the spot where the wire usually connected him to cyberspace. The tiny metal socket embedded in his skin behind his ear burned his fingertip.

He yanked his hand back, his palm covered in blood. Too out of it to feel worried, he rubbed his thumb back and forth over the slick red liquid in an attempt to disbelieve his eyes. *Dammit.* At least he had a stash of tissues within reach of the workstation. He closed his hand around material as coarse as absorbent sandpaper. Astonishment at having the ability to feel every individual fiber gave way to wonder at the overpowering smell of coffee from the empty cup on the desk. A solitary fly on a stack of take-out food containers cleaned its mouthparts. The raking scratch of insect legs ended when it sensed him staring.

Boom.

Eric recoiled into a ball and trembled, trying to overcome the reflex twisting him into an impression of a yogic master on his chair. A woman stood in the doorway, her feminine silhouette outlined by the nuclear glow from an over-amped sun behind her. She slid inside, closing the door behind her as he lowered his arm.

"Crap! Sarah," rasped Eric. "You scared the shit out of me."

He uncurled, stretching his legs out in search of carpet. For a moment, she stood a half step from the door. She gave him the same disdainful frown she always did whenever she caught him after he'd been up all night. He stared transfixed at her legs, covered in sheer black stockings. Sarah moved with feline grace past the bed to stand beside him, arms folded. Eric lifted his gaze from her legs to the sleeves of her grey skirt-suit. The fabric creaked as she moved.

"You didn't sleep at all, did you?" Her disapproving smirk relaxed to an expression of doting concern. She tapped the flat silver box to the left of the holo-display, causing a blinding flash of teal light to appear above it. "You've got to be at work in two hours. Why do you keep doing this to yourself?"

Eric curled and relaxed his fingers, idly scratching at his bare chest, wondering if he hallucinated the creaking sound from his ribs trying to force their way out through his skin. How long ago had he eaten anything? He'd become too thin. His black and white striped pajama pants would fall off him if he stood too fast.

"Thanks." His raspy voice hurt his ears, yet still sounded as though it came from far away.

He looked up. Sarah curled her violet lips into a frisky smile, her green eyes glinting. She slid into his lap, hiking up her skirt and tilting her head. The left side of her hair, maraschino red, dangled past her shoulder. The white half glowed from the horrible fiery thing in the sky. He squinted, trembling as the devouring glow seeped past the window, consuming the walls, the apartment, the woman he loved.

Vertigo overcame him. He struggled to lift his leaden arms as she leaned in and kissed him. Silver gleamed in the periphery of his vision, a small datapad on the desk. *The codes. I got them. What happened? I don't remember logging out. Something must have ambushed me; that explains why I'm so messed up.* He dug his fingernails into the armrests.

Sarah reached under his pajama pants and grabbed him. Her touch sent a lightning bolt up his spine, so painful he couldn't move or scream, merely gasp as she caressed him. Hypersensitive neurons screamed as if his skin peeled away.

She stopped, scrunching her nose at him. "What the devil's wrong with you? You're looking at me like I'm about to tear it off."

Pins and needles accompanied his exhale, as if flakes of solid matter peeled away from the inside of his lungs and whirled around inside his chest. "Cortical bloom. Senses on overdrive. Your hands... so cold they burn."

"So, touch me then..." She took his hand and guided it up under her skirt.

A trail of blood tickled down the left side of his neck. *How can she not see that?* He touched her. He kissed her. She moaned. Her scent flooded him. *Is this what it's like for dogs?* Eric covered his face before the overpowering aroma made him sick, but his fingers carried her fragrance. He loved her scent, but not at a thousand times intensity. He heaved.

Sarah pushed him away and stood. "Dammit, Eric. Are you still high?" She twisted his arm over, staring at a row of four thumbnail-sized onyx hexagons lined up below his wrist. "You idiot! You know this shit will kill you." She flung his arm back at him and adjusted her clothes. The numb limb bounced off his chest and fell into his lap, unresponsive. "You know I love you, but we can't go on like this. You have a real job, a good one. Why do you insist on throwing your life away into cyberspace? Those boosters are gonna kill you."

He stared at her as she tapped her foot, waiting for a reply he couldn't provide. It's not as though he didn't want to... he did—his voice disobeyed.

"Don't do this to me Eric. Dammit, you look like you got your ass kicked in there this time. Do you want me to call you out sick?"

"Nmmm," he mumbled.

"Okay then, well... you better not be late. Do you need me to help you shower?"

"Nmmmm." Eric slouched forward, elbows to knees, palms to

forehead. Her scent clung to everywhere, cloying, nauseating. He'd be inhaling her all day. He scrunched up his face and breathed. *Progress. I can't hear my alveoli screaming anymore.* "I'm… ngh. Sorry. Some cutty bastard musta snuck me from behind." His eyes opened to slits. The angle of his head brought the interface plug into view. It dangled off the desk, a pendulum swinging inches above the carpet, smeared with blood. He didn't remember pulling it out.

"We can talk over dinner." Sarah crossed the tiny apartment back to the door. "Eric…"

He looked up, squinting at the glaring light framing her silhouette. "Ngh?"

"I love you; please don't get yourself killed out there." She sighed. "Think about what losing you is going to do to me, okay? You really need to stop using that crap before it kills you."

"Yeah, I know. If this works out, I won't ever need to plug in again."

He forced a smile until she ducked out, letting it fade as the door squeaked closed on pneumatic rails. Grumbling, he grabbed the desk and wobbled to his feet, purposefully walking out of his pajamas and leaving them on the floor. Naked, he stumbled over some forty feet of cobalt-hued carpeting to the bathroom. The white tile floor may as well have been dry ice. Stepping on it hurt marginally less than walking over razor blades. He clenched his jaw, focused on the idea the pain was a lie, and trudged into the shower. The frosted glass panel slid closed automatically.

"Wash, on. Temp preset three."

Water erupted from four holes in a diamond pattern on a mirror-finished square above him. Rivulets of blood wound their way down his chest in the warm spray. The sight of it made him crave vanilla ice cream with cherry syrup. The thought of food hit him with the force of a gut punch. He grunted again, clutching his stomach. Crimson faded from the flow. He stared at the jet-black hexagons, tiny panels adhered to his flesh. Water beaded on them. Each one contained a dot of Corbo, a military grade stimulant officially known as Parietal-Occipital Cortex Booster F91C. Eric laughed, or at least the impulse to laugh formed in his brain. Only a weak smile made it to the end of the nerves. *No wonder they shortened it to Corbo.*

He hooked a fingernail under the dermal patches and flicked them off, making gunshot noises each time one fell away. Faint pink hexagonal marks remained. He stretched, yawned, then grabbed the soap gel. It didn't choke him with an overpowering stink of artificial pine. At the lack of fragrance, he held the canister to his nose, sniffing. Now he couldn't smell anything at all, nor could he feel the water striking him. He fixated on the bright green soap gel, trying to recall what it *should* smell like. He remembered a muskiness overwhelming him, a woman. The soap should be many times more pungent a fragrance than her, but had no scent whatsoever.

This is new. Senses should fade back to normal, not go away. He rubbed his eyes and grunted. *She's right. I gotta lay off.*

Eric twisted, peering out past the frosted glass at his empty apartment. It felt like an hour ago he'd walked to the shower chamber. *Was someone here?* He pressed a hand to the glass, unable to tell if she'd really been there. *Sarah?*

FOR THE THIRD TIME, ERIC VISITED THE MIRROR TO VERIFY THE BROWN, DEAD hedgehog on top of his head looked at least somewhat presentable. Satisfied—rather taking 'as good as it will get'—he went outside. The door chimed to indicate the security system came on. A weak AI voice wished him a pleasant day at work. He jogged down a long flying stairway on the outside of the building. At the bottom, he glanced up at the individual slabs protruding from the wall. *I'm amazed I haven't fallen off yet… I need to complain to Hargreaves about getting a railing put in.*

The fireball in the sky no longer burned the retinas out of his eyes. The birds had gone silent. Intense sunlight washed the color out of the street before him, paling everything to weak ghosts of their natural hues. Traffic seemed unusually light, causing him to keep checking the time, fearing he'd overslept far worse than he had. Marko didn't meet him standing on his usual corner.

Eric scrunched his hands and rubbed the datapad in his breast pocket. He'd used the last of his Corbo stash to get the precious data in his pocket. Being out left made him anxious. The chem didn't cause addiction in the brain, but it had become a crutch. Taking on defense programs in cyberspace without it felt like trying to beat a car in a footrace. The latest generation software countermeasures were too much for his rig. Even *with* Corbo, he barely got past them. Then again, if things worked out, he wouldn't need much of anything from a chem merchant ever again. Sarah would like that. They'd have to leave the country, but who cared. Every country had become more or less the same. Only the food and slang changed.

Dingy apartments drifted by for two blocks until he ducked into the turnstile of the nearest Mantra station. Eric rolled his eyes at the marketing weasels who mined the gem of a name from *Humanity Transporter*. A little girl seated halfway up the steps to the monorail platform held out dirty hands as he approached. Barefoot, in a tattered grey dress, she looked as though she hadn't eaten in days.

Eric stopped in front of her, fumbling around his pockets. In his suit coat, he found a static bankstick he didn't recall having. The display read 34 MU. He handed it to her. "Here, kid. There's still thirty-four cows on it, should be enough to at least get one breakfast combo."

She leapt up to stand, took it, and clutched the tiny plastic device to her chest. "Thank you, mister!"

He took two more steps before he realized she had Sarah's face, an adult head on a nine-year-old's body. Falling into the railing, he whirled to look at her as she darted off toward a McKing. He couldn't see her face from behind; long, black hair trailed after her. *Not Sarah. Maybe she's right. Maybe I should lay off the boosters for a while. My brain's playing games on me. Too much info comin' from a plug instead of meatspace.*

The monorail slid to a halt within a second of his arrival on the green-tiled platform a story and a half above street level. It looked about three-quarters full, but he found a door and boarded without bumping shoulders. An older black gentleman adjacent to the nearest open seat didn't even look at him as he sat down. Eric set his briefcase across his lap, leaned back, and closed his eyes.

"Sir," said a pleasant female voice before he could take a full breath. "Sir, this is your stop."

Eric jumped. A shimmering woman in a railway uniform stood in the aisle next to him. Sporadic image shifts as well as her glowing radiance made no secret of her being a hologram. He glanced to his right. The old man was gone; the scene outside the window appeared to be the monorail station inside his office building. He glanced back to the attendant, mouth opening to speak, but stopped. None of the people on the tram when he boarded remained. Everyone around him looked entirely different.

"Uhh, thanks. I must've nodded off." He smiled at the disappearing ghost and stood up. "Sorry for the delay, everyone."

As soon as he stepped onto the platform, the Mantra took off. He gazed at it until the last car vanished into the blackness of an engulfing tunnel. *Did I even sleep?*

Cinnamon. The smell hit him hard, not for what it was, but because he smelled it. He clasped his hand once more over his face. A passing woman glanced at him; flash of maraschino red. He blinked.

"Sarah? Weren't you wearing grey?"

The woman spun to give him a quizzical look. Chinese. Black hair.

"Oh, sorry. Thought you were someone else. I just woke up. My fiancée is wearing the same outfit."

She offered a nervous smile and took a few steps faster away. *Cinnamon.* He looked up and to the right at a small kiosk selling cinnamon rolls and coffee. He got in line as a subconscious reflex, no conscious thought involved. The malaise lurking in his gut since he awoke morphed into a desperate craving for food. He didn't make eye contact with the teen girl behind the counter while staring up at the board, vaguely aware of someone with red and white hair and green eyes in front of him.

Keep it together, man. Bad trip. It's not Sarah. "I'll have a cinnamon roll, regular, and a large coffee… black, please."

"They're watching you, sir."

"What?" Eric jumped.

She leaned closer. "Thirty-two MUs, sir."

Fear gripped him. Fear he would look down and find *her*. *She even sounds like Sarah.* He closed his eyes, extending his right hand; the wristwatch-sized faceless device on his arm chirped with a tiny digitized voice.

"Transaction approved, thirty-two monetary units transferred to CinnaCrave Corporation."

"Your order will be ready in a moment, sir. New batch just came out. I'll give you one of the gooey ones."

He smiled, still not looking down from the menus. "Your name's not Sarah, is it?"

"No, sir. It's Kelly."

Eric lowered his gaze. Barely five-foot tall, pale, round face, jet-black hair with streaks of violet, deep blue eyes capable of devouring a soul. She appeared to be sixteen, if even. *Is she that pretty or am I that happy I'm not seeing Sarah?*

The smiling girl slid a paper carton and cup over the counter. An hour ago, the scrape would have been deafening. It barely registered over the din of the station.

"Thanks, Kelly." He took his food then followed the crowd to the moving staircase.

Cinnamon flooded the air as the escalator carried him to the lobby along a pale titanium-green tube awash with the life-sucking glow of fluorescent light. A handful of people rode the other half downward. A flash of red, stark against the blandness, caught his eye. Sarah glanced at him from the descending side. He locked eyes until distance moved her out of his field of vision. Sweat trickled down his face. He spun and searched, but found no one with red-white hair. Shivering, he faced forward and shoved the coffee cup against his mouth. Too hot to enjoy, but he wanted the pain—and the caffeine—more than the flavor.

At the top, Eric walked through a lobby of faux marble and gold without taking his eyes off the dark forest-green tiles. Navigating by memory, he made it to the elevator with minimal collisions and jabbed the button, his finger doing an impression of a woodpecker.

"Yo, Morris... You okay?"

He glanced to his left at a dark-skinned man in a pale beige suit, Ravinder, from the compatibility team. A cyan strip of light hovered in midair in front of the man's eyes, the newest wearable internet. Eric pitied him; how it must suck to work tweaking someone else's code to make it run across multiple platforms. The poor bastards on the compatibility team didn't get to be creative.

Eric slouched, staring down. "Yeah, fine. I had a late night."

Ravinder chuckled, letting him in the elevator first. "You look paranoid, man. Shaking, sweaty, all edgy and stuff. If I didn't know better, I'd think Sector Patrol was after you."

Mention of Sector Patrol wasn't the kind of thing Eric wanted to hear while carrying the kind of information he had in his pocket at that moment. He played it off with a weak smile. "I had a late night... Was close to making level and just kept going."

"Heh." Ravinder clapped him on the shoulder. "Been there. You should join me over on the Tao server. So, did you get the codes?"

"What?" Eric jumped into the wall. Scalding coffee splashed on the back of his right hand. "W-what are you talking about?"

Ravinder blinked. "Uhh... Codex? You know? The last you told me, your ranger was level 43. Level 44 is when you can get the Codex and unlock the winged mount."

"Oh." Eric laughed—a noise so sudden and harsh it made the other man jump. "Yeah… I got the Codex last week. Had it in inventory before I made level."

Ding.

The elevator opened. Eric ducked away and down the row of cubes and peered through an opening in the tan cloth-covered partitions at a desk. Ed Jones, all three hundred ninety pounds of him, smiled back at him from a desk portrait—with his arm around Sarah.

He spun away. Three quick steps. Another opening, another empty chair. Gina Alvarez had a dozen photos on her desk, most of her kids. Eric stared at the big one in the center, two women embracing: Gina hugging Sarah.

Not good. Not good. Coffee wobbled out of his cup from a shaking hand. *The drugs should've worn off by now.*

He walked faster, but the urge to look overwhelmed his panic. Every desk he passed, Sarah's face put itself in place of every woman in photos, even the cartoons hung up on cube walls. Only Adam, who had married his companion Nathaniel a year ago, had a workspace free from Sarah's presence. He lingered for a moment there, staring at some of the powder-blue ribbons from the office party. Adam's '2064 Employee of the Year' trophy mocked him. The skyscraper-shaped block of angle-cut crystal looked heavy enough to beat a man to death with. It reminded him of daydreaming about doing it.

Five grand and an extra two-week vacation. Not Adam's fault Robert's a backstabbing asshole.

The cinnamon roll was getting cold, but the coffee had finally reached the perfect drinking temperature. *What is wrong with me? Why do I want to run away from her? I… We're going to get married. Is that it? Am I having jitters? No. I want to see her—just not everywhere, not where she shouldn't be. Shit. It's been an hour. I shouldn't still be seeing her. I should take Adam's trophy and have a chat with Marko.*

Eric wandered two desks down the aisle and fell into his chair like a tossed corpse. Sensing his presence, his desk terminal lit up with five holographic screens bathing his workspace in a pale glow. Email, spreadsheet programs, incoming financial data feeds, more numbers than he had ever wanted to see in one place. Ignoring it, he opened the carton and stared at the gooey treasure. A strong wave of cinnamon flooded his nostrils. *Shit, I forgot to grab a fork. I can't eat this mess with my hands.*

He got up and took a step before his stomach roared; he doubled back and grabbed the precious confection to carry with him. *Someone will swipe it if I leave it undefended.* The break room waited half a floor away, less than a minute walk. He scurried, clinging to the baked precious as though it would save the world. Head down, he refused to look into any more cubes. Once he reached the café space, a frenzied rummage of drawers began in earnest. *Fork... Fork... Fork...*

"Eric?"

"Fork!" he shouted, whirling on the source of the voice with plastic utensil and eyebrows raised, lips curled back.

Nosferatu of Cinnamon.

Colleen Michaels screamed. The somewhat heavyset blonde tipped back into the wall, fanning herself. Eric held the black plastic utensil even higher, like a holy relic capable of warding away any threats.

"Fork." He relaxed his stance. "I... needed a fork." He tapped the utensil on the paper carton. "CinnaCrave. Got a gooey one. Too messy to eat without a fork."

"They know. You'll never get away with it," said Colleen, her voice seemingly echoing over the entire building.

He bared his lack of fangs again. Tension pulsed in his forehead. "What?"

"Earth to Eric? I said 'that blows, you need to get laid.'"

He flashed an insincere smile at her. "That an offer?" A hot flash swept over him. *Shit. She's gonna go to HR. Dammit! Why did I say that?* He changed to a cheesy smile, hoping she took it to mean 'just kidding.'

She smirked. "Are you completely nuts? My husband would kill you."

"Sorry. Know you're married. Lame joke," he muttered.

Clinging to the cinnamon roll, he remained motionless. She wandered off, shaking her head. Once she vanished behind lifeless grey cube walls, he checked both ways and began the long hundred-meter scurry back to his cube. Halfway there, a flash of maraschino red caught his eye. On the other side of the office, beyond two long rows of pane glass, Sarah walked in slow motion among a crowd, gliding as if everyone around her existed in slow motion. She stared at him, flashing a faint smile. Her violet lipstick caught the light, gleaming. Her clothing had changed—a dark pantsuit with a broach made of five silver spheres. Anita Brown, CTO wore that. Eric blinked. Sarah's legs turned dark, chocolate poured over ivory. He looked up, caught like a deer in the headlights of the older executive's quizzical look.

Oh, shit. She's going to think I'm crazy. She can't know. None of them could possibly know. He smiled, keeping his gaze on the floor the rest of the way back to his desk, eager to enjoy his cinnamon feast.

ONLY A BITE-SIZED NUGGET REMAINED OF THE GARGANTUAN CONFECTION AN hour later. Eric picked at it while sifting through Monday morning emails and getting back into his routine of code grinding. The office terminals didn't allow users into the normal VR world of cyberspace, but plugging in allowed him to generate programs much faster than typing. He slid the wire into the socket behind his ear with a *click* that echoed in his skull. Slumped in his seat, he stared at holographic terminals, watching program lines appear as fast as he could think them up.

His latest assignment was investment optimization software for the banking industry. Robert Carlson, his immediate supervisor, had come up with some fancy algorithm to predict ebbs and flows in the market, and wasn't sharing it with anyone. The rest of the team worked on the skeleton of a software package to interface it with dozens of different financial systems. When they finished, the big man got to put the star on the top of the tree. If it worked, the company stood to make billions and most of the employees wouldn't see a bit of it. If it tanked, they'd all be out of work.

He didn't plan to be around for it either way.

Eric patted the datapad in his breast pocket. Code formed on screen for as long as it took him to enjoy the last of the coffee. Two hours after arriving in the offices of Echelon Capital Management Corporation, Eric Morris finally felt ready. He tossed the empty cup into the trash, making an easy basket. He rose out of his chair enough to prairie-dog over the cube walls and look around. Sounds of office work surrounded him, yet no one in sight. No one watching. Ten years of rule following would come to a sudden end.

Perfect.

Out came the datapad. The programming interface slid to the left. A login screen, green on black, appeared. He liked the retro look. Lines of text formed in front of him; the voice of his supervisor spoke them in his mind.

Echelon_Login: RCarlson

Password: ********

"Good Morning, Robert." A woman's voice replied in his brain.

I've just broken the law. Eric covered his mouth to stifle a nervous giggle. *That's why I'm seeing her everywhere. Freaking out with nerves.*

The monochrome terminal flew forward, appearing to burst out of the holographic screen. Eric sailed headfirst into a kaleidoscopic tunnel of light that led to the Junior VP's workspace. His attention focused on an icon in the shape of a safe. He reached down the illusory tunnel into his drawer, grasping a secondary wire while again rising up only enough to stare over the cube walls. Still, no one in sight. He sank into the chair, a wasted husk of a man in a suit two sizes too big. Grinning, he unplugged the wire from his head. All the pretty lights and shifting images vanished in an instant. Eric snapped the first lead into the datapad, the other, he ran from the little device into his head. Two lines of left-shifting image crawled up his intangible display screens.

Again, he concentrated on the tiny safe. This time he blinked at it.

The female voice spoke into his mind again. "Authentication Required. The requested file has been secured via Neuronal Map. Please wait."

Eric whimpered. *The AI sounds like Sarah.* He squeezed the little pad until his knuckles whitened. The code he obtained last night, almost died to get, contained a false brain print. It had to work. If the system detected the forgery, they would trace it to his login point and he wouldn't be safe anywhere in the NatUnion; he'd have to go to the third world.

A rainbow image of a brain appeared on the two-by-two-inch screen in his hand, rotating.

"Neuronal Map Accepted. Please speak the access code for voiceprint validation."

He resisted the urge to wipe the bead of sweat trailing down the left side of his head. Irrational fear said it would flow into the wireport and cause a fatal shock. He blinked. *No. They don't do that.* Hand shaking, he tapped one finger at the datapad to play the passphrase identification. A green line wavered on its little screen as another man's voice flooded his brain.

"Robert Carlson – Junior Vice President, development. Big fish eats little fish. I eat the big fish."

You conceited fucker. Eric scowled. He'd half expected it to be 'I hate Eric.'

"Access granted."

A sudden high of adrenaline killed his hesitation. Eric mentally dove into the safe. The icon expanded to fill the screen, then extended out into the world around him. Due to office policy, the simulation took on the appearance of transparent illusion rather than solid VR. Shelves full of file tags slid past him on both sides. *I know you've been skimming, Robert. Your prize algorithm is a load of shit. It's a worm.* File after file passed by his searching hands until he found one that felt right. *There you are...* An object resembling an old cigar box morphed into a treasure chest when he brushed the 'dust' away from it.

The ornate container opened. Eric passed through the tiny opening, falling downward into a spiraling tornado of numbers. He floated into the company accounts. The routine he had written six months ago for this moment leapt out of the datapad and slithered away into the network. Five minutes from now, the bulk of Echelon Capital's... capital, would be swimming into a series of carefully hidden bank accounts, all disguised under false names and identities he'd spent over a year putting together to appear as legitimate as possible. His program would transfer the money around in small amounts, filtering it over 200,000 individual identity records before it trickled into a single pool he and Sarah could live like royalty from. It would take the authorities ten years to follow the money. By then, they'd be long gone. He'd take everything the company had plus the twenty-three billion Mr. Carlson had been nice enough to skim from clients.

I always said if I was gonna break the law, I'd do it big. Big enough to never have to work again.

When the dust settled, they would be rich. Him and Sarah. Somewhere in the Islands, perhaps Cuba. Maybe Central America. They'd go to a place they could disappear. She was fond of Jamaica, even if she had the complexion of a ghost. Eric sat back in the chair, picking at his lip and grinning. Anticipation dulled his paranoia. A vurp refilled his mouth with the taste of acid and cinnamon. Three minutes from now, he wouldn't have a care in the world.

Ding.

He disconnected the wiring and tucked the datapad back into his breast pocket before leaning up out of his chair. On the far side of the break room, the elevator doors parted. Sarah walked in, now in a black jacket over a white shirt. Her matching knee-length skirt and flat shoes had Sector Patrol Investigations written all over it. The four men behind her, also in black suits and sunglasses, marched in military step.

He felt as though he'd been shot in the heart. *Sarah, working for the SecPats... how long? Did she ever care for me at all?* Tears rolled out of his eyes. The faint beep from behind him, the beep signaling he had become a rich man, meant nothing. Images of the two of them on a beach, clad only in sunlight, evaporated one after the next. He clasped the edge of the cube wall to keep from falling over and pulled himself up. What did it matter now? She was a lie. The company could have its money back; it would make them go easy on him at sentencing. Without her, nothing had any purpose or meaning.

Eric wept until his forehead hit the partition. A press of cold to his forehead hit him like a reset button to the brain. *Get a grip, man. That's not Sarah. I'm fucked in the head. I'm hallucinating.* He grabbed his left forearm, the place he always put the Corbo. *Damn drugs.*

He frowned at the desk across the narrow walkway. The photos of Tito and his wife now looked normal. Sarah's face had vanished. Tito's wife, whatever her name was, smiled at him with the same innocence as Sarah. One of the security men pointed at him. Eric sucked in a breath, hoping they would take him without the usual trouncing SecPat officers had a reputation for doling out.

Sarah's face isn't in the photo anymore.

He sprinted, hauling himself out into the walkway by a two-handed grip on the cloth-faced cubicle wall. The men split up, taking different paths across the cube farm to herd him toward not-Sarah. Sweat rained off his cheeks as he cornered around the end of the row. Poor Colleen never saw him coming. Her legs were in the air before she knew what hit her. Her lunch container rolled off to the side as he recovered his balance and went for the fire door.

A SecPat officer sprinted at him from the right, suit-jacket billowing in the air behind him, flickering azure light glinting from an earbud. Eric blinked, frozen with terror for a nanosecond. The man leapt. Like a sack of wheat, Eric dropped in place. The agent careened over him, committed to a tackle that claimed a small folding table.

Shrill wailing alarms erupted as Eric shoved the emergency door out of his way and bolted into a stairway of bare cinderblocks and grey-painted railings. The walls blurred; the horrible electronic screeching sickened him as if someone let off an air horn right at his ear. He moved as fast as he could stumble, hanging on the railing to avoid rolling down forty flights. At the bottom of the first landing, time dragged to an inexplicable crawl. A glint of copper caught his eye, a bullet descending amid a billowing cloud of black smoke and orange light. The agent's shouting drowned beneath the alarm.

Eric's mind, freed from the moment by the strange effect, focused on the spiraling projectile gliding butterfly-like toward the banister. Rather than land on it with gentle grace, it burrowed into the steel tube. Twisted, warped metal blasted forth as the railing warped in the direction of the bullet's flight. He couldn't get his arm up fast enough. A sliver of pain caught him in the cheek.

Time crashed back to normal like a slingshot launching him into the wall. The agent continued shouting, though the alarm made it impossible to understand him. *I have to find Sarah.* Eric ran down the stairs around corner after corner. He hugged the outer wall, trying to prevent the agent from getting a shot at him down the central shaft. Floors passed in a blur. Eventually, the scuff of his shoes on stairs overtook the siren. The sound carried louder and longer than he thought normal.

The smell of mold and rubber assaulted him when he burst through the door at the bottom into the parking garage. His third breath tasted like coolant from electric cars' power cells. He spun and slammed the door behind him, gazing around in search of something heavy enough to block the door with, but saw nothing.

It smashed open, driving him into the wall. Squeezed between the steel door and unpainted cinderblocks, he gurgled. Cinnamon and coffee mixed in the back of his throat. The SecPat agent took a few steps, somehow missing him there—likely assuming he had run off.

Beep.

"Hey, hon, it's me. Why aren't you picking up your desk phone? Guess you're in the bathroom or something. Gimme a call if you still want to meet for lunch." The sound of an air kiss ended Sarah's voicemail.

Shit. His throat dried out. *SecPat knows it's me. They're tracing me by phone.*

The massive agent whirled. Square-jawed, his head gleamed with the shine of polished chocolate. The incredulity in his eyes at finding his quarry right behind him lasted all of two seconds before it became rage. Eric curled his fingers around the side of the door and waved, offering a sheepish smile.

"Hi."

Growling, the agent flung himself into the door, crushing more cinnamon into Eric's throat before whipping the metal to the side, smashing it closed with a *boom* that reverberated across the parking deck. Eric, wheezing, wobbled to the side. Reaching for something, anything to grab so he did not fall on his ass, he wrapped his arms around the man. His fingers found purchase on a hard, rubbery object at the same moment the agent cracked him over the head with the handle of a giant pistol.

Eric slapped into the floor, his cheek skidding over the smooth concrete for several feet. Whatever he had grabbed remained in his hand. Adrenaline propelled him onward despite the throbbing pain in the back of his head. He crawled forward, avoiding a stomp by a fraction of an inch. When he rolled over, he found himself clutching a synthetic baton.

A sense of vertigo overtook him. The humble weapon inspired him like a magic artifact. Eric imagined himself online, calling on what he'd learned as a half-elf ranger. He rolled to the right as the big man kicked at him, winding up on his feet holding the weapon out like a broadsword. His opponent raised his gun; Eric lunged. Manic-eyed, he screamed and brought the baton around, striking the agent's gun hand. Fingers snapped, caught between the handle of the pistol and the carbon-fiber rod. The agent's scream of agony sounded like a barbarian war cry. The pistol clattered to the ground, bouncing along the inclined floor toward the street exit. Eric attacked again, striking the man on the chest and the head, but the giant agent seemed oblivious to his assault, hesitating only until the pain of broken fingers seemed to fade.

Eric thought it odd his strikes didn't cause damage numbers to appear in midair. The agent showed little reaction to the hits aside from a deepening sneer. Despite Eric's perfect form, he spent far too much time slouched in a chair exploring cyberspace to have any real muscle tone. The agent ducked the third swing, coming back with a left-handed uppercut to the chest. The hit lifted Eric off his feet and knocked him into a backward flip. He landed flat on his front, stunned and sliding. The baton skittered away into the parking garage.

Gasping in a desperate attempt to get some air past the cinnamon-coffee slime in his mouth, Eric patted at his chest, trying to activate a healing potion. Severe pain made it impossible to breathe or even remember his own name. He couldn't understand why the command to use a healing potion didn't do anything. His delirious gaze fell upon a jet-black handgun lying within arm's reach. Reality came crashing down. There would be no healing potion. No flying horse to get him out of here. *I really did steal billions of cows.* Today would either be the best day of his life, or the last one.

As soon as he went for the gun, the agent dove at him. Eric's hand hit the weapon as the enormous man landed on top of him, hauling him back and grabbing for his arm. Eric tucked into a ball, cradling the pistol to his stomach. A rain of fists tenderized his shoulders and back. With all his strength, he shifted, sliding the barrel between his side and left arm—and pulled the trigger.

Whump. Whump.

Clothing and bodies muffled two shots, but they still seemed loud enough to attract every Sector Patrol agent within fifty miles. Almost three hundred pounds of dead man slumped on top of him. His ribs hurt where the slide nicked him; his back burned from flakes of gunpowder burrowing into his skin. He lacked the will to move.

Well, I'm right fully screwed now. I gotta find her.

Holding his screams behind clenched teeth, Eric fought his way out from under the corpse. He kicked the body to distance himself from it and scrambled upright before running amid the cars and columns. He'd never been in here before. Only the wealthy bothered with personal cars. Insurance alone cost more than he made. *Well, not anymore.* He allowed himself a silly grin as abject terror became euphoria. For a few brilliant, blazing seconds, he was free of the corporation. How many people stumbled from one day to the next, always thinking about 'doing something,' but never having the balls to break routine. He'd broken routine in the biggest way possible. No more rat race for him. He had the nerve. He had the balls.

"Balls!" yelled Eric. He cackled and shot the window out of someone's e-Lexus.

If I live, I can afford a car. But I won't need one, not on the beach. He slid to a halt behind a large white vehicle halfway between SUV and car, and took out his phone. Fog rolled out from behind the tire, surrounding his knees in an otherworldly mist. A leak in the superconducting e-cell's cryo tank. *As much as these damn things cost, you'd think they'd not make pieces of garbage. Even cars had been designed to become obsolete in five years. Consumerism demanded constant upgrading, constant replacement. Nothing lasted. Everything disposable. Quick, cheap, use it once, throw it away, replace.*

Shoes scuffed across concrete. More agents arrived, two from an elevator, one from the stairs. His brief stint as an adrenaline junkie crashed, leaving him trembling. *They're going to find the dead guy. I can't stay here.* Eric squeezed his phone, trying to call Sarah. *Come on, pick up.* The device vibrated against his head. Vid mail. She didn't answer. Steps came closer. Crying, he held the phone out in front of him so Sarah's four-inch holographic head could appear, and raised the gun next to it. Time stopped, his breathing as loud as thunder.

"Hi, missed me," chirped Sarah. "You know what to do."

When the SecPat man came around the edge, Eric fired.

A massive slug spiraled out from the barrel of his weapon, every curved scratch from the rifling clear and distinct in the copper jacket. The spinning nugget crept forward and burrowed into the chest of a much smaller security man, closer to his size. His white shirt turned red, pulled into the wound in the projectile's wake. A spent casing leapt from the huge gun, tumbling as the slide slammed back. Shock ripples spread across the skin of Eric's hand. An explosion of blood spattered from the man's back.

Time resumed its flow. The slide racked forward.

I'm nuts. That's it. Too much Corbo baked the noodle. I'm dead. This is all happening in the last two seconds of my life.

The man collapsed in a gurgling heap. Shaking, Eric wiped his face on his left sleeve. Pain in his arm made him gasp. The spot he always put his boosters hurt to touch as if the skin had been flayed off.

A shower of glass bits pelted him as bullets riddled the vehicle he hid behind. Whimpering, he ducked and curled into a ball. At a pause in firing, he scrambled up and tried to run. He slipped in blood, but managed to avoid falling, loping up to an ungainly run that ended with a collision against a column a few yards later. He clung to the concrete to stay upright. A white pockmark blasted out of the dark grey stone three inches from his head. Eric screamed and sprinted, barely staying a few inches ahead of exploding car windows. Eight vehicles later, he ducked behind a black van, then jumped through a gap in the floor by an access ramp, leading one story down.

His shoes hit the concrete with an echoing *slap*. Eric let momentum take him down to a roll. He somersaulted and managed to crawl into a run a second before two more shots ricocheted behind him. *Stupid. Now I'm underground. What's the plan now? Kill them all? Stealing was bad enough. Oh, screw it. I've shot two SecPats already. They won't execute me any less for killing two more.*

Light flicked on up ahead, a small window in a booth. A short black woman in a company security guard's uniform, a massive spray of hair beneath her cap, emerged with her hand on a stun pistol. Still running, Eric raised his right arm up, waving the ridiculous, oversized handgun in her general direction.

"You, out," he shouted. "Get lost."

She froze. A second later, she jumped back into the guard station and slammed the door.

Beyond the security office, sunlight gleamed on shiny concrete floor. The building's south face sat one story lower than the north due to a steep hill on the cross street. Salvation. He sprinted away from the sound of oncoming SecPat officers, racing into a light crowd of pedestrians outside. A familiar voice shrieked to his left. Sarah. He spun; there she stood in a low-necked bright red dress almost too short to be worn in public.

"Sarah!" He grabbed her arm and pulled, but she resisted. "Come on, we have to go."

Something hit him in the side of the head. The scent of imitation leather came out of nowhere. A purse swung like a hammer, smushed into his cheek, hung motionless for one second stretched to ten. Time resumed. Sarah melted into someone else: black hair, dark, possibly Indian. The woman reared back to club him a third time.

He put a hand to the side of his cheek, startled back to real time by the slap of dress shoes on concrete and distant sirens. "Sorry... Thought you were someone else."

He ran, not waiting for her to respond—or hit him again. People screamed whenever they noticed the gun. He cringed and considered tossing the thing, but decided against it and tucked it under his arm, hiding it under his jacket. He looked a mess, but at least the black clothing concealed the blood from a casual glance. Men shouted behind him, the usual phrases 'stop,' 'freeze,' and 'drop the gun.' *Come off it, lads. You'd shoot me if not for the crowd in the way.* Eric glanced over his shoulder at the four men fighting pedestrians. They certainly looked as though they wanted to kill him.

Surprised they haven't started shooting already.

A block over, left turn, two blocks straight, right turn—down a hundred step escalator in an open-air mall, he pumped his legs until they burned. Out of complete randomness, he vaulted the counter of a steam-filled noodle bar in the food court, fleeing from shouted Cantonese as he barged across the tiny kitchen and out an alley door. He made it another half a block before his legs gave out, lungs ready to quit. The cooks' cursing petered out to a faint echo punctuated by the slam of a door. Hands on his knees, Eric gasped for breath while gazing at clouds of fog drifting over the trash-covered ground.

The taste of cinnamon burbled back into his throat.

Fifty-six billion MUs waited for him in a secure patch of network managed by the Swiss Financial Consortium. He had only to get of the NatUnion alive—and find the real Sarah.

He staggered onward for as long as he could force his body to go. Eventually, he collapsed, crawling between a dumpster and a large cardboard box. He sat with his back to the wall, cold handgun pressed to his face, elbows on his knees... and sobbed. All that work, all that planning. How could they possibly have known? How long had SecPat been watching him? Did they get Sarah? He pressed his thumb to the release. The magazine slid out. He held it up, examining the three remaining .50 cal bullets—two in the mag, one in the chamber. Light gleamed from the metal as he turned it, half inserting the magazine back in the weapon. *What am I doing? I killed two agents. They're not going to arrest me anymore.* He slid the mag into the handgrip; a palm-strike locked it the rest of the way.

Click.

"Eric?" asked a familiar woman.

He snapped his head up, letting his gun arm sag limp over his leg. Sarah emerged one alley down, wearing the black skirt-suit of a Sector Patrol detective. Maraschino red touched her shoulder on the left, a cascade of snow on the right. Despite the dimness, her eyes shone like emeralds, as if they had tiny LEDs embedded inside them. He let out a nervous laugh, crying and smiling at the same time.

"Is that really you?"

She walked closer, arms stiff at her sides. "You don't look good, sweetie. What happened?"

A glop of spit flew from his teeth, lofted by a sudden, strong cackle. "I'm havin' the worst day."

"You'll never believe what happened at Echelon, hon. Robert has been stealing from the company." She stopped two paces from him. "The Sector Patrol wanted to interview anyone who worked with him."

Sweat and blood mixed in trails down his face, beading on his upper lip. *They blamed Carlson? They just wanted to interview me, and I've shot two of them. I got away with the money, but now I'm boned.* A kicked-chicken cackle came out of him. Twisting his forehead into his left hand, he continued laughing like an insane man for almost a minute. Sarah stood patiently, still two steps away. At last, his face reddened, and he sucked in a great breath, lunging to his feet.

She backed up a step. "Easy, sweetie. There's no need to do anything rash."

"So all this then"—he waved the gun back and forth—"all this is some kind of misunderstanding? Some giant fucking cocked-up misunderstanding." Laughter. "Look, I don't know who you really are." He pointed the gun at her face. "I've been seeing you... seeing Sarah's face on everything female all damn day."

"Eric, you need to relax." She took a slow step closer; the click of her high heel on the alley seemed to echo over the entire city. "I told you, you're spending too much time on the net. It's not healthy. The Corbo's done damage."

He lowered his weapon, face twisted in a suspicious sneer. "What's your name?"

"Eric, it's me, Sarah. You're sick. Please, let me have the gun before you hurt someone."

"I don't think you're really Sarah." Eric punched himself with his left hand. When he looked up, she still stood there, still Sarah.

She flinched at the sudden motion. "Please, Eric. You're in way over your head now. I don't want them to kill you. They were after Carlson. We can say you had a stress breakdown. Toss the gun. No one will hurt you."

Tears ran down his face, sobs and laughter came in equal measure. She drew closer, the scent of her perfume washed over him.

"Why am I seeing her face on everyone?"

The woman who looked like the woman he loved leaned up and kissed him on the chin. "Calm down, sweetie. Breathe. Everything is going to be fine. You weren't in the mood this morning. We can do whatever you want right now."

A facial tic twitched his cheek. "You're not Sarah—you just look like her."

"It's me, Eric. I work for SecPat. It was supposed to be a surveillance operation. We were after Carlson. The job was never about you."

He cringed, shaking.

"Sweetie..." She reached for him, but he leaned back. "It was never about you. What we had is real. We can go back to that. You need to give me the gun and calm down."

She leaned in. Her lips met his. Her eyes closed.

Boom.

Blood leaked through her teeth, metallic on his tongue. Eyes popped open; sadness and betrayal mixed. She gasped and crumpled to the alley. A tiny silver pistol slid out of her right hand. The faint breeze teased her hair; eyes stared lifelessly at the clouds above. Crimson spread across her shirt, joined by a growing puddle on the pavement below her body. Eric stood over her, gaze fixed on the small gun. *She was trying to trick me.* All emotion left him. He stared into her eyes, waiting, watching, expecting her face to change.

It didn't.

Still Sarah.

He collapsed to his knees, limp arms dangling. A trickle of blood ran from the corner of her lips to join the pool.

"Sarah?" he whispered, breaking into sobs. "Sarah?"

Gathering her arm in both hands, he pressed the back of her hand to his cheek. Still warm.

"Sarah!" he screamed, and fell over her.

He touched her face.

"Fifty billion… I don't want it… I want you. Please come back. Undo. Load save game. You said it was a misunderstanding."

Eric sat on his heels, pulling Sarah's lifeless body into an embrace, apologizing in an endless cascade of blubbering pleas. He cradled the back of her head, stroking her hair. *Was she trying to warn me?* His mind raced to the little girl on the steps… with Sarah's face. All the pictures in the office, everyone he saw. They all stared at him with the same fearful eyes. They all knew what he would do.

His gaze fell to the street, to the small silver handgun lying amid a puddle of her blood. He pushed her upright, kissed her full on the lips, and eased her to the ground. Minutes passed. Still, he waited. Still, the body before him remained her.

He pressed the hot muzzle of his pistol under his chin.

"I'm sorry, Sarah."

Boom.

SHOCK.

A splintering of electrical impulses spread over Eric's brain, prickling needles marching in endless waves. Blue lightning arced across a world of glossy silicon black, shimmering into a brilliant oblivion at the distant horizon. The ground shattered into a thousand onyx shards.

Silence.

Eric shot upright in his well-worn chair. The presence of reality crashed into his sensorium, a paralytic cascade of sound, as oppressive as if he'd surfaced out from a silent lake into an unruly crowd. Painfully loud squeaking came from the ceiling fan overhead. The whirring of distant electronics hurt like a wood chipper gnawing on his skull. Even the wind outside seemed loud enough to strip the skin off his body. The holographic panel in front of his face offered no information, merely a devouring black void.

He pressed a hand to his head behind his left ear, squinting at the excruciating brightness in the window. The pine trees wavering on the far side of the street shifted to silver before the radiant glow engulfed them. It hurt too much to continue looking. He tentatively probed around the spot where the wire usually connected him to cyberspace. The tiny metal socket embedded in his skin behind his ear burned his fingertip.

He yanked his hand back, his palm covered in blood. Too out of it to feel worried, he rubbed his thumb back and forth over the slick red liquid in an attempt to disbelieve his eyes. *Dammit.* At least he had a stash of tissues within reach of the workstation. He closed his hand around material as coarse as absorbent sandpaper. Astonishment at having the ability to feel every individual fiber gave way to wonder at the overpowering smell of coffee from the empty cup on the desk. A solitary fly on a stack of take-out food containers cleaned its mouthparts. The raking scratch of insect legs ended when it sensed him staring.

Boom.

Eric recoiled into a ball and trembled, trying to overcome the reflex twisting him into an impression of a yogic master on his chair. A woman stood in the doorway, her feminine silhouette outlined by the nuclear glow from an over-amped sun behind her. She slid inside, closing the door behind her as he lowered his arm.

He stared at her in shock. Numb, he reached up to disconnect the wire from the socket behind his left ear. Sarah rounded the corner of the bed. He twisted the plug between two fingers as she neared. When she stopped, he let go, dropping the wire to fall against the side of the desk. He glanced down at his arm. Four Corbo hexagons formed a neat line upon a strip of angry purpled skin and open sores.

Part of him wanted to say *you scared the shit out of me.* He couldn't do anything more than stare, trembling.

"Eric?"

"Holy shit. You're alive!"

"You were online all night again, weren't you?" She shook her head, then surveyed the clothes strewn about the floor. "I can't keep going like this. You're killing yourself." She touched the flat silver box left of the holo-display and recoiled. "You've gotta be at work in two hours. I don't understand why you keep doing this to yourself. Robert's already looking for an excuse to fire you."

Eric glanced at the datapad, the precious codes.

He shifted his gaze back to Sarah. More precious.

She tilted her head; maraschino crept down her shirt. "What the devil's wrong with you, Eric?" After a moment, her look of concern shifted amorous. She slid her hands over his thighs toward his crotch. "Come on. We have at least twenty minutes."

He stood, not caring that his pants fell, and lifted her off her feet. "To hell with Robert. Got a feeling he's going to have a bad day. I'm calling out sick."

IV

A MESSAGE OF FATE

ABOUT A MESSAGE OF FATE

This is a quick story I wrote years ago as an introduction to my first fantasy roleplaying game system manual. Prior to me writing *Chronicles of Eldrinaath,* I'd developed a game simply called "Epic" that started in 1996 and monopolized most of my creative energies until 2014 or so. It is, alas, somewhat of an unwieldy beast mechanically speaking (the roleplaying game rules I mean) – but the setting is ripe for fiction writing.

Argathia is the same setting as my Epic (pun intended) fantasy novel *Of Myth and Shadow.* The tone of the story came from using it originally as an introduction to a never-published game manual. I wanted to set the stage for 'endless adventures' and it's a slight spin on the classic tale of an epic adventure about to begin.

I've added this story to the *Far Side of Promise* anthology at the suggestion of my editor since it's related to *Of Myth and Shadow,* which she quite enjoyed and wanted to read more stories set in that world.

4

A MESSAGE OF FATE

ldgar stopped walking, contemplating how in the lands he could have been talked into embarking on such a foolish endeavor as this journey. He couldn't explain how he, a Marn warrior with not too shabby a reputation, ended up playing travel guide to a bunch of toplanders trying to find some ancient hidden tomb or some such. The surface-dwellers who entered the mountains always had delusions of grandeur, always believed every little legend that filtered down into their tiny, exposed villages.

Chief Sargor Stonebeard must have seen something different in these outsiders in order for him to send Aldgar to take them up through the Boneclaw Range. For all the gems in Gharog Keep, he wished the job had gone to someone else.

"Why have we stopped?" asked Kaldoran, from a few paces behind.

Aldgar remained silent, rolling a pinch of his dark mahogany beard back and forth betwixt his thumb and forefinger. The wind at this altitude blew with the ferocity of a Marnish woman. He didn't much care for being out under wide-open skies, and would rather stay among his people, especially with his wife. For what reason had Sargor sent him out here to escort the foolish surface dwellers?

After a painfully long pause, Aldgar turned his gaze backward. Kaldoran, a Knight of the order of Arakain, watched him with a pensive expression of curiosity. Twice the Marn's height, the Aeron's already large presence seemed even more so thanks to a huge pair of bronze wings framing his form in a shimmering aura of coppery light. The man's armored helm hid most of his face except for his red eyes.

Perhaps he is a capable warrior. Aldgar locked stares. The eyes easily betrayed many a wet-nosed boy, but the Aeron showed no sign of fear, hesitation, or doubt.

"Just waitin' fer tha lass to catch up," barked Algar, gesturing at the slender Isian bringing up the rear of the group.

Generally, Marns respected Isians, as both groups lived primarily underground. Unfortunately, the Isians had too much in common with elves, being slight of body and—in his opinion—feeble in battle. This woman in particular, named Isa, happened to be a wizard or such, and soft. She didn't complain or protest, though her slow progress proved her unsuited to the rigors of overland travel, especially high in the mountains.

Behind the Aeron, a man named Cyric broke up into fits of snickering while watching Isa struggle to make her way up the mountain trail. The snicker brought Aldgar's attention once again disdainfully on the human member of the group who had yet to prove himself capable of being useful for anything more than wasting food on a pointless existence. How could a man well into his twenties not wear a shred of real armor? Aldgar grumbled to himself at how a man could call himself a warrior and parade around with only leather as a defense.

Cyric didn't even carry a real weapon, only an assortment of daggers. He also never seemed to be around when things got rough. Yet, he had the gall to laugh at the short, slender Isian for being out of her element? Even in an ordinary robe with only a giant stick for a weapon, the woman hadn't run off to hide when the frost wolves set upon them hours ago. Aldgar hadn't seen Cyric once during the fight.

He grumbled in quiet contempt at the human before returning his impatient gaze to the Isian.

A mere slip of a girl, Isa stood barely taller than him, her skin as white as new snow, hair the color of the night sky. Aldgar had seen his fair share of Isians before. They descended from ancient Ashanar elves that parted ways with their king and went underground. Centuries of living in the dark and some interbreeding with humans eventually caused them to diverge sufficiently from true elves to become a people unto themselves.

She too had red eyes, though they held nowhere near the confidence the Aeron's did. Then again, he had the unwavering confidence borne of serving the god Arakain. While traditionally underground-dwelling, Isians didn't often explore the surface world, especially the high peaks. Aldgar couldn't fault her too much for her discomfort navigating such harsh terrain. She'd spent her entire life in comfortable surroundings, studying magic.

Isa continued to step carefully around the collections of needlelike rocks congregating hither and yon along the mossy trail. Whenever she placed her foot wrong, she'd emit a faint squeak and stumble to catch her balance. Eventually, she noticed the other three had stopped, all waiting on her. She stopped walking and scowled, seeming equal parts furious and mortified. She traced her hands around in a graceful pattern while intoning words too faint to hear from the distance. In a moment, her small figure lifted from the ground, hovering a few inches above it. She glided forward, catching up to the group without stumbling or struggling to move.

Aldgar snorted at his disapproval of magic. Cyric whistled in awe.

Isa flashed a smug grin as she floated up the trail like a phantom. Fierce winds whipped her long, black hair around and threatened to rip her cloak off.

The sooner he got these fools where they needed to be, the sooner he could return home, so Aldgar resumed trudging up the path. Cyric stood still, content to watch Isa for a little while longer, though a somewhat less than gentle nudge from one of the Aeron's wings got him moving.

They continued to climb along the mountain trail, each passing step more arduous than the last. Cyric whispered to Kaldoran, amazed the Marn's short legs could withstand such a trip. The human's whimsical mood gave way to a grim expression. The exertion of the climb sapped his apparently limitless cheer.

Levitation magic made the hike quite easy on Isa. She glided along behind Cyric, seemingly unconcerned with how long their journey would take. After the first hour she'd touched down again, needing to re-cast the magic. Aside from invoking the spell again, nary a sound came from her, neither of protest nor urgency. She did occasionally smile in a wry manner whenever Cyric stumbled.

The warm oranges of an afternoon sun eventually faded to the iridescent blue of the moon Vyrra, rare for the season. Midway through the Time of Suns, the warmest months of the year. For the first time in two centuries, the blue moon of magic appeared first in the summer. If it meant anything, Aldgar didn't know. Marns seldom paid much attention to the heavens.

Within the hour, the other two moons broke past the horizon, Kalindor, the red moon of fury, and Myrnaxis, the green moon of avarice. Perhaps an hour after the full lunar triad appeared, they reached a spot where the treacherous trail widened out to a flat ledge. There, Aldgar decided to pause their journey on a nearby precipice for rest.

The mountain face here had no cave entrance, nor did anything hint at a possible reason for the widening of the trail.

"This place feels unnatural." Isa approached the stone wall on the uphill side of the ledge, gazing around as if trying to sense the energies in the rock.

"What do you feel?" asked Kaldoran.

"General malaise." She sighed. "Nothing specific."

Cyric clapped. "Grand. So, we don't need to be concerned."

The group decided to make camp for the night as it had become obvious they would not reach their destination any time soon.

Aldgar eased himself down to sit, still grumbling to himself. Mostly, he begrudged the slow moving toplanders for taking so long to travel the early bits of the trail. A party of all Marns should have been able to make the trip in one day. Granted, the Aeron could do it in a few hours by air if he only knew where to go.

"Why the groan?" mused Cyric. "It's not like you have very far to go down..."

The human appeared to be the only one amused by the remark. Aldgar had heard his share of tallness jokes, and they long ago lost any effect on him. Kaldoran scanned the skyline for any signs of trouble. Isa made no secret of being thoroughly annoyed at Cyric's very existence. It occurred before they met Aldgar, but he'd evidently been quite rude to her, assuming she'd happily jump in bed with him. She hadn't. Since then, tension had been thick between them. Quite unlikely he could do anything to make her laugh short of hurting himself.

The sorceress canceled the levitation spell and floated down to her feet. She removed her cloak, folding it over itself into a cushion she spread out on the ground near Aldgar. The woman appeared to be fond of him, not in a romantic manner. She trusted him to keep her safe despite his making it clear in no uncertain terms he did not in any way trust magic.

Nonetheless, she sat next to him, perhaps because she viewed his calmness as reassuring. She acted wary of Kaldoran as well. No surprise. Sorcerers studied certain paths of magic the minions of gods tended to disapprove of. Unlike Cyric though, at least he didn't leer at her.

Cyric wandered to sit by the mountain face, as far as possible from the edge of the trail. He slumped to the ground like a sack of grain. As much as he attempted to conceal his fatigue, even a blind Marn could tell the trip demanded more of the human than he'd been accustomed to. Within minutes, the somewhat muffled sound of stealthy snoring came from him.

Aldgar snorted again, unsurprised the human went to sleep with no consideration for being involved in a watch rotation. Even high in the mountains, dangers could still present themselves without warning. The Aeron continued looking off at the distant sky, perhaps longing for some time on the wing, frustrated at having to walk.

For no particular reason, Isa began talking. She confided in Aldgar she'd been sent to live among humans from a young age and knew little of the mountains, the tunnels beneath them, or even her own kind. Humans regarded her with distrust, and she suspected they sent her on this quest, not too concerned if she survived it.

Kaldoran whirled away from the edge. "To arms!"

Cyric startled awake.

Aldgar pushed his helm up and cast a disinterested glance at the Knight. Isa scrambled upright, gripping her staff. Though she looked confident, the Marn scoffed in his mind. Anyone who trusted magic to protect them instead of good, solid steel had to be a fool.

Cyric sat up, making a face as if he prepared to complain about being disturbed, but upon noticing everyone else readying weapons, kept quiet.

Kaldoran eased his large sword from its sheath, trying to keep quiet. The faint scraping did more to convince Aldgar a problem approached than a verbal warning. He pushed himself up to his feet and pulled his battle-axe over his shoulder into a two-handed grip.

"Wot ye see?" muttered Aldgar.

"A wyvern headed directly at us," whispered the Aeron, still staring into the sky.

"Where? I can'ae see a thing," barked Aldgar, fed up with whispering.

Kaldoran pointed, yet the Marn couldn't make out anything in the air. He could see just fine in complete darkness, though not well at long distances. He almost called the Aeron daft, but remembered they possessed unusually keen eyesight.

Cyric vanished among the shadows at the back of the ledge. Isa looked into the sky. Her expression said she didn't see anything, either.

All the more reason she felt lost and alone, her own heritage could no longer call her daughter, and everywhere she went it seemed that she wasn't welcome. Now this imminent threat approached, and she felt more helpless than when she was a small child being sent off to live in a strange place.

An indistinct blur moved in the sky. A creature winged its way towards them, dragonlike in shape, though it had only two legs tucked beneath its body. Its malevolent head pointed at them, unmoving, while its serpentine body undulated up and down in rhythm with its flapping wings. A stinging barb jutted from the end of the tail, violet scales glimmering.

Aldgar widened his stance. Wyverns preferred to attack by strafing in hopes of knocking people over, then pouncing on them. He focused on the tail barb. Its stinger represented the greatest threat, as claws or fangs could be remedied with bandaging.

Isa whispered under her breath. A glowing shell of silvery blue light appeared around her, then faded. No doubt, she'd enchanted herself with some type of magical armor or defense. Aldgar shook his head. He trusted forged metal, not the hope inexplicable energies might protect him.

Unsurprisingly, the human disappeared again. He seemed to avoid confrontation as much as possible.

The creature loosed a horrific reptilian shriek and flashed by above, too high to strike. The leathery ruffle of its wing membrane offered a disconcerting reminder of its weight. It circled back and went by again, still too high to attack.

Kaldoran's wings twitched in anticipation. He evidently wanted to confront this creature in midair, but held himself back for some reason. Perhaps he felt a need to protect Isa. Aldgar watched the wyvern circling, remaining focused on its tail. When it committed to an attack, he'd be ready. The barb couldn't penetrate his plate armor. His axe would chew through its scales easily. Though the force of the collision would probably knock him on his seat, he'd swat the beast out of the air if it came close enough.

The creature swerved around again. This time, it dove toward them. Aldgar raised his axe. Kaldoran positioned himself to attack the creature's wing. A loud metallic clang echoed over the mountains as the wyvern's talons crashed into Aldgar's chest plate. The weight of the creature moving so fast knocked him into a tumbling roll, though his axe tore a hefty gash along the beast's side.

Kaldoran's sword bounced harmlessly off scales. The Aeron remained on his feet, as the brunt of the strike hit Aldgar. He emerged from the backward somersault on his feet and charged after the fleeing wyvern, though it had already gone past the ledge, out into the air.

Isa pointed at the diving beast. A ghostly image of a large amber sword appeared in front of her and rocketed off toward the Wyvern. The creature hesitated, staring confusedly at the blade's approach. Its head made small circles to match the spinning magical sword—until the spell struck it between the eyes. The phantom blade appeared to be impaled through the creature's skull, sticking out from both sides.

The wyvern's entire serpentine neck jerked back, pulling its dive to one side and making it more of a fall than an attack run. Out of control, it crashed into Kaldoran, crushing him flat before bouncing away and tumbling end over end while flailing its talons at the ground. Lucky for him it appeared nearly unconscious from the spell. It neither bit, clawed, nor tried to sting him.

Aldgar charged at the stricken creature, bringing his axe down into the beast's gut with a sickening crunch. No sooner did hot black blood strike him in the face did its tail career up and slam into his shoulder. Its dagger-sized barb bounced off his Marnish steel shoulder guard, splattering a sickly green ichor all over the metal. He grunted in annoyance and proceeded to hack at the tail.

Cyric emerged from the darkness, seemingly attempting to sneak up on the wyvern.

Amazing. The fool shows himself before the beast is dead.

Kaldoran breathed a wheezing gasp and fought his way upright. Having a whole adult wyvern fly-crash full speed into him had knocked the wind out of him for a moment.

The Wyvern flipped over onto its legs with cat-like speed, despite the gash in its abdomen. It snapped its jaws at Aldgar, simultaneously whipping the tail stinger at Cyric.

Isa pointed both her arms at the creature. A gout of fire sprang up from between her hands, twisted into a ropelike stream, and singed across the back of the Wyvern. The beast turned on her, hissing. Cyric, clutching a wound in his side from the tail, leapt at it and jammed his dagger into the wyvern's back. It whirled on him, shrieking.

Cyric dove away from its biting maw and tumbled behind a rock. The creature returned its attention to Isa. Aldgar moved in between them. Kaldoran fly-jumped over the wyvern to land beside Cyric. He mumbled a quiet prayer. A sublime golden light bathed his hand, which he placed over the poisoned wound.

"Thanks," whispered the human. "Leg was going dead already."

"Thank Arakain." Kaldoran smiled.

The wyvern snapped its teeth at Aldgar's face. He blocked, swatting its head aside before whipping his axe around in a counterattack. Screeching, the wyvern rotated away, sliding sideways and snapping its tail stinger at Isa.

She yelped in alarm, raising her staff in an attempt to defend herself. The wood struck the stinger an instant before it plunged into her chest, redirecting the barb into the stone wall. Aldgar gave a determined grunt and swung again. Kaldoran rushed at it from the other side. Ducking and weaving, the wyvern backpedaled from the men, inching toward the ledge, and a mile-long dropoff.

Aldgar's axe scored low along the leg, sending a spurt of steaming black blood into the air. Kaldoran struck it true on the neck, almost decapitating it. The creature staggered dizzily backward, dragging its head along the ground. Cyric darted in to recover a pair of throwing knives embedded in its back.

A fiery blast exploded at the creature's chest, flinging it off the ledge. After a moment of silence, a crunching splatter echoed up from below.

Cyric stood and adjusted his shirt as if he had done all the work. Smiling proudly, he went back over to recline by the mountain face. Aldgar grunted in satisfaction, then sat in his former position and began cleaning his axe. Kaldoran resumed scanning the sky. Isa curled up atop her cloak, though she appeared nowhere near close to being able to sleep.

Once Aldgar finished cleaning wyvern gore from his axe, he settled in for the night. By then, Kaldoran no longer stood like a sentinel watching the sky. He sat, leaning forward, head down, his wings curled forward around him almost like a tent. The ability to fly would be considered a tremendous gift by some. Aldgar preferred being able to recline in a bed. Trying to sleep with huge wings looked frustrating and uncomfortable.

ALDGAR SNORED NONE TOO QUIETLY. THE METAL HELM ATOP HIS FACE ONLY made it louder.

He snored at such volume, he woke himself up. The warmth of sunlight made further sleep impossible. After righting his helmet in place, Aldgar sat up. Cyric lounged against the mountain face, gnawing on a ration.

Kaldoran knelt at the edge of the flat area, facing the cliff. It took him a few minutes to finish his morning prayer routine. Once done, he returned to the camp and invoked Arakain's magic to summon food for everyone. Aldgar raised an eyebrow in surprise at the sudden appearance of a bowl of cave spider and mushroom stew—his favorite. For the first time since he'd been ordered to escort these toplanders, he didn't feel the need to grumble, happily taking the bowl and tucking into his feast.

Everyone ate with due haste. Soon after, the group resumed making their way up the trail. Thankfully, they covered most of the distance the previous day. Though everyone appeared fully aware Isa's lack of experience and difficulty trekking difficult terrain prevented them from completing the journey in one day, no one complained. Even Aldgar gained a modicum of respect for her. She may have been a 'soft' city dweller used to a pampered life, but she held her ground during a wyvern attack. Considering she did so wearing only a fabric robe—no armor of any kind—meant either extreme bravery or foolishness.

A merciful hour or so later, the trail leveled off to a flat path over rocky tundra. A breathtaking view of land stretched out in all directions. From atop the Wyvern mountains they could see all the way to Northumbrook and south to the grassy Kargorath Plains. The land of Argathia glimmered like a multicolored gemstone set in a sapphire band of ocean.

Aldgar didn't bother admiring the landscape. He preferred the quiet solace of a deep mountain cavern. To him, the only beauty to surpass multicolored striations of various minerals in rock took the form of expertly crafted armor. Kaldoran also didn't appear terribly impressed. Isa and Cyric, however, gazed in awe.

"I wish I could see such views every day," said Isa.

"Aye." Cyric whistled. "But if ya see it every day, it'll lose it's luster. Look at Kal over there. Bored. Just like flyin'."

The Aeron chuckled.

Upon spotting the entrance to the cave ahead, Aldgar pointed. "Here we be. Keep the sightseein' fer later. We go' ae job ta do."

The group hesitated a few steps shy of where the trail met a large clearing in front of where the giant cave should be. An acrid stench, part charred meat, part sulfur hung in the air. Fumes scorched the inside of Aldgar's nostrils, making him cough once. Cyric gagged. Isa covered her mouth and nose.

Cringing, Kaldoran moved closer to the end of the path. Aldgar disregarded the stench and moved up alongside the Aeron. A pair of ogres sat camped out at the entrance to the cave the toplanders had been so insistent on finding, that his chieftain charged him with playing guide to.

"Ogres. Tha' would explain the smell," mumbled Aldgar.

Cyric winced.

Isa couldn't get any paler, being an Isian, though her eyes widened. One hit from an ogre would be the end for her.

"You ha' ae problem wi' attackin'?" Aldgar eyed the Knight of Arakain.

"Not in the least. Ogres are a threat to innocent people." Kaldoran drew his sword, rose to his full seven foot plus height, and flared his wings. With a cry of, "defend yourselves," he stomped out into the clearing.

"Blimey," muttered Cyric as he scurried about to find a hiding spot.

Aldgar rushed alongside the knight, eager to give his battle axe a taste of ogre flesh.

The ogre on the right stomped toward Kaldoran, the other roared at Aldgar.

From the trail head at the edge of the clearing, Isa gestured at the ogre on the right. It let out a sudden, startled yelp and smashed its club over the head of the other ogre, compressing its skull into its shoulders. The second ogre grunted heavily, swooning.

After hitting its friend, the ogre blinked confusedly between it and Kaldoran as if wondering how the two so rapidly changed places. Aldgar rushed in and swung at the dazed ogre. The twelve-foot-tall monstrous humanoid brought its huge club around in time to block, though the crude weapon splintered under the force of the Marnic axe. Aldgar spun into an immediate follow-through, burying the axe head in the ogre's shin.

Much like a tree, the giant creature fell over sideways with a low guttural scream of pain.

Kaldoran's first attack nicked his ogre above its eye, sending a trickle of blood down its face. The stunned ogre flailed uselessly in a horribly mistimed attempt at defending itself. Kaldoran deftly slashed his blade into the monster's ribs. Seeming more annoyed than hurt by the wound, the ogre bellowed and raised his club.

Kaldoran grabbed his sword in both hands, raising it to defend. A heavy sideways swing knocked the enormous club aside but knocked the Aeron a few paces backward, his blade ringing.

The other ogre flailed around on the ground in agony, emitting an ear-splitting wail of anger, frustration, and pain. Aldgar rushed in to finish it off. Cyric shouted, hanging off the back of Kaldoran's ogre by a grip on two daggers he'd jammed into its upper back. The ogre spun in circles, trying to reach him.

"Just die already, dammit!" yelled Cyric.

The felled ogre grabbed a head-sized rock and hurled it at Aldgar. The tiny boulder bounced off his helmet, knocking him off balance for a second. It gave the ogre enough time to grab him like a child picking up a ragdoll. Aldgar roared angrily, his arms pinned at his sides.

Faint amber light danced around the ogre's head. Before it could smash Aldgar into the ground, it screamed in terror and threw him aside. He tumbled like an armored ball into the mountain face, bounced off, and landed flat on his chest. The ogre cowered away from something invisible, screaming in terror. Furious, Aldgar sprang to his feet and rushed at the insane ogre.

The beast didn't even react to his approach. He sank the battle axe into its forehead, slaying it in an instant.

Cyric screamed as his daggers came free from the other ogre's back and he went flying from the creature, spinning around and around. Kaldoran swooped in and ran the ogre through the chest. He gave his bastard sword a twist, then yanked it loose.

The monster's giant club slipped from fingers thicker than a child's arm and thudded to the ground.

Kaldoran crouched to wipe blood from his sword on the ogre's loincloth. Aldgar slung the axe to the side a few times, not wanting to make it dirtier by touching the ogre's garment. Cyric picked himself up, dusted himself off, and put his daggers away. Isa walked over, cringing at the stink wafting up from the dead half-giants.

Aldgar started into the cave mouth with nary a word. The others followed. Soon, the air grew hot and steamy. The cave walls gleamed, slick with moss and an unidentifiable slime. A few hundred feet in, eerie amber light became visible up ahead. A deep echoing rumble vibrated the earth, something huge in the distance breathed.

Though the old writings spoke of the dragon who had lived in this cave for thousands of years as a being of reason, Aldgar kept his axe at the ready. "He knows we be 'ere."

No one moved for a moment. Aldgar advanced cautiously, entering the outer reaches of a vast, underground chamber. Dragon or not, he preferred having solid stone around him. His Marnic eyes pierced the darkness, revealing a massive gold-scaled dragon curled up in a pose similar to a sleeping cat. Its head appeared larger than some human hovels. Surprisingly, the dragon did not recline upon a bed of treasure, coins, or magical artifacts, rather, vast shelves of books, orbs, potions, and bizarre magical devices.

Isa gasped in awe, as Isians also possessed true night vision.

"Who disturbs me?" asked an inhumanly deep voice.

The Aeron stepped forward. "I am Kaldoran, Knight of Arakain. I and my friends bring a message from the archmages of Ga'ron, grand one. Will you give us counsel?"

Cyric squeaked. A subtle shift in color told Aldgar the dragon had somehow created light, illuminating the entire chamber so the human and Aeron could see.

The dragon sat up into a regal posture, its shimmering golden body framed by gargantuan wings, also seemingly made of gold. "Very well, knight. Approach and present your message."

Kaldoran stepped forward, removed a large scroll from his pack, and held it out to the dragon. "We come seeking your aid, oh great wyrm. An unknown sect has appeared in the countryside, invoking powers even the archmages are unable to decipher the origin of. "This scroll was taken from their camp without their notice."

Cyric puffed out his chest.

The dragon stroked his chin whiskers. After a moment, the scroll floated up toward the dragon's face, where it unfurled itself. He stared intently at the scroll for some moments before his massive eyes widened. "Fools! I've known humans to be reckless, however this is beyond even the idiocy I thought them capable of. They cannot comprehend the forces they seek to set in motion will guarantee their own destruction. They seek to reawaken Nightwing."

"Wow." Cyric whistled, then whispered, "Sounds pretty bad."

Isa glared at him in disbelief. "The whole world in flames? Legions of undead roaming everywhere?"

"Oh, aye." Cyric nodded once. "Tis bad."

Aldgar pursed his lips. This situation sounded… important. Perhaps the chieftain had been wise after all. Something told him he wouldn't be going home to his forge any time soon.

The scroll flew back to the Aeron's grasp.

"I must alert the others." The dragon stood. "King Lowyn of Aegaan must be warned. The pact must be honored."

Everyone stepped aside as the great golden dragon walked toward the chamber exit. "I will take word to the others of the flight. Tell the mages we shall meet at the hallowed circle in two weeks' time."

Kaldoran nodded.

"You and your friends should make your way to Aegaan. Bring word to King Lowyn with all due haste."

With that, the great dragon leapt into the air–distancing itself from the cave in a thunderous rush of air. Cyric wandered into the chamber, gazing around at the shelves.

Kaldoran caught him by the shoulder and steered him back to the entrance. "Dragons have magical wards on their hoards. Don't think it would not notice you borrowing things. And do not dare steal from this dragon."

"No harm in looking, is there?" Cyric smiled.

"Yes, there is." Isa narrowed her eyes. "From here, I recognize at least three artifacts capable of killing you in a second if you touched them incorrectly."

Cyric swallowed.

They hurried out of the chamber, down the cave, and out to the clearing by the dead ogres.

"Curious the dragon allowed these filthy beasts to remain alive," said Kaldoran.

Aldgar snorted. "They hadn't gone into the cave."

"You have my thanks, Aldgar." The Aeron bowed. "We must make our way to Aegaan to warn the king."

Aldgar grinned. "Ye nae git rid o' me that easy, lad."

Kaldoran smiled. "If what we fear is afoot, we shall certainly need your blade."

"Alright then, I suppose we have room for another." Cyric saluted him.

Isa took in a deep breath, also smiling at Aldgar.

He nodded once, then proceeded to lead the group back down the precarious trail. It would take them two days to leave the range and another week to reach Aegaan.

They ought to make it on time. For the first time in his almost four-hundred-years, Aldgar thought he might be able to tolerate being away from the mountains for a bit.

Can'ae go lettin' a black dragon devour the world, now kin I?

V

A QUEEN'S LAMENT

ABOUT A QUEEN'S LAMENT

This story is older than the anthology call, originally written for fun as a bit of character background. The setting is the same universe as my Tales of Widowswood (Emma) series, a fantasy kingdom called Eldrinaath. This is a world I developed starting around 2015 or so for a new fantasy roleplaying game system. Having a 500-ish page sourcebook to reference helps quite a bit for world-building.

When I wrote this way back when, I never expected to be a published writer or for anyone who didn't know me face to face to read it. A Queen's Lament is a bit of backstory to one of the characters my players met in a campaign I ran for the Chronicles of Eldrinaath roleplaying game. When coming up with short stories to submit to the anthology call, I happened upon it and figured I'd submit it as well. It's a peek into the same world as Emma and the Banderwigh, only not a middle-grade story.

5

A QUEEN'S LAMENT

G uilt weighed heavy upon Queen Myrana's heart.

She gazed into her bedchamber's full-length mirror. The light of the twin moons imparted a phantasmal radiance to her dress, the only source of illumination. Shadow figures, patrolling guards, crept across the walls on the distant wing of the castle. Night held the world firm in its grasp. Not even the sound of her breath pierced the veil of silence. The ebon marble floor caught her glow, amplifying it enough to perceive the walls of her expansive bedchamber. One hand caressed the obvious burden of motherhood upon her delicate body.

Her hair, black as midnight, hung loose and draped wherever it cared to fall. She ran her fingers through it, longing for the days when she had been young enough not to care about 'looking presentable'. How it seemed like a void against the nightgown—a seep of ink staining the pure white silk. The effort it took her to walk to the side of the room still lingered as gasping breaths, evident in the air as fleeting clouds of mist.

She mocked her own appearance, so thin and so pregnant; she resembled a twig with a spider's egg sack at the midpoint. A shiver took her at the memory of a nightmare she'd suffered weeks before, her belly rupturing to birth ten thousand arachnids. She found it a wonder she could still stand at all. The past month had been exhausting, yet the priest Handren could offer no explain for why she had not yet delivered. Rumor surely spread by now within the castle about the unusual length. Her handmaidens whispered when they thought she could not hear.

Myrana covered her mouth to stifle a sob at the worry her husband knew the baby was not his. The priests believed she should be in pain by now. Such pain would have been a welcome harbinger of an end to this ordeal. Whatever her baby did sapped her strength, leaving her scarcely able to get out of bed. She rubbed her stomach with both hands.

What are you waiting for?

A hint of motion drifted within the infinite darkness surrounding her in the mirror. The shadows behind her writhed as if alive. With downcast eyes, she broke the silence with a timid whisper.

"Lorinath?"

No reply came, not that she expected one. *Foolish. Why should I expect him to be here?* The Niltharien mage will never return to the Kingdom of Ondremmar. He'd taken what he came for—and she had not been his prize. She drew shaking fingers to her lips as if to pull back the word, trembling with dread that Eodil may have heard another man's name pass her lips. Her husband's kingdom sat at the crown of the world, as far north and west as could be. She envied the simple life of the clansmen in the Bannoc Tarn to the south, or the wild ones from the Plains of Tyrem to the east. Ondremmar had the advantage of steel and magic, but her king was as cold as his land.

Eodil, distant as ever, had not shown any reaction to her growing belly —he couldn't possibly have failed to notice by now, even with them using separate bedchambers and spending barely an hour in his presence each week. She knew Eodil had not fathered this child. The baby had been inside her for far too long. Myrana never imagined one moment of weakness with a dark elven man could result in a child, but had no other explanation for carrying so long.

Handren would likely have been less worried if she admitted what she had done, but she couldn't bring herself to tell him. Myrana shivered. If she couldn't tell the Priest of Vaoren, how could she tell Eodil? If she could not seek the forgiveness of her family's patron god, how could she ever ask it of her husband?

Even as her swollen womb grew, he said nothing. Eodil went on about his life as though her pregnancy simply didn't exist. For once, she was grateful her husband occupied himself with matters of the kingdom and afforded her so little attention. She clung to the illusion he may not have noticed she carried this child for fifteen months.

She glanced in the mirror while clinging to the bureau for support. Instinct cautioned her the birth would be soon. Perhaps Eodil chose not to see it. He was quite good at that—situations he deemed unworthy of his attention received none of it. They had been married for three years. Short of the eve of the ceremony, the nineteen-year-old queen had scarcely been touched. They *had* been in love, but after his father died... he'd become so busy.

No one could accuse Eodil of being an unattractive man, nor did he wield a cruel disposition or possess of any true flaws of the soul. Lately, he seemed more interested in matters of politics than matters of love. She tried to be there for him when he needed her, most notably during the guildsmen's crisis, one of the few times the stress of the crown showed upon his face. Rather than his wife, he favored the company of his advisors—Lady Neasa in particular.

One little crack of doubt had given the Niltharien all the opportunity needed.

Myrana shuddered at the memory of the mage, wondering if his seducing her had been part of some greater plan. Everything she knew of his kind claimed their hearts were as black as their skin, yet he had been kind to her—despite rumors of their contempt for humans. If not for Eodil's suspicion about wizards, she would never have laid eyes on him. She smiled to herself at the one bit of power she held over him. Eodil believed she'd spent her tenth year apprenticed to a mage in the city of Eastmarch, dismissed soon after for being a poor student. Fortunately, as a prince, he'd been free with his contempt for magic so she'd kept her tongue. Eodil didn't need to know she'd completed her studies. While far from an archmage, she considered herself at least a full wizard.

Believing she had apprenticed for a year gave him the only excuse he needed to relegate the task of dealing with a *wizard* to her. The Niltharien showed little reaction to the intended snub by a meeting with the Queen, something oft reserved for matters of frivolity, charity, or art. He'd traveled to the Kingdom of Ondremmar intending to stay for only a short time. Over the course of their meeting, he told her how he hunted another of his kind who had stolen fragments of an ancient scroll, and sought the ruins of an abandoned temple that predated human settlement in the area. According to him, the Niltharien formerly occupied this area, many thousands of years ago.

They'd spent hours poring over old texts, trying to figure out where this place could be. A striking, exotic figure, he lurked at the edge of her wanting—a forbidden elixir. Queen Myrana leaned on the bureau, smiling as she recalled his face. Tall and regal, clad in the ornate robes of a high-order wizard, Lorinath was entrancing to stare at, even in a memory. Of course, her slight build could let her pass as one of the Astari; perhaps he didn't notice her rounded ears and mistook her for a one of the forest-dwelling elves?

Myrana blushed. *No, my attire is far too modest for him to have made that mistake.*

She closed her eyes and remembered him whispering in her ear as she gave herself to him on the same bed she spent the past two months trapped in.

He spoke at first in the Niltharien tongue.

Your language is beautiful. What did you say?

Lorinath's eyes glittered, dark violet gemstones aglow with an inner light that made his already jet face seem even darker. In her daydream his voice sounded lustrous and silken. "Never in my days could I envision a human to be gifted with such grace. It is beyond tragic you shall only enjoy it for a fleeting time."

Myrana looked again at her roundness and covered her mouth to stifle a wistful laugh. She'd almost screamed, taking such a statement from a Niltharien as proof he meant to kill her. To a man who would live ten thousand years, the lifespan of a human amounted to a candle flame in the dark.

The baby kicked. She put a hand over her belly. *I will be a mother soon. I must tell Eodil.*

She feared how her husband would react to the truth. Yet with each passing week he continued to ignore her growing womb, Myrana worried more and more he already knew. Her trepidation turned to anger and jealousy at how he always sought Neasa for advice. If the king ignored his own wife and spent so much time in the company of his only female advisor, what conclusion would any reasonable person draw?

Perhaps he knows already and merely waits to see how long it takes me to confess.

Justifications circled in her head one after the next as she wobbled toward the bed. Bare feet peeked under the hem of her gown with each step, glowing bright against the floor. Noises from the hallway betrayed the approach of her handmaidens. She didn't care to suffer the nuisance of their fussing over her for being out of bed and hurried as fast as her body allowed. She had spent the past two months in it more than out and grew weary of lying down.

"What are you hiding from, child?" She patted her belly.

Uncomfortably cold, the floor had been a welcome sensation to disrupt the monotony of spending so much time under blankets. No sooner did she grip her bedding than a rush of hot fluid ran down her legs, leaving her standing in a warm puddle. More still flowed from within her. Myrana heaved forward, crying out as a painful cramp clenched her insides. She fell against the side of the bed, scrabbling for a handhold at the blankets, but her weight dragged her to the ground. Time slowed to a haze amid wracking pains unlike anything she might have imagined.

The creak of the door preceded a commotion spilling into the room. Figures in pastel dresses of pink, green and blue surrounded her. Women's voices swirled into a meaningless warble of noise. Agony, as if tooth and claw shredded at her from the inside, lit fire to her abdomen.

Cold marble touched her cheek; the fire inside her belly worsened to the point she no longer felt it, and the room swirled into nothingness.

———

A WOMAN'S SCREAMS ECHOED OUT OF NUMB DARKNESS.

Myrana floated on her back, weightless. The distant girl shrieked again. *I know that voice.* The scream came a third time, and she knew the voice belonged to her.

Two women on either side held her hands. A male figure in a white robe drew a knife across her distended belly. The sensation of being sliced open struck her as pleasant compared to the torrent of anguish going on inside. The ceiling spun. Handmaidens squeezed her wrists, apparently expecting her to fight to get away, though she lacked the strength to bother.

"I call upon the grace of Vaoren to restore your humble servant," said a blurry male voice.

Handren, the priest. Gold-yellow light welled up below her vision. Myrana struggled to lift her head, to look around. The radiance flared, taking with it every scrap of agony. Her pain-addled mind rebounded at the placid tranquility, and she blacked out.

———

MYRANA'S EYES FLUTTERED OPEN.

Fleeting glimpses of faces hovered in the darkness between her and the ceiling. She wore a different gown, this one dark burgundy and plush, but had no memory of putting it on. Myrana clutched at her belly, finding it flat. For the first time in months, she could see her feet tenting her blankets. The baby was gone, replaced with a dull ache. The priest must have attended to her, restoring her body with divine magic.

Did I dream the past year? Was I with child at all?

She stared at her hands, pallid and glowing, uncertain if her one-night affair and the baby had all been some bizarre nocturnal flight of fancy, a game of the mind. Myrana traced her fingers over her stomach, finding it tender, but nowhere near as sensitive as it should be. She let her arms lay at her sides, searching for answers in the decorative carved ceiling. None of the little winged babies offered as much as a hint. The increasing need to believe it had all been a strange dream ended at a clank from the door. Beth, her eldest attendant, entered the room carrying something. Myrana struggled to sit up, and the sudden onset of soreness brought tangible truth to the past few hours.

Without a word, Beth approached and handed her a baby wrapped in pink. At first, she thought it a perfect porcelain doll of a child, until the infant's warm breath touched her cheek. The sleeping baby appeared even paler than her mother, with skin of chalk white. Wispy black hair already covered the tiny head in dense swirls. After giving the queen a strange glance, Beth backed away. Myrana gazed at the woman, wondering what the look could have meant. Beth didn't glance back. The woman slipped into the hallway and eased the door closed behind her. Judging from the color of the blankets, she'd borne a daughter. Myrana cradled the infant, sizing up the feeling of motherhood.

Perhaps I shall not care if Eodil disregards me. Myrana smiled at her child. *I have you to love now.*

What she had dreaded had not come to pass. Myrana had pale skin. Lorinath had been the color of midnight. The child, she feared would turn out stone grey. Pure white *did* seem slightly inhuman, though nowhere near as much so as ink black or slate. She kissed the infant atop the head, astounded and relieved at the baby's coloration. She would not have loved her child less had she been another shade, but like this, passing the girl off as Eodil's blood might be possible.

The din of distant activity in the castle faded to silence, almost on cue. The child fidgeted and awoke, looking up as she squirmed in the blanket.

Mother's love upended itself into a tangle of confusion. The baby's eyes shone bright violet, luminous like fireflies—as Lorinath's had. In the quiet dim of her room, they cast a patch of amethyst upon her chest. Her feelings changed to dread fear. The tiny being she now held ceased being her baby—*it* had become an unknown creature.

As she thought about Lorinath, one night's weakness of a lonely queen coalesced into fear for her soul. Her mind swam with stories and legends of the dark elves, their traffic with demons and treacherous tales of forbidden sorcery. Had she lain with a demonic creature? In her mind, the baby's stare shone malice into her heart. Feeling panic, Myrana placed the child upon the bed and ran to the door. Beth and several of the other handmaidens clustered a few paces outside her room, whispering. They turned at the sound of the creaking door. Their stares accused the queen. Now she understood what the look in Beth's eyes meant—she must have seen the demon's eyes. Myrana's imagination ran away, adding whispered words to unmoving mouths in the voices of her handmaidens as her gaze drifted from one to the next.

"Our Queen lays with demons."

"Traitor."

"The child is not of Eodil."

The youngest servant girl turned away, unable to meet her gaze.

"Summon Handren!" Myrana tried to yell, but managed only a breathless gasp.

The crowd of women dispersed in different directions like mice caught by a cook. Myrana fell into the doorway, clinging to the wall to remain on her feet. The priest had been present at the birth. She clutched her stomach. *He had to have seen her.* It was unnatural for a mother to be unconscious during the delivery. Everything about this felt like an aberration. She held tight to the doorjamb, afraid to look over her shoulder at the *creature* lying at the center of her bed.

What will I see if I look?

Would it still be an innocent baby? Would there be something darker grinning at her with fangs and claws? Her mind raced to a point of panic. A foreboding heaviness sneaking up behind her made her whirl, arms held up to brace for an ambush. Only a helpless baby lay in the middle of the bed, blinking back at her with a confused expression as if perplexed by the woman's reaction of fear.

They stared at each other. Myrana froze in place, shivering as she imagined the sun's emergence imminent. The baby kicked a few times and grew discontent, making grunting unhappy noises a touch short of full on crying. Myrana recoiled from the sound, knowing her affect toward the child was causing it. Terror at what the *thing* would do when it became irate made her cringe away.

She backed into the priest as he entered. With a startled yelp, the strength left her legs. Handren's arms wrapped around her, preventing her collapse. Realizing who held her, she clung to him like a scared child.

After a moment of shaking and whimpering, she pointed at the baby and rasped. "Look at its eyes!"

Handren guided her into the room without fear. The child kicked her legs at his approach and began to cry.

"What do you make of the infant's eyes, Handren?" whispered Myrana. "Do you think she fears a servant of Vaoren?"

She and he both made a hand gesture of reverence at the mention of one of the gods.

His dour expression said he noticed its features did not carry any traits of Eodil's line. "I do not mean to speak out of turn, my lady, but this infant bears no resemblance to Eodil."

Myrana's fear gave way to shame. She stared at the floor, no longer able to bear her lie to the gods—or those that serve them.

"He was a visitor to my husband, not of this land." Her voice dripped with contrition as she folded her arms over herself. "Eodil wished not to be bothered by the ramblings of a wizard. He tasked me with assisting him." She sniffled. "I do not recall at what point our meeting turned away from a discussion of maps and crypts, to things forgotten. He said I was too beautiful to be neglected like the relic he sought." Her grip on the priest faltered. She felt unworthy to touch him, and took a step away. "For three years, I yearned to know the touch of my husband, which had been so long absent to me." She cringed at the thought of her deed, unable to fathom how she had come to be seduced by such a being. "Eodil knows not that I dwell within his house; he lives as if we had never loved. It was the Niltharien, Lorinath. He must have sensed the void within me and ensorcelled me."

Handren rubbed his chin.

"No." She sobbed. "It was my fault. I could have resisted him, but chose not to."

"Niltharien." Handren's face twisted with disdain. "The infant has the blood of demons within it. You were right to be concerned."

He stepped closer, comforting her with a hand on each shoulder.

"Niltharien seldom deign to suffer the attentions of a human woman, even one as radiant as you. I do not mean to take away from your exquisiteness, but to them, we are mere beasts. I suspect more behind this tryst than simple lust." Handren's eyes welled with sympathy as he beheld the shivering queen. "I blame you not, my child—you were as much a victim of the dark elf's charms as you are of Eodil's coldness."

Myrana shuddered at the thought. Had she been used? What had been Lorinath's true motive? Could this baby be a threat to the Kingdom of Ondremmar, to Eodil?

"What should we do?" she stammered between hesitant gasps.

"This creature may very well pose a risk to the crown, the land, and to your soul." Handren sighed. "While I cannot suggest the course of action of a queen, I dare say that this abomination is potentially a threat."

Myrana shifted around to look at the baby, who continued to fuss and cry, louder now as if she could comprehend the meaning behind the priest's words. Myrana's mind swam with fear. Surely, the gods knew what she did. Her soul was damned already for consorting with the abyss. She could not bear the thought of being responsible for the downfall of her homeland to demons.

I am already condemned for laying with a demon. There is only one thing I can do to spare my kingdom.

Eodil would learn about her treachery; she knew what it would mean for her. She would do what she had to do, and then send herself to the gods for mercy. The second part, she could not tell Handren of. He would try to stop her. She couldn't bear the weight of Eodil's contempt. A momentary daydream of being bound and laid over the executioner's block, searching the audience for Eodil, brought her to tears.

He would not be there to watch.

The baby emitted a series of grunts.

Myrana froze, staring at her child. *How can I consider what it is Handren implies I do? I am no mother if I cannot protect my... demon.* Despite the infant's nature, the idea of slaying it made her recoil inside. Bile welled up in the back of her throat. She closed her eyes, squeezing tears free. Only if she immediately took her own life after the deed could she suppress her mother's instinct to protect the baby, fiend or not. *I will follow her into the arms of the abyss. The citizens of Ondremmar do not deserve to be slaves of demons because I am too weak of will.* She drew a breath and steeled herself. *My life is mine to surrender, not Eodil's to discard.*

The child stilled as Myrana picked her up, seeming pleased at her mother's touch. Weight burdened Myrana's heart at the silly smile on the girl's face; she felt detached from herself, moving as if an outside force worked her limbs like a puppet. The blanket loosened around the girl's head, revealing ears with cute peaks, partway between the sharp points of the Niltharien and the roundness of humanity.

Handren remained quiet as Myrana carried the baby to a small table and set her upon it. The young queen walked to the bureau and removed an intricately decorated scabbard of white and silver from the drawer. She clutched it for a moment in shaking hands before she drew the blade apart from its sheath. The long, thin trefoil edge gleamed in the moonlight. Delicate patterns engraved upon the weapon made of fine Ondremmar steel and ivory marked it as the queen's ceremonial blade—never meant to taste blood. Tears dripped from her chin. One struck the blade, sliding down the edge before gathering at the point. When she lifted her gaze to the child, the infant calmed and smiled.

Clever little thing.

A small puff of guilt rose from the smoke of her mounting terror. She wondered if the little demon tried to endear itself to her to save its life, or genuinely experienced happiness from her presence. A twist of nausea filled her as motherly feelings welled up. She raised the knife over the baby, staring past the tip at the child's heart. For the sake of her people, she could not suffer this abomination to live. Myrana tensed her arm, but couldn't summon the will to drive the weapon downward into her own child. She averted her gaze and grasped the knife in both hands. The breath she took to prepare herself leaked through her teeth at the infant's cooing.

What are you doing? She is still your child!

"Handren..." Myrana shuddered with fear and guilt. *I cannot do this. She looks so innocent. A deceit?*

The priest moved to her side. "Yes, my queen?"

Myrana clutched the dagger to her breast in a feeble effort not to tremble. "The will of Vaoren... can your prayers mend the flesh of demons?"

Handren blinked and stammered. "Certainly not!"

"Forgive me." Myrana raised her hand, no longer shaking. "I needed to hear you say he would not."

The baby kicked randomly and reached for Myrana; her wide smile faded to confused worry.

She senses my fear. Wants to know why her mother is afraid of her.

Myrana focused her attention on the infant and spread her arms to the side while chanting in the language of dragons. Arcane phrases focused the intent within her mind, tapping the ancient power of the plane of aether. The invocation was a basic one, often taught to apprentices. A wisp of white light slipped from her hand and fell upon the squirming baby, who stilled with sleep.

Handren raised an eyebrow. "You have not cast a spell in some time, my lady."

"I cannot bear the thought of what I must do." She unwrapped the bundle to bare the infant's arms and grasped the baby near the left wrist. "If your prayer has no effect, I will ensure the safety of my husband's kingdom. Then, I shall follow her. I ask that you preside over my service afterward."

"As you wish." Handren bowed.

Myrana used one finger to open the baby's hand. She shuddered from guilt at the thought of even a mere exploratory bloodletting, but forced herself to use the razor-like trefoil to draw blood from the baby's palm.

The child's eyes snapped open with a look of alarm. Handren whispered a prayer to Vaoren. Golden light gleamed along his outstretched arm and surrounded the baby's wound. For a half second, the infant's expression twisted in preparation to wail, but it seemed her pain ended before she decided it worth screaming over.

Myrana smeared blood from the child's palm with her thumb. No wound remained.

"By Vaoren's grace..." Handren rasped. He staggered back and caught himself against a small table, blood draining from his face.

The knife slipped from Myrana's grasp and hit the floor with a clatter. *I was about to murder a baby... My baby.* She gathered the infant in her arms and sank to her knees, clutching her child tight to her breast and sobbing.

Handren edged closer, white robes fluttering over his dark shoes. After a moment of silence, he cleared his throat. "Vaoren has blessed you with great wisdom, my queen."

"I am not worthy to have her. What mother could dare conceive such an act as I nearly committed?"

"A mother whose mind has been twisted by fear." Eodil's voice rolled like thunder across the silence.

"Your grace." Handren shifted to his right and bowed.

Black suede boots stepped into the spot of floor Myrana stared at.

"Leave us," said the king, his commanding voice echoing off the stone walls.

Without a word, Handren moved for the door.

"Priest." Softer and bereft of threat, the king's words caused the man to pause. "If this infant's blood coursed with the taint of demons, would Vaoren have seen fit to intervene?"

His tone made it clear he already knew the answer.

Handren hung his head. "No, your grace. The infant is no more demon than I."

Eodil did not speak or look back as the priest made his way out into the hall, but paused at the threshold. The sound of whispering handmaidens crept in from the open door. Myrana risked a peek up. The look on Handren's face betrayed his worry for Eodil's wrath, though none came. The king remained silent until the priest pulled the door closed.

He stooped to grasp Myrana by the left arm, above the elbow, and pulled her to stand. His grip closed with uncomfortable strength, though he didn't inflict pain as he guided her to sit on the edge of the overstuffed mattress. Hard eyes stared into hers for a moment, swirling with anger and bewilderment.

"Wife, not only do you offer your virtue to a stranger in my house— now you plot to murder your own child?"

Myrana cradled her baby, staring at her lap, unable to endure Eodil's painful gaze.

"We..." Words failed her.

KING EODIL STARED AT THE SLENDER WEEPING FIGURE ON THE BED.

At three and twenty years of age, he had no heir. The closest thing his wife produced was a half-human bastard—and a girl at that. *I have shut myself away from her.* If Myrana wanted to make a plea for attention, this had certainly worked. A glimmer of the joy he had once known in her presence poked out from beneath his anger. Her rebellion, defiance, risk-taking reminded her of the girl he fell in love with. He had allowed his father's death to overwhelm him.

"Do you recall the look on my father's face when I announced our intent to marry?"

Myrana shivered. "His face became so red, I thought he would burst."

"He wanted me to marry Rowena of Evermoor, or Alisandra of

Ralithir." Eodil stooped to retrieve her blade and slid it back into the scabbard with a muted *click*. "For political alliances."

"He thought I had ensorcelled you."

Eodil raised an eyebrow. "You had." Her head snapped up, fear in her eyes. "But, I do not think you used your magic to do so."

He left the blade upon the round table before taking a seat at her side. The infant squirmed to look at him. Within her innocent, albeit glowing, eyes, he recognized the reason he disregarded his father's command. "He intended to forbid us to marry."

Myrana smiled. "You asked Handren to marry us before your father could make a public decree."

"I did." He took and held her hand, but his smile lasted only another moment. "I regret he was so bitter to you. Only that I knew his motivation was borne of greed, did I defy him."

What is to become of me? "I have betrayed you." Myrana stared at the floor. "Whatever failure of mine made you cast me aside, I cannot make excuses—"

"We have betrayed each other." Eodil exhaled. "After two years, and no sign we were any less in love, the old man had only one way left to spite me... dropping dead on the throne."

She squeezed his hand. "I know you loved your father, despite how he treated me."

"I became consumed with guilt. The last words I spoke to him were forged of anger. I told him he was a blind old man with an iron heart, who could not see love was greater than politics... and yet I allowed politics to drown my love for you."

"Your duties consumed you." She bounced the baby, eliciting happy chirps. "The burden of the crown has aged you. Are you still the man I once loved?"

What will become of my daughter when he sends me to the dungeon?

"I have not been. To become so again, I must divest myself of my anger. It is too late for me to convince my father to change his ways." Eodil grasped the infant's hand between two fingers. "This girl is no demon. Let this child live as a reminder of the failings of your loyalty to me."

"I allowed another to..." Myrana's tears thickened with shame. "A reminder? I am not to be ex—"

"Of course not. I am not my father. I could no more order your death than tear the moons from the sky with my bare hands."

Relief leaked out of her eyes. She leaned against him and cried on his shoulder.

King Eodil pulled his wife's head to his chest. "She shall also live as a reminder to me of my failings as your husband. Each time I look upon her, I will remember how I failed to attend to you, as my wife, and as my queen. It is a mistake I shall not repeat." He allowed a faint smile. "Have you yet named her?"

"Vymarra." Myrana pulled her nightdress down and offered the baby a breast. "Do you think it possible to love as we once did?"

He lifted her hand, tracing a thumb over her fingers. "I know only that it is not *im*possible."

She bowed her head. "I ask too much that you forgive me what I have done."

"I have heard even the pure blooded Niltharien are not born tainted." Eodil's voice soothed her as it did when he'd been courting her. "They cultivate the evil within their dens. Enough of your blood dwells within her to spare her the corruption. See to it she knows not of darkness. She will not become what you fear. Perhaps you should teach her your art, so she does not gravitate to the sorceric nature of her half-kind."

He knows? She stared over at him with a look of surprise.

"I am King of Ondremmar. Not a breath is taken in this land I am unaware of. Our Queen is a wizard, and no mere apprentice."

She tensed.

"Yes, I am aware of your skill." He kissed her. "I shall try to unseat my distrust of magic, though I do understand enough to understand arcane magic and demonic power are different paths. Guide her to the arcane and away from the lure of the abyss."

Myrana couldn't bring herself to look him in the eye again and kept her guilty stare upon her contented baby.

"For how I have been to you, I make no excuse." Eodil's voice lost some of its grandeur, becoming sincere. "If you will still have me, we shall no longer be strangers dwelling within an empty castle. I bid you return to the royal bedchamber from this night and evermore."

Myrana spoke after a long pause, though her voice a mere scratch upon the silence. "I can hardly fault you—"

He stalled her protest with a polite kiss.

She stared at him in disbelief.

"No small part of what happened here tonight is my doing. Think no more of the dark elf, or Handren's hasty counsel."

"Yes, your grace," she said, managing a normal tone.

"It pains me when you speak to me thus. We are husband and wife. King and queen. Equals."

She held her chin higher.

He smiled.

Myrana gazed into the dark as he stroked her hair, wondering to what extent he might think of her as betraying him in the days and years to come. Genuine love once burned between them, when he had been only a prince without the weight of a kingdom upon him. She could not abandon her guilt with the haste that Eodil desired.

Queen Myrana cradled her baby close to her breast, vowing to shield the child from the evils of the world. She beseeched the gods the day would come when she might earn her daughter's forgiveness for doubting her—if ever she could bear to tell her the truth behind the little scar on her hand.

VI

THE FAR SIDE OF PROMISE

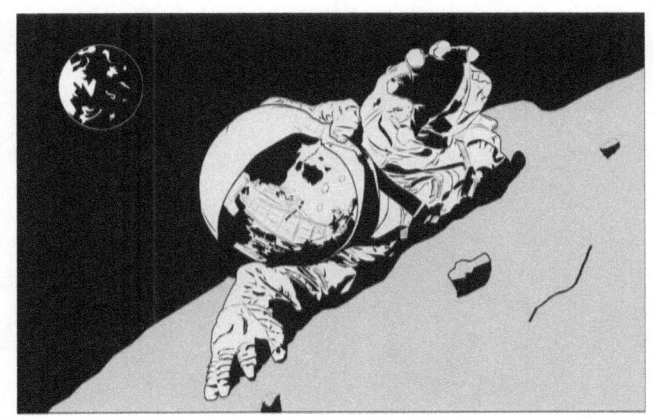

ABOUT THE FAR SIDE OF PROMISE

This is the first bit of fiction I ever wrote in first person. The inspiration for this short came from a writer's chat room I used to participate in during the early stages of my writing journey. Someone had asked a question about using real products in their story—if it was allowed or not. At some point during the discussion about making up fictional brand names or products, I randomly thought of the Wongo bar (Wellness on the Go) and started spouting off a bunch of cheesy marketing slogans.

I'm not honestly sure where the idea to frame the story on a distant planetoid came from. The Wongo bar thing came wrapped up in a heaping pile of corporate dystopia and cynicism. The persona of Jek, the main character, started talking to me in this gritty, dry unimpressed voice... probably my subconscious mind invoking the narrator from the video game *Full Throttle*. Anyway, it ended up being a 'space noir' story I intended as dark humor. For some reason, even though I had never written first person before, this story demanded it. One man, one planetoid, too many damn Wongo bars.

6

THE FAR SIDE OF PROMISE

Futility was something I had long gotten used to since arriving on Planetoid R1840M. Some nimrod in a fancy suit, impressive office, and ridiculously expensive chair decided to name it 'Promise'—as in a 'bright new future with Far Horizon Mining.' The only thing a day here promised was another fourteen hours of ass busting work extracting Mithrinium ore from an obstinate lump of rock. The surface consisted mostly of hard rocky stuff as brittle as glass, some large swaths of softer dirt, and the occasional patch like driving a seventy-ton collector into a lake of wet baby shit.

Yeah, paradise.

That's what the M stood for, by the way. Mithrinium, the highly volatile metallic salt somehow vital to the process of faster than light travel. I'm no chemist; all I know is the crap is worth a fortune, and the last guy to light up a butt within twenty meters of the stuff is probably back to Earth by now—without a ship. Either way, my ass fell for their bullshit story of a better life. Sure, the money isn't bad, but it's all waiting Earthside. Not like there's anything to spend it on out here in the ass end of nowhere, anyway.

Hell, even Pluto has whorehouses.

Like every other day out of the half a year I'd been stuck on this beige lump of shit hurtling through the void, I got into a staring contest with my friend—the Wongo bar. Six inches long, one inch wide, half an inch thick, these things and me... we go way back, almost seven months back. I don't even remember what the hell real food tastes like anymore. The only sensation my tongue registers these days is cardboard with an aftertaste of sweaty foot. Shit, I probably insulted the flavor of cardboard.

Some degree of cruelty beyond the normal levels of ordinary human suffering must be responsible for the three smiling faces staring back at me. What kind of asshole puts the recruitment posters that fooled us into coming out here on the walls of the ready room we wind up stuck in? Someone wanted to remind us every morning how stupid we were. Orange planets behind smiling men and women in space suits without a scratch on them; thumbs up for Far Horizons Mining Company. Find your Horizon... The future is you... Adventure among the stars...

The damn ad jingle still rattles around in my head.

It came down to just me and the Wongo bar. Again. Like every goddamn morning for the past seven months. Best I could remember, it'd been a week and a half since I took a decent dump that didn't involve screaming, swearing, and sweating like I had done a two-hour stint on a treadmill.

"Yo, Jek, you gonna eat that?" asked Nabo as he walked in.

Am I gonna eat that? I turned the Wongo bar in my fingers, making the wrapper crinkle. Most people ask that question in regard to *food*.

It occurred to me I really had forgotten what real food tasted like. Steak. Beer. Shit, even fish right now woulda been like manna from Heaven. Fuck, I'd kill someone for a PB&J, heavy on the PB.

"Yeah," I muttered, still searching for the willpower to tear open the wrapper. "You're up early."

"Couldn't wait to get started," said Nabo, side-fisting the dispenser box and catching the bar it spat out before he trudged in defeat to sit on a facing bench.

At least I had one good thing to say about Far Horizons. They didn't make us pay for the nutrient bars. I'd heard other companies put 'em in credit-operated vending machines. That's like takin' a whizz down a dead man's throat—after stealing his woman. There's no point locking them up or rationing them out, we only eat them because we have to. Even the damn rats won't touch these things. That's gotta say something. A man doesn't want to starve, although lately I'm not so sure.

Nabo leaned his elbows on his knees. His turn for a battle of wills. No one eats a Wongbo bar willingly. Takes a bit of psyching up. The overhead light faltered, leaving me in the dark for a moment with him. He disappeared except for his eyes. Barry called him Marvin once; Nabo in an e-suit did bear a likeness to that old cartoon alien—two eyes floating in a field of black. Can't argue truth. The dude *was* midnight dark, and Barry was dead. Nabo didn't much care for the Martian joke—after I explained it to him—but he had nothing to do with the man's demise. Barry didn't mean it as a racial comment, just one of those stupid ideas that pops into sudden clarity after weeks of mindless drudgery. Heh. Barry thought I was gonna hit him too for getting' racial, but I didn't take it that way. Clarke's stupid idea got him killed.

Nabo glared over his bar at me. "The hell you smiling at?"

"Nothin'," I mumbled, peeling back the silver wrapper. Today's justification for opening it was less time spent looking at the word 'Wongo.' "I can't wait to eat."

"Bullshit." Nabo grinned, and bit the end of his bar through the wrapper.

"Plastic give it any more flavor?" I asked.

He waved his hand in a side-side tilt. "Not really, but the plastic helps scrape the walls clean on the way out."

Kara, the only female on this rock, came out of her room, naked and carrying a large spanner wrench in one hand and a towel in the other. She had her ways. Six miners and a manager shared two showers. Neither one of them had curtains; none of us had much privacy. Guess curtains cost extra. Only Jon still bothered to even attempt it. Course, now with Clarke and Barry gone, mornings ended up being a little less of a cluster. We almost had enough time before our shift to enjoy a moment of shared discontent at the Wongo bars. Nabo and I watched her go by, wordless, the same routine as every other morning. Both of us had the same question on our mind.

Had we been here long enough yet?

Pretty is a highly subjective term. Many things can make a woman attractive. Genetics, cosmetics, sexy clothes, alcohol, long stints in a penal facility—or being stuck on an asteroid mining colony at the edge of explored space. Kara got that hint as well, which probably explained why she always carried the spanner to the shower. Being the only woman anywhere within a hundred thousand miles tended to make a person paranoid. Can't say I blamed her much. Course, that didn't explain why she walked to the shower naked in the morning—I never will understand women. Maybe she figured saving the four calories she'd burn to get dressed would let her go longer before she had to endure another eating another damned Wongo bar.

Maybe she wanted an excuse to kick someone's ass.

She vanished through the hatchway. Water valves squeaked a minute or so later. I bit into the damn thing; crumbly bits of fibrous matter broke apart in my mouth. If you let it sit there, sucking on it, it almost tasted like it attempted to be chocolate. If you just chewed it to get it over with as fast as possible (as I usually did) it had about the same flavor as damp paper seasoned with sneaker soles. If you got an old one past its 'freshness' date, it took on a subtle undertone of some kind of vegetative matter. Got a fresh one today. Lucky me.

Lin scooted out of the shower area, wrapped in a towel, and claimed his punishment from the Wongo dispenser.

"What's wrong with you?" I asked, due to the seen-a-ghost look on his face. "Don't usually see your eyes open all the way."

Nabo laughed. Hypocrite. Political correctness had been one of the first things to die out here, right after self-respect.

"What you mean?" He flopped on a bench to my left. "My eyes always open."

"Probably tried to play grab-ass with Kara again." Nabo ate half his bar in one bite. "S'why she carries that spanner. Pound your skinny little ass into wonton if you touch her again."

"Fuck you too, Nabo."

Nabo pulled his towel aside. "It's here if you want it, little man."

I looked away. "Damn, man, cover that thing."

A half-coherent voice muttered from Sleeping Room 2. "Hey you two, you know fraternization is against company policy. You boys want to get romantic, save it for your day off. And can it with the racial jokes or you'll have to take another sensitivity module."

Nabo and I chuckled.

Lin shouted, "No romantic, Jon, this one being racially insensitive to me."

Nabo's laughter shook the walls. He closed his towel. He leaned at Lin, devouring the last of his Wongo while making his eyes bulge. Lin got up and hurried to his locker. Jon shot a disgusted look at the dispenser, seemed like he might skip it today.

"Staring at the damn machine won't turn 'em into tacos," I said, then laughed. I'd straight up kill someone for a real taco at this point.

Jon shook his head and punched the machine hard enough to dislodge a bar. Rumor had it he came from South America. Clarke once tried to joke, saying Jon made it across the DMZ with a backpack full of the good stuff. Wonder what rock Clarke lived under... Earth had like four governments left. Guess he's been out here way too long. Jon did look like he could've been from there, but Promise didn't exactly get a regular flow of information flowing freely. Jon's a hard guy to read. We're still waiting for him to show any kind of emotion at all.

He had a habit of skipping showers too, which was fine with Terry, the manager, as it saved energy. It was less fine with Lin, his roommate. Of course, with Barry and Clarke gone and presumed dead, Jon now had his own room. Maybe it had been his plan all along, stink everyone out so he had some privacy. He also frequently slept in his jumpsuit, which carried the reek of Mithrinium wherever he went.

Kara, dripping wet, walked in from the tiny shower space. No one but Lin paid her much notice as she dried her hair in front of a room full of men before putting her jumpsuit on. The company-issued white boxer briefs didn't do much for her image of femininity.

"Watch your eyes, Nabo. I saw you lookin'." She wandered over and punched the dreaded machine, which spat out another Wongo bar.

Damn corporations... at least scientists would've given us a maze to run before we pushed the bar.

"Two more months." Nabo flung off his towel and went over to his locker.

"You only got two months left?" asked Jon.

Nabo smiled. "Nah, man. 'Nother two months out here and she might start lookin' good enough."

Kara ignored him.

"You angry she beat you arm wrestle," snapped Lin. "She pretty."

As if it wasn't hard enough to choke down the damn bar, doing so while laughing hurt.

Nabo twisted around to grin at her. "I think he likes you."

Kara gave him the finger.

"I think she got that feeling when he grabbed a handful in the shower," muttered Jon.

Nabo slammed his locker, making Lin jump. "Kara would break him in half."

She tossed her boots to the ground and sat on the right-side bench, next to Jon. I swung my legs over and grabbed a pair from my locker. The pod connector opened. Terrence Earle, supervisor, manager, and general corporate face, ducked past the bulkhead. Dealing with him required a nuanced sort of experience. He always had the same plastic smile so disingenuous his eyes appeared to be in a permanent state of half-closedness. Made me wonder if the company sent him rubber masks he pulled over a mannequin skull whenever he needed a different expression. He even had the gall to wear a miner's jumpsuit, only his looked like it'd just come out of the wrapper. Not one scrap of dust or wear.

"The fuck flavor is it this week?" asked Kara.

"Wongo flavor," I muttered. "I think I'd rather lick Nabo's fuckin' foot."

"It beef." Lin nibbled at his. "Maybe chocolate."

"The wrapper accused it of being chocolate." Kara didn't look convinced.

Nabo waved his second bar at Terrence. "What the hell are these things made out of, anyway?"

Jon eyed his half-eaten one. "Last year's miners."

For a moment, I thought Jon was in trouble. The whites of Terrence's eyes became visible.

"That is nothing more than a demoralizing rumor," said Terrence. "The Wellness-On-the-Go nutrient bars contain everything a body needs to maintain optimum functioning in extreme conditions."

"And they have a shelf life of forty-two years," I added.

"That ain't what I asked, man." Nabo stood.

Terrence was tall, something like six-eight, but not Nabo tall. Nabo's chin stopped at his eye level.

"Uhh," muttered Terrence, no crack evident in the rubber smile. "Standard flavor."

"Fuck these things." Kara grumbled. "Standard what? Recycled toilet paper?"

"Don't think about it, just eat it," I said. "We've been here six months, six more to go 'til we rotate out."

"I have an announcement, everyone." Terrence folded his arms over his chest.

"They're shipping you a new facial expression?" I asked.

He chuckled and pivoted side to side so everyone could bask in Managersmile™. "That's a good one, Jek. What I wanted to say was, corporate has announced a bonus incentive for this quarter. They sent a new batch of productivity goals. If we can meet or exceed—"

"You crazy, Terrence? We work fourteen hours day now." Lin kicked his locker closed. "What more productivity we can have?"

Jon let all the air out of his lungs past flapping lips.

"Got some productivity for them, right here." Nabo grabbed himself through his jumpsuit.

Everyone but Lin laughed, even Terrence.

Our manager tapped his fingertips together, still smiling. "Well, I just wanted to put it out there. They said there would be a food bonus involved."

"What, like actual food?" Rubber-man had my interest.

Jon's eyebrows went up. Kara let a half-eaten Wongo bar dangle from her lower lip.

"I'm not privy to the details. All I know is they said it would be a dramatic improvement in the quality of your rations."

"Nabo's damn underwear would be a 'dramatic improvement in the quality of our rations.'" I shook my head.

"Yours if you want 'em." Nabo shoved his ass in my face.

"Freeze dried steak?" asked Jon.

"Shit, I'd be happy with damn oatmeal," muttered Kara.

Terrence started out the pod hatch, but paused. "I imagine it would depend on the degree the team exceeds productivity goals. The better we do, the better the reward."

"What the hell else can we do?" asked Jon. "We're two men short, one collector short, and already working fourteens to cover the slack. They want more productivity, they should bring us back up to full staff."

Nabo nodded. "Damn right. This 'no free time' shit ain't right."

"Planning to go to mall sometime, maybe catch movie?" I slapped the last fastener on my left boot closed.

"You know what I mean." Nabo slammed his locker.

We had three video game consoles and fourteen terabytes of movies, but the monitor took a shit three months back and the replacement has been 'on the way' ever since. Lin being right about there being nothing to do here except masturbate, sleep, eat, and work only made Nabo angrier. Of those, eating felt less and less appealing. Suppose sex counted as an optional activity, regs or not, but we only had one woman, plus three men and a manager. Even if she was into it, the station had nowhere to go to avoid an audience. Everyone would at least hear it.

Not to mention she still had at least two months left.

I hadn't realized I was drooling all over myself until she glared at me.

My head pointing in her direction didn't help matters. I had a spanner rattled in my general direction.

"Damn, Barry…" Kara kicked the bench. "Figures he'd lose the new machine."

I kept a chuckle to myself, thinking about Barry's little trick with the fuses.

"That collector only start for him." Lin grumbled. "He know secret."

"Nah, Kara. I'm just thinkin' 'bout freeze-dried steak. I'm gonna go after that collector."

"You crazy, Jek." Lin laughed. "Clarke took it out by The Wash. He not back by now, he not coming back."

Nabo waved dismissively. "Man, The Wash doesn't even exist. Probably a snot blur on the scanner lens."

"They must've found something out there," said Jon. "Their last transmission sounded thrilled."

"If so happy, why they stay gone?" Lin shook his head. "I no going. I like alive."

"Look, Jek." Terrence raised Managerhand™. "I can't have you go traipsing all over R1840M in search of a lost crew that's been missing for a month. You need to be operating your assigned unit to keep up with our output quotas."

I stood, hands on my hips like some kind of space gunslinger… only I didn't have any guns. Lucky for me. "There's no indigenous life on this ball of shit. What if they threw a track and got stuck?"

Terrence heaved that specific sigh of feigned regret they must train managers how to do. The 'I care but I can't do anything' line of bullshit capable of making an ordinarily reasonable man want to choke someone out. "Their attempt to locate this… Wash was done outside of company approval protocols. We received no distress transmission."

"They're sending the bill for the lost collector to the next of kin," muttered Jon.

Kara laughed. Nabo had no reaction until Terrence's face hinted Jon could be right, at which point he whistled.

Jon blinked. "Seriously?"

Terrence waved him off. "I have no control over what corporate does."

"Look, Terry." I advanced on him, pushing him into the wall by mere presence alone. He had like an inch of height on me, but one of my biceps was worth two of his. It helped he feared anything remotely physical, including work. "What if I got the collector back? Even if The Wash isn't real, I can find the machine. That'll push us over prod goals and make you look good. Even if I waste a day, we're already behind. Doesn't matter if we miss it by four percent or five percent, does it?"

Terrence tapped all his fingertips together. "Well—"

"I'll go with him," said Kara. "I'm so sick of these damn bars."

"Wait just a minute, people." Terrence held up both hands. "We can't shut down the operation for this. Even if he *does* recover the lost collector, I can't authorize a full stop for the day."

"Hold on," said Lin. "You fine with him going for collector, but when going for crew you say no?"

"Crew's cheaper to replace," muttered Nabo. His glare challenged Terrence to say anything.

"One person going alone is asking for trouble," said Kara. "Need at least two."

"I'll go too. Nabo and Lin are the most proficient operators. It'll be slower, but they can both handle a collector solo. We only have two machines anyway, unless this works."

Terrence stared at Jon, as did Lin.

"Less you want to go out there instead, Lin." Jon winked.

Lin shook his head, pointing. "No, I operate collector alone for day. You want be fool, you be fool."

I put my other boot up on the bench and slapped the fasteners closed. "We'll take a Six-Six out heading on their last course. Station control still shows their position as a weak signal trace out of the relative northeast."

"There's no telling how far off the glass that is." Terrence stared at me, head tilting. As far as he cared, this planet didn't exist beyond what showed up on his precious map table. "What?"

"I'm marveling how your smile never changes, wondering what kind of material they molded your face out of."

He let out that same noncommittal chuckle he always made when he found something insulting, but was too afraid of HR to get angry. "I'm not authorized—"

"Eight hours, tops. If we don't get a good signal trace by then, we'll turn around. We're so far behind already they won't notice. If it works, if I find it, we can run all three collectors on fourteens 'til the quarter is over and make up the loss."

Terrence thought for a minute. "Okay, fine. You got eight hours."

A Six-Six was an open-topped rover vehicle with six giant tires and six seats, arranged in three pairs. Its actual designation consisted of a jumble of numbers and an overstuffed mythological name like Basilisk some cheesedick in a lab coat back on Earth thought sounded intimidating. The only thing threatened by a Six-Six was the unlucky ass planted in those unforgiving seats for more than twenty minutes at a shot.

We'd gotten out of there fast, before Terrence could change his mind. Since I had the idea to take this crazy chance, I wound up driving with Kara in the passenger seat and Jon catching up on lost sleep in the middle row. Kara was a beat-you-at-arm-wrestling, chug-beer-and-fart kind of girl —and smart too. She had the rover's onboard navigation computer up and running in four minutes, and patched into the outpost system in six, a feat not supposed to be possible. After seven minutes, a map appeared on the wire-gridded glass console.

"Damn, that's a neat trick." I leaned over.

"I'm not just a pretty face."

I couldn't tell if she tried to be sarcastic. We teased her about her femininity, but from the neck up, she looked fine. Neck down, solid as an ore collector. All muscle. Somehow, the tiny bit of static at the end as the comm cut off made her sound cute. I guess I *had* been on this rock too long. Maybe the faint blur caused by the dark amber helmet visor made her look good, or maybe she seemed more attractive because she left the spanner back in the locker room.

I made a course correction, heading a little bit farther to the right. "Well, that bettered our odds."

There's something to be said for driving over an endless field of dark grey rock with nothing but the emptiness of space above you that can put everything in perspective. The operations manual of the Six-Six cautioned against doing more than 54 MPH on a planetoid with .32 Earth gravity. One poorly placed rock could turn the land vehicle into an unsteerable spacecraft. Yeah, screw that. Forty is just fine.

The readout on the arm of my e-suit showed at least 61 hours of air left. "It's a damn miracle."

Kara held on as I struggled to keep it in a straight line over some ripples in the planet surface. "What is? That Terrence gave us the okay?"

"That too." I started to laugh, but grunted as we hit some rough terrain. "No, that the e-suits work. NHM is so damn cheap."

Jon chuckled over the comm, not bothering to sit up. "They *are* cheap. The collectors are sealed, but you know all the maintenance tasks send us

EVO. If they didn't give us decent suits, they'd get less Mithrinium out of us. Suits cost less than full-service bays or delicate remote optics."

I couldn't argue. "You've got a point."

A rough bump shot straight up into my tailbone, knocking my spine into my skull. Kara bounced out of her seat, clinging to the overhead bar. The irony was, I bet she could have lifted the Six-Six, at least in .32 Earth gravity. Hell, I probably could too. Nabo could throw it.

"Hey, Jek, watch the bumps. I'm trying to sleep here."

"So glad you came along to help out." I tried to glance at him over my shoulder. The corner of the air scrubber backpack made it impossible to see behind me. "You mind giving us a hand looking once we get closer?"

"No problem. Wake me up when we get there."

Kara glanced at me without a word. I stared through two visors' worth of fog. I never noticed before; her eyes were blue. Blue eyes and brown hair didn't happen too often. I started to figure I'd been out here too long. Yeah, definitely going to be my last tour. Hell, if I had a choice between sex and steak right now, I would've gone for the steak without a second thought. That's when I stopped figuring I'd been here too long and *knew* it.

The ground shook.

"What the hell was that?" shouted Jon.

I looked around at flat, open grey landscape. "I have no damn—"

The ground shook again, harder.

Another vibration rattled the Six-Six. A plume of dust rose out of the dirt to the left, spraying us with small rocks and sand.

"Meteorite shower!" Kara shouted, pointing up and to the right.

Like a miniature Ring of Saturn, a hail of stones ranging from pea-sized to five feet across fell directly at us.

"Gun it!" she yelled. "Go, go, go!"

Driving too fast on this planetoid will launch us into space if I hit a bad bounce. In the nanosecond mental math following her screaming, risking it seemed like a better option than having a ten-ton meteorite smash us flat. At least if we floated out into the endless black, I'd have a little time to be happy I'd never eat another Wongo bar again. Inspired by that logic, I shoved forward on the accelerator. I imagine in any kind of atmospheric condition, the electric motors in each wheel would have been whining their little hearts out. Promise had no atmosphere; it didn't even have the courtesy to have a poisonous one. No sound. Nothing but Kara screaming and Jon snoring over the comm.

Snoring?

A rock easily the same size as our Six-Six cratered the ground about ten yards ahead and to the left; glassy shards sprayed over us, some sticking into the front end. A barrage of clicking and snapping filled my helmet during the debris shower. Two spear-like crystals hit the tire, but broke off when they hit the ground. Thank whoever decided to put solid wheels on this damn thing. I swerved, going into a slide. A peppering of little clanks followed. I wasn't worried at first until I remembered that whole 'no sound' thing. That's when I realized more rocks hit me on the helmet.

Talk about motivation.

Another impact covered us with dust as I turned toward it quite by accident—trying to avoid another falling titan. It worked out though; only silt hit us. Pulverized glass, rock dust, whatever this ridiculous place is made of. I'm no geologist. Best I figure, this planet is made of solidified disappointment and shattered hope—maybe the crystallized tears of former miners.

*The ground bucked from a*nother big rock slamming down right behind us. The ass end of the Six-Six left the ground, tilting us up on only the two front wheels. I got lucky; out of instinct, I accelerated rather than stomping the brakes. Brakes would've flipped us. I must've looked somewhat competent. Kara cheered as if I did it on purpose. Works for me.

"Jon, how the fuck are you slee—shit!"

The rear end came down, giving me steering back in time to avoid a cloud of head-sized rocks falling in a row like some giant machine gun aimed for the rover, tracing a line of bullets across the ground. One landed in the back seat, crushing the Six-Six down on its shocks. I held on. Jon woke up. Kara screamed.

When the suspension bounced back, we caught air. Not little air either —big air, 'we're going for a ride' air. I conducted a reassuring tensile strength test on the control sticks. For once, I was thankful for Wongo bars. When you shit once a week, it's harder to mess yourself. Even if I did, it would've been a diamond-hard nugget the size of a cherry.

Kara, however, kept enough of her cool to dive over the seatback to the emergency air tank in the center. She struggled to stretch forward and grab something.

"Come on, come on." She yelled, "Gotcha!"

They say 'In space, no one can year you scream' (at least not without radios), so none of us heard the hissing from the billowing cone of white vapor. I imagined it, though. Our rapid ascent slowed, and then became a rapid descent thanks to our new source of thrust. The change in trajectory shoved all of our stomachs up to say hello to our throats. The Six-Six came down hard, crashing into a twisting slide that gave me a good close up view of the console. In fact, I had such a great view of the navigation screen I decided to take a short nap.

———

"JEK!"

Jon's voice intruded on my blissful repose. Never realized how comfortable a pillow glass and steel could be.

"Jek! Are you alive?"

"Five more minutes, Mom," I mumbled.

"Get up, asshole. We're boned."

Who the hell is he to bitch at me for sleeping?

A flood of memories crashes into my half-awake brain, like a nugget of half-chewed Wongo rounding the colon. Meteor shower. Amateur space launch. Crap. I shot upright, staring out past the narrow, sloped nose of the Six-Six. The rover dangled over a crevasse, the central wheels right on the edge, caught on a ridge of tight-packed rocks. The front tires spun free, the rear set off the ground. Lucky thing for those rocks, probably the only reason the whole thing didn't go over. That, and like my ex, the Six-Six carries most of its weight in the ass.

No sign of Kara. I turned, trying to peer over the seat to the center row at Jon, but couldn't see past my rebreather.

"Jon? Where the hell are you?"

"On the fuckin' nose," he yelled.

I started to stand up, which caused the vehicle to slip an inch and Jon to scream like a tween girl. I froze. Ignoring his barrage of contradictory commands to 'don't move a damn muscle' and 'do something,' I twisted in the seat to face the rear. The meteorites still fell, but they came down far enough behind us to go from pants-staining scary to a thing of beauty. Moving at the speed of a governmental agency, I eased myself over the seatback and made my way to the rear. My shifting weight tilted the Six-Six back. Jon stopped yelling at me, which likely meant he'd become a lot happier.

Balancing in the rear seats, I stretched over the end hull and rifled through the storage compartments. One of the benefits of being with a mining operation involved having tools made for dealing with rock. I located a B11 in short order, a shotgun-like device about as big around as my arm with a huge, angry three-pronged grappling hook on the front end. Even in .32 Earth gravity, the bitch was unwieldy.

After managing to level it off at the ground behind the rover, I pulled the trigger. Nothing happened. Crap. Oh, right—the safety. My second try worked better, and the hook bored into the surface about fifteen meters from the back end. As if some dickhead engineer foresaw this exact moment, the Six-Six had a mounting clamp for a B11 on both bumpers. Didn't take me long to have the rover moored to the ground. No way would this bastard thing fall over the edge.

I grabbed a roll of cord and moved to the front end, sliding on my chest until I could see past the nose. Jon had a two-handed grip on the grille protector, trying not to look down thirty or forty meters to a bubbling silver mass. I hesitated, staring down at what had to be a lake of molten aluminum. For the second time in a day, I felt rather grateful Far Horizons Mining didn't skimp on our suits. Granted, falling into that mess would surely overwhelm the e-suit's thermal compensation, but at least the suits could ward off the solar radiation. It did get pretty damn hot here during the 'day,' so maybe the suit could withstand the lake for a little while. At least until the planetoid rotated into the dark. Then the aluminum would turn solid. That would suck. Hmm. Would people float on molten aluminum? Probably. I really didn't want to find out.

"Jek, the hell are you doin', man?"

"Thinkin'." I lowered the cord to him.

"'Bout what?"

"How much I don't feel like going swimming right now."

The moment I started to haul him up, I spotted Kara. She'd landed on the opposite side of the crevasse, about halfway down on a ledge. The crash must have catapulted her right out of the seat. I pulled on the cord while not paying much attention to Jon, too busy trying to think of how the hell we'd get her back up here. When Jon grabbed my arm, it startled me so much I almost leapt off the hood. Fortunately, the gold visor prevented Jon from seeing my face. I twisted, using gravity as well as my entire body to pull him up onto the rover.

We landed in the front seat on top of each other like two lovers. I'm glad no one saw that.

"You should shower, Jon. I can smell you through two e-suits."

"Fuck you too, Jek." He patted me on the helmet. "Thanks, man." He rolled off me and jumped to the ground.

"Ugh, I should've brought Nabo. He could have dragged this damn thing off the ledge himself."

"You wouldn't have been able to lift his ass off the bumper."

"Heh, you got a point." I looked over my shoulder again. "Give me a hand here. Pull."

Jon stood, looking at the B11. "Winch it back?"

I shifted the drive mechanism to reverse and eased forward on the throttle. It's pretty damn hard to gauge motor strain when you can't hear them whining. The vibration in the frame couldn't really convey the same information. "I don't want to rip the damn hook out of the ground. Sudden loss of tension will throw us over the edge. The B11's motor is way too weak to winch a Six-Six around and if I accelerate too hard, the wheels will chew the edge apart."

"Son of a bitch." John grunted, trying to pull the rover back by hand.

It took some doing, but we managed to get the Six-Six off the ledge by the time Kara woke up and moaned over the comm.

"What happened? Shit, I think my leg's broken." She drew in a gasp. "Is... that mercury?"

"It's molten aluminum... I think." I scrunch up my nose. "Mercury would be boiling."

"Okay, that explains the thermal warnings... Umm, where the hell are you guys?"

I bundled the B11 and tossed it into the middle row. "We just got the Six off the ledge. It almost joined you down there. Hang on, gonna come around the other side."

Jon stared off at the meteorite pummeling as I drove the length of the crevasse, rounding the corner almost a quarter mile away from where we hit it. Fortunately, our landing made enough of a mess of the edge, the impact point proved easy to spot from the other side.

"We're running out of time, man." Jon muttered over a private channel. "We're going to get caught in the dark if we don't haul ass. We don't have the time or the equipment to get her back."

I blinked at him, not that he noticed past the visor. "You can't be serious."

"This is why it's a bad idea to send women up here, even ones as rough looking as her. Stupid macho bullshit. You wanna save her, don't you? Think you'll get some?"

"If it was your smelly ass down there, I'd want to haul it back too. And she ain't 'rough looking.' She's just not scrawny." I grabbed the B11. "And yeah, maybe there's a little chivalry left in here somewhere. Look, I got an idea. Be ready to back up."

"Fuck, man. This is a dangerous waste of time."

"So was this whole goddamn trip. And I don't only mean today." I waved at the planetoid. "This *whole* goddamn trip."

"Hah. Yeah, no shit." Jon shifted into the driver's seat as I glided to the ground and stomped around front. Okay, maybe the trip wasn't a total waste. Jumping in .32 Earth gravity is fun.

After tying the grapple end to the bumper and triple testing it, I attached the B11's housing to the mounting brackets on my e-suit's chest and patted it into place. It would rip the suit in half before it came off.

"Kara, you still awake?"

"Yeah. Just sunning myself down here, all I'm missing is a Wongo-rita."

The mere thought of that almost painted the inside of my visor with brown sludge. "Uhh, I'll forget you said that. Comin' down."

I tensioned the winch in the B11's handle and stepped over the edge. I'm not sure what made Jon even consider winching the Six-Six back with one of these. This thing's motor had less power than Terrence's quarterly motivational pep talks. It would barely lift *my* ass up in a vertical ascent; it couldn't take two people, much less a rover. Either way, I had the situation sorted already.

Heat tingled in my legs through the e-suit. "You're right. Damn, it's hot down here."

The ledge Kara sat on crumbled as my boots touched it. She forced herself to stand on one leg, unable to hide the primal panic in her eyes at the feeling of the ground shifting under us. I managed to get my arms around her before it gave out completely and chunks of rock went floating off in the aluminum lake, some sinking. Good thing the girl had serious upper body strength. Good thing the e-suits were rigid, too. I hit the locking lever on the B11, freezing the winch.

"Jon, you there?"

"Yeah."

"Back it up slow. Three to four MPH tops."

The Six-Six had no trouble lifting the two of us. Kara's right leg probably broke at the shin. I figured it had to be her right since she let off a scream like someone tried to remove hemorrhoids with a power drill as soon as that leg scraped the top of the crevasse. Come to think of it, I've never seen her cry before. Well, not literally see. Damn gold visors. Could hear it in her voice over the comm.

"You okay?" I asked.

"My damn leg."

I stood, pulling her upright with me. "E-suit should be rigid enough to act like a splint. Come on."

"How the hell did you break a leg without cracking the suit?" asked Jon.

"Just talented, I guess." She grunted.

We limped to the rover, and I lifted her over the side. After stowing the B11 in the back, I reclaimed the driver's position from Jon and shooed him into the passenger seat. He looked at me. Despite the expressionless gold ball facing me, I imagined a blankness to his face and assumed we both considered saying 'screw it' and turning around. We exchanged a nod. The instant I reached for the stick, Kara leaned past the gap in the front seats, and pointed.

"Look!"

Her gloved hand hovered between our visors. I leaned forward, searching the land ahead of us where she pointed. On the horizon perched the unmistakable fat-roach shape of a collector, beside the edge of a long strip of sparkling pale grey silt.

"Son of a bitch," I said.

"Ha! We're golden." Jon stood in the seat, pounding one hand on the frame of the windscreen. "Go! Go!"

So, I went. A long, smooth patch of glass-like beige ground led to an immense smear of silvery-grey. Mithrinium, in its powdery glory formed the shape of a great non-moving river. I drooled as if we'd found an ocean of prime rib. This much pure Mithrinium meant productivity; it meant food.

Like a suckling piglet, our missing collector tucked nose first into the side of the silt-stream. I drove right up behind it, imagining Terrence's rubber face changing shape at the productivity numbers we could pull off with something like this. It had to be eighty-five percent pure, compared to the usual twenty-something we managed from the denser ore. I wonder what genius back on Earth decided to set up the mining operation where we did. I was so taken by daydreams of steak, I didn't notice poor Barry until all three wheels on the left side of the Six-Six ran him over.

"Aww fuck." I brought us to a shuddering stop, wheels sliding on the slick ground.

Jon hopped down and went for the collector while I headed for Barry—or what remained of him. The enormous wheels didn't do much damage.

They were wide, fat, and soft, and he was already dead. I could tell because of the way the body bounced when I ran him over. He tumbled like a life-sized action figure, rigid. Arms and legs stuck in the position they'd been in when he'd taken his last breath. After plodding to where he came to rest for the second time, I nudged him over on his back with my boot. The faceplate of his helmet had been smashed. Bloody threads trailed out of his mouth, frozen solid like a macabre jelly donut squeezed too hard.

Rapid depressurization really sucks.

"Jon, somethin' got Barry."

Thirty yards away, by the rear end of the collector, Jon faced toward me. "What do you mean 'got' Barry? There's not supposed to be anything on this planetoid."

"Helmet smashed out. Poor bastard's frozen solid." Hmm. Guess the molten aluminum bubbled up from below. Can't be hot out here if he's an icicle. Oh, wait. We're in a shadowed valley, out of direct sunlight. Yeah, that'll do it.

"Maybe he caught a little meteorite in the face," said Kara.

"No," I said. "His whole head would be gone if it was a rock shower."

Kara shrugged. "Could be a little one, like the size of a grape."

All three of us fell silent, having an near-orgasmic moment daydreaming about tasting actual grapes.

"Dammit, they swore nothing lived on this rock." Jon shivered, worry clear in his voice.

Crap. He sounded emotional. Now I knew we'd stepped in deep shit.

"You see tracks or anything in the silt?" asked Kara. "Any sign of what did it?"

"There is no indigenous life on Promise." A calm voice I recognized as Clarke's crackled over the radio. Too calm for a guy who'd been stranded for weeks out here without food and only a dead operator to keep him company.

Kara gave me a look. I couldn't see her expression nor did I know a hundred percent sure what she thought, but I had an inkling we were close to the same wavelength. The 'two plus two equals nine' wavelength. Jon peeked around the edge of the collector as I reached into the cargo hatch on the Six-Six. Holding the B11 like the plasma rifle it wasn't, I crept toward the giant machine.

"C-Clarke?" said Jon. "How the hell are you alive? What happened?"

I sidestepped to my left to get a better field of view. Clarke's ass hung out of an open hatch about halfway along the left side of the collector.

"The silt is too fine. It gummed up the system," said Clarke. "Barry encountered a hostile entity. I'm trying to get this thing running again so I can get back."

Jon leaned in closer. "I thought there wasn't supposed to be anything alive on this rock but us?"

"Careful, Jon." I eased closer, sighting over the grappling gun. "Something's not—"

"I said hostile. I did not say indigenous." Clarke whirled out of the opening, swinging a long wrench.

It caught Jon on the helmet before he could move. The splintering crack echoed over the comm link as he careened over backward and hit the ground, skidding into the silt wash. Clarke turned on me next, but I had the B11 ready. Firing it knocked me back two steps, but the hook (mostly by luck) nailed him in the face, shattering his visor. One of the three-pronged stone-boring tips sank into Clarke's left eye as the momentum of the hit pinned him against the collector. The other two tips skimmed the outside of his helmet and stuck in the hull.

Kara screamed. Clarke's body twitched in a series of spasmodic jerks before it hung limp.

Jon pawed at his helmet, gloves a blur. "Shit, it's cracking. It's cracking! Jek, do something It's—"

I turned toward Jon. He started to scream over the comm, but his voice drowned in a deafening hiss. He clutched his the visor, trying to hold it in as the pressure differential forced a tiny break to become a catastrophic failure. Half-inch-thick polycarbonate resin, and most of Jon's guts, exploded through his desperate fingers and froze into a bloom of gore. I imagine if our e-suits had been flexible, he would've been mostly compressed into his helmet.

For the better part of ten minutes, I stood there staring at Jon. Perhaps shock or disbelief led me to try to figure out which of the crystallizing blobs were which organs. Maybe my brain needed something to distance itself from the reality of killing Clarke. An odd mixture of gratitude and guilt came over me. Jon's laziness had been a thing of legend. Only his desire to get out of work made him agree to come with me. He figured we'd be driving around in aimless circles for a few hours, then go back to the outpost with nothing to show for our time.

More sleep.

In actuality, he saved my life. If he hadn't come with us, it would've been me there screaming my guts out. Honestly, in some sick kind of way, after seven months of Wongo bars... the frozen bloom of gore coming out of his faceplate struck me funny, as if his panicked scream took on solid form.

I really needed to get off this rock.

"Jek?" Kara's voice came out of the black like an angel. The sound snapped me out of the trance I'd slipped into. "Are you okay? What just happened?"

I ambled around so I could see her. She tried to pull herself up in the rover's seat to get a better look at me. "Yeah... I guess. Clarke killed Jon. I shot Clarke."

"Oh, my God..." she rasped. "W-we should get back before something else happens."

"We came this far. Jon's dead, Kara. We shouldn't make his death for nothing and all that bullshit," I muttered while trudging over to him. Two kicks broke the mass away from the helmet. I dragged both to the Six-Six and put him in the rearmost seat, setting the gore in his lap like a bouquet of flowers. "The least we can do is ship him back home for a decent burial."

I belted kung-fu grip Barry into the seat next to him.

"Kara, you think you can drive the Six back?" I stomped past where I'd stapled Clarke to the machine. "I'm gonna see if I can get this beast moving."

"Yeah." She growled in pain as she pulled herself into the driver's seat.

I climbed the boarding ladder to the cockpit of the two-story tall collector. Frost covered most of the screens, a sign someone opened the doors without recovering the atmosphere first. I brushed a gloved hand over the console, tracing smears in the flaking white. The whole thing looked dead and dark. None of the systems would turn on, not even warning lights. For some minutes, I poked and prodded at buttons trying to bring the behemoth online, but got the distinct impression the electronics were toasted.

Leaning back to unleash a torrent of creative invectives at the stars, I managed to scream myself dizzy before something unusual caught my eye. Four two-inch fuses gleamed at me from their perch tucked into the elastic strap on the sun visor. Standard operating procedure called for three spares. I reached under the dash to the panel. Sure enough, the master fuse socket was empty. It must have been Barry's trick; he liked to 'reserve' the newest collector for himself to pad his numbers. No one managed to notice how he always seemed to get the 'stubborn' one to work. Then again, no one else was bored enough to actually read the Standard Practices and Procedures manual. Sometimes we had fun reading parts of it it in cartoon voices while trying to shit unsuccessfully for the third time in a week.

Wow, I *really* needed to get the hell off this rock.

"Guess Clarke never read the SP&P Third Edition." I plucked one of the fuses from the visor and snapped it in place. The dash lit up like the red-light district of Venus City.

"External lights are on." Kara cheered.

Clarke's body swung a little on the hook as I backed the collector out and turned it to face home. He and Barry had already filled the bin with silt from The Wash. What we had on board already would be enough to send our production high enough for the company to ship Terrence a 'shocked' rubber face to wear for the announcement meeting.

"What about Clarke?" asked Kara. "He's swinging on the side."

"Clarke can fucking drift."

I hopped out and shimmied down the ladder before jogging over to where I'd stapled him to the side. When I grabbed the end of the grapple, fully intending to kick Clarke off into deep space, his remaining eye snapped open. Sparks lapped from his face to the B11's grapple prong. I staggered back, trying to convince my heart not to stop dead in its tracks. Clarke reached up and grabbed the hook claw, twisting it back and forth until he pulled it free. The last of his visor crumbled to fragments of amber. His face, exposed to the nothingness that was Promise's lack of atmosphere, wrinkled around his remaining eye as he grinned.

Where the plasma drill rod had impales his skull, a sparking tunnel of circuitry, silicon, and metal gaped.

"He's a goddamned android..." Well, at least now I understood how one hit from a wrench shattered an e-suit helmet—and how he survived out here so long alone.

"You are rather observant, Jek." Clarke punched me dead center in the chest.

I hit the ground so fast I didn't remember going down. One instant Clarke stood in front of me, the collector behind him, and then I'm gazing up at a star field with no air in my lungs, vaguely aware of sliding.

"What the hell?" I croaked.

The soft silt arrested my skid. I managed to sit up right as Clarke kicked me across the face. I flinched enough so his foot caught the solid back of my helmet rather than visor. The hit lifted me off my ass and flung me face-down a few feet away, as if I'd been run over by the collector.

"Kuromori-Hanford was interested in this rock, but they didn't want to make a full investment. They desired scouting data, data Far Horizons was all too willing to provide, unbeknownst to them."

"Y-you were a plant the whole time?" From the ungainly sprawl I'd landed in, I leapt into a wild right cross—and almost broke my hand on his helmet.

Clarke smiled as I stumbled away, shaking my glove. My punch barely moved him.

"I should thank you for coming out here. I never expected them to send a search party. I am grateful to you for fixing the machine."

"Heh." I looked at my empty hands. "All I wanted was some damn real food. Don't give a shit what company mines this place."

"Well, I can at least offer you respite from those dreaded ration bars." Clarke raised his fist, but hesitated as a shimmering orange beam scorched a black line in the ground behind him, surrounded by the intense teal-green fire of Mithrinium burnoff.

He whirled about, lifting an eyebrow above a silver tunnel full of sparks. Kara stood in front of the collector's nose in a fog of aerosolized silt. Her stance tilted heavy to the left; the weight of the supplemental mining unit (corporate doublespeak for big ass laser) seemed a little much for her broken right leg.

Shit, the SMU a challenge for me to lift and maneuver. The sudden thought of Lin trying to use it made me laugh. Maybe I *was* going crazy. Being moments from death has that effect, I guess.

"Don't touch him, Clarke. I'll shoot the Wash. I'll blow us all to shit." Her voice carried a hint of nervousness, vulnerability I'd never heard come out of her before.

I knew damn well she shouldn't need to struggle with that coring laser. Her, me, or Nabo could all use it without an exo-suit. The heaviest part was the cable bundle tying it to the collector. However, she appeared to be unable to lift it and aim at Clarke. She growled, struggling with the weight. Her voice sounded close to tears. Of course, even if she shot him with it, the slow burn might not kill him before he ripped her head off.

Clarke turned, ignoring me. Yeah, right. I'm no threat. What could I do to an android with my bare hands? Nothing but crack jokes.

"You're not going to shoot that silt. It runs deep through the core of

R1840M. If you fire into that, the entire planetoid will explode. Look at you. You can't even lift it."

She slouched to the side as the mere act of staying upright drained her. My eyebrows shot up. I realized she faked it. Kara wouldn't sound so vulnerable, and she'd only suffered a broken shin. She *was*, however, right in front of the ore pick up grinders—the machine's mouth. I dropped into a three-point stance as Clarke charged at her. I sprinted, following the android's bobbing helmet. A second before he reached her, she chucked the laser at him and dove to the ground. The android involuntarily caught the SMU, unmoved by the weight, and promptly tossed the laser aside. Before he could sneer at her, I hit him full on in the back with all my weight, a body check that launched him headfirst into the grinders. The mechanism sucked him in up to the chest in seconds, winding down to a laborious crunch when it bit into the rigid backpack.

I leapt for cover an instant before the air tanks exploded.

"Fuck!" Kara screamed as I landed on her broken leg.

We both laid there as Android Clarke's twitching e-suit lurched inch by inch into oblivion. In a little over a minute, the largest piece of him was about the size of my thumbnail. Her breathing calmed. In some odd sort of way, this hostile place felt peaceful for a time.

"Guess I owe you one," I said, after a good while of silence.

"Just returning the favor." She pointed at her leg. Couldn't see her face, but her voice smiled.

"Still good to drive?"

Kara laughed, rolled over, and crawled back to the Six-Six, dragging her right leg. I hauled my sore body up the ladder into the collector and fell into the driver's chair.

For most of my life, I had a thing for petite little delicate women who giggled no matter what lame ass joke I cracked. For the past month, Kara set about changing my mind at least once every other day. Being with a girl who could throw *me* around made for quite a different experience. We'd moved into the same room, leaving the other two with private staterooms... at least until more personnel arrived. I think I'd wound up on Lin's shitlist. He denied it, but he had a serious crush on her. Nabo still gave me a 'better you than me' glance whenever the subject of Kara came up. He hadn't been out there... he hadn't *seen* her. I dreamed about her face, imagined what she looked like under the visor, glowing like an angel before the black of space. Yeah, I'd been harsh on her before only due to her not being petite. She's a beautiful woman.

"Hey, wake up." Kara bonked me on the head.

She'd gotten out of bed early and already had her usual morning outfit on: spanner wrench in one hand, towel in the other, and nothing else. I pushed myself up, glared at the chrono on the wall and squinted at her. "We still have six minutes we could be sleeping."

"The supply shuttle commed in. Terrence said they'll be landing in five minutes."

"Food bonus…" I flew out of bed and grabbed my jumpsuit. "You should put something on. They're gonna have a 'ceremony' for Jon and Barry."

She rushed into her jumpsuit, not bothering with boots she'd have to take off again to shower, and we made our way across the outpost to the docking bay. Terrence met us there, leaning on the cargo box subbing as a casket for Jon. Lin and Nabo walked in a minute after us. The big man gave me a disbelieving smirk and laughed. I got a hostile glare from Lin.

"Good morning, everyone." Terrence flashed Managersmile™. "As you all know, thanks to your efforts recovering the collector and making subsequent trips to The Wash, we have shown a six hundred percent increase in productivity. As a result, our outpost has qualified for the food bonus Far Horizons promised two months ago."

We all clapped with varying degrees of enthusiasm.

Terrence faced toward the shuttle. "Without further ado, allow me to present you with"—the massive rear ramp door whined apart from the hull and settled on the floor with a heavy, metallic scrape—"new *cherry flavored* Wongo bars!"

The sound of a flea farting would have been deafening.

"They even sent us a double-shipment, so we won't have to ration. Eat as much as you want!" Terrence turned back, still with the same near-closed-eye smile.

"Kara?" I stared at the grinning cartoon cherries on two decorative red and white shipping palettes, then at Terrence.

"Yeah."

"Can I borrow that spanner for a sec?"

Terrence's eyes opened all the way.

VII

THE TOWER

ABOUT THE TOWER

The Tower is one of the few stories I've written based on dreams. It's also one of a handful of times I've pictured a well-known actor as the main character. In this case, I pictured Alex Grant played by a late-fifties Michael Douglass.

I still have no idea what inspired the dream as it's a bit outside my usual genre. It left me with such a Twilight Zone mood, I needed to jump on the computer as soon as I woke up to write it down. The story is pretty much the exact sequence of the dream as if I'd watched a movie of it.

7

THE TOWER

F oggy glare blurred in a streak of passing headlights and screaming horns.

Steady pinging came from the dashboard. Static crackled from the car radio. Pixies of reflected glow smeared over the wood accents in the dash from another vehicle hissing by. Alex Grant focused his gaze on the hand hovering before his eyes. Starched white cuff with blue lines, grey suit jacket, Yale class ring, crimson smears. The fingers blurred as raindrops on the outside of the windshield came into focus. Red taillights glimmered within the beaded water, making them sparkle like rubies.

It took him a moment to realize the hand belonged to him.

The fragrance of coffee teased at his awareness.

On the floor, passenger seat side, most of a small caramel latte pooled on the mat. A lake of java surrounded the rubber Mercedes logo. He peered between his splayed fingers at a tilted world. Smoke swirled past his headlights. The sky appeared darker than he remembered. He looked down. On the flap of a Brooks Brothers coat, his phone, cracked and spattered with blood.

As soon as he touched it, a bright flash erased reality.

He sat in traffic, a standstill, yelling at someone. The cell phone squished into sweat on the side of his head.

"I'm sorry, Mr. Grant. It's too short notice," said the man on the other end. "The audit committee is going to be here in two days. There simply isn't enough time for that."

"Look here, Simons." He pointed over the steering wheel, thrusting his finger with each word as if stabbing someone. For an instant, he hesitated at the lack of blood; *why do I think there should be blood on my hand?*

"Mr. Grant?" asked Simons.

Alex shook off the confusion. "Those parasites from the SEC are like any other government tool. All they want is to keep their job, their nice, cushy, government job. I want you to spin a web of BS thick enough to gum up a congressional inquiry. Bog them down and give MacManus a chance to get the Bank Austria situation under control. The last thing we need is to have those bloodsucking rats sniffing around our Unicredit arrangement. I don't care who you have to throw under the bus to do it, you keep the board clean, you keep me clean, you keep yourself clean—but you keep them the hell off of BA-UNI, you got that?"

"Uhh… Yes, sir."

"Dammit!" Roaring, he slammed the phone into his thigh. Another flash, and the world became dark.

Alex remembered the phone striking his leg. The raindrops had returned, the sunlight and traffic gone. He squeezed the brown leather-covered wheel, mystified at the noise of it creaking. A trickle ran down his head, drawing his touch. His fingertips came back bloody. Matching red on the wheel, two o'clock. Fog rolled past the windshield, aglow from one working headlight.

"Did I go off the road?"

He stared vacantly at the wheel, then glanced right at the radio controls. A little phone-shaped light flickered. Alex reached for it, but froze, his fingertip hovering, eager and terrified to push the button. He hesitated only a second, then pushed it.

A flash of white blinded him.

Daylight. The scenery changed. Back in traffic, midway across the Brooklyn Bridge. Old ladies with walkers could have beaten him to the city. A digitized ringtone filled the car. He clicked the answer button on the steering wheel. Soreness spread along the outer edge of his left hand, pinky numb. A distant memory said he'd punched the console, angry at the congestion.

"Got some good news, man."

A different man spoke, familiar, yet he couldn't drag a name out from the depths of his mind. Alex responded on autopilot, as if watching the scene unfold from the outside. "It better be frickin' amazing news." He rubbed his upper lip to work the stress out of his face.

"I got the arrangements all set, man."

He shifted from rubbing to squeezing the bridge of his nose. "Can you *please* stop calling me 'man.' I'm old enough to be your damn father, Rick."

"Sorry, Mr. Grant. Hey, anyway… I got a guy inside customs. Your old lady's due back in the States in two days, right? Flight 818 out of Managua?"

"Yeah, the bitch is all into that 'save the Third World' crap. Pisses eighteen percent of my net worth into the jungle. Two days, right."

"Perfect. Look, we got a guy on the Nicaragua side gonna slip something in her bag. Hector's my man at JFK. He's gonna find it for us. Then you and the kidlet won't have to worry about your old lady for at least ten years. And, she won't get half your money."

Alex chuckled, a few seconds of freedom from anger. "I don't think Michael would appreciate being called 'kidlet.' He's an old man of ten now. You sure this is gonna work?"

"Pretty sure. The guy down there said they could make double sure. Little bonk over the head, motel room, force-feed her some balloons. That's harder to claim as an accident when they get an anonymous tip she's muleing heroin."

Alex Grant stopped pinching his nose. "That'll get her twenty-five at least. She'll be my age when she gets out."

"You bagged a twenty-year-old when you were forty-five? Nice, man."

He made a fist at the annoying three-letter word. "These 'friends' of yours… If they stuff her like a Thanksgiving bird, you can guarantee my boy's safety?"

"Probably."

Alex tapped fingers on his cheek. Traffic slipped forward two car lengths. Hard braking sloshed a caramel latte. Two droplets hit the console. "Son of a bitch!" He roared, fumbling with a handkerchief. "How much would that cost?"

"Ten large, plus the cost of the product if I can't back-door it out of the evidence room. Worst case scenario, about sixty."

He frowned at the white cloth, balling it up and pocketing it. "Forget it; go with the original plan."

"You got it, boss."

His thumb flicked the button to hang up. Traffic, sunlight, and sound vanished with a whooshing noise.

Dark again.

Headlights glided past him in the dark, accompanied by the wet rush of rubber on rain-soaked street. A blurry pedestrian walked by, not bothering to peer in the window. Alex squinted at the console in the center of the dashboard. The clock displayed --:--, the words 'no signal' scrolled across the radio.

He looked up out the sunroof at a green awning fluttering in the wind. Mild pain twinged down his back as he sat up straight. Rain fell in waves, a thousand tiny sticks playing snare drums on the roof and hood. He wiped at his face and looked toward the passenger-side window. His Mercedes had to be half up on the sidewalk. *Explains the tilt.* He reached out and pushed the start button on the dash. Another blinding flash took reality away.

When the light dimmed, he found himself again in traffic. Shadows of tall buildings muted the noonday sun. Anger filled him. He tapped a rhythm of discontent into the steering wheel. He'd finally made it off the bridge, somewhere past Spruce Street. If he could get to Beekman, he could swerve down Theater Alley to Fulton.

"Come on, you damned idiots!" He punched the horn. "Why is everyone standing still?"

A few drivers gave him the finger. Heat swam over his face on a rush of blood when he checked his watch. He had a meeting in twenty minutes, a mere thousand feet away, but it would take an hour to get there.

Impatience ran down his leg to the gas pedal. He cranked the wheel and jumped the car up onto the sidewalk. Another white flash; He squealed the tires around a corner. The grille of a sanitation truck filled the driver's side window; headlights, horn, and screeching tires. Alex crossed his arms over his face. Crunching metal and breaking glass devoured his screams.

Silence, save for the purr of a running engine.

After a moment, he lowered his shaking arms to find the window dark and intact. The scent of car tire air surrounded him, mixed with caramel. He looked at the backs of his hands, flipped them over, and checked his palms—intact. When he gave up trying to explain things, he let off a one-breath chuckle.

A hit-and-run is all I need. Idiot in the truck didn't even stop.

After a few rapid breaths, he gripped the wheel and spun it left. The car lurched off the curb, rocking as he straightened out along the road and stepped on the gas. Empty streets let him drive fast. His Rolex had stopped at 7:14 and ten seconds.

"Christ. Ten thousand for a damn watch and a bump kills it. Unbelievable."

He pulled up outside the building, got out, and poked his phone.

"We're sorry, all circuits are busy. Please hang up and try your call again later."

"Screw you too, Betty. Or whatever the hell your name is."

Alex stuffed the phone into his coat pocket, frustrated at the large device's inability to slide in with one smooth motion. He growled, shoving at it almost to the point of tearing the coat. "Good grief. *Must* they make these lousy things the size of bibles? Who needs a phone this big?"

Fussing to neaten his coat, he shoved the car door.

Kachunk. It echoed as if a vault slammed.

The glossy black Mercedes S550, looked perfect. Right eyebrow cocked, he walked an orbit. No dents, no dings, no cracks. The car had suffered only a coffee-soaked floor mat. He put a hand to his face to rub away the confusion. Headlights rushed at him from the left. He gasped and jumped back, but when he found the nerve to look again, saw nothing.

He checked his watch again. Still 7:14.

Nah. I'm imagining this.

Alex stepped up on the sidewalk, the rarity of getting a street-front parking space hit him three strides later. He glanced around at the usual assortment of cars parked too close to each other and stared at his. *Huh. After the morning I've had, I'm due a little luck.* Alex faced the building—a pillar of dark grey stone stretching into the clouds. Six stories up, leering gargoyles around the structure glared down at him. The sense of malice in their carved eyes felt too real. One seemed to smile at him. He averted his gaze.

"I'm losing my God damned mind." He rubbed his eyes, then looked up again. The stone creature had a grim frown, not looking at him. "Too much stress. Most of it will be gone soon, stuck in Nicaragua for the next twenty-five years."

A blood-red awning over the entrance ran most of the way to the curb bearing the words, "The Tower" in plain silver letters. His phone rang, startling a cloud of pigeons into the air. The motion of birds, more than the sound of the incoming call, made him jump back against his car and shield his face.

When the birds passed, the phone continued ringing.

He pulled it out. "Grant."

Static wheezed at him for a few seconds before a woman's voice came through. "… are you, Mr. Grant? …ecided to postpone the meeting until Wednesday. Your wife called… Nicaragua. Michael wanted to say…"

His assistant.

"Amanda?" Alex shook the phone. "Amanda? I'm getting a bad signal. Why do you sound like you're at the end of a tunnel?"

"…oming in today?"

"No, I'm gonna take the day off. I got stuck in traffic, just got to Midtown. Look, I'm at that place I was telling you about."

"…partment?"

"Yeah." He glanced at his gleaming car. The deep grey of the sky left him unable to tell if it was late morning on a crummy day or early evening on a nice one. A powerful horn blared in his memory. Why did he believe he'd survived a near miss from a trash truck? *Too close. What would happen to Michael if I….* "Amanda, are you still there?"

"…es Mr. Grant."

He touched the sore spot on the side of his head, then examined two bloody fingertips. "Get a hold of Rick Rosenthal. I changed my mind. Tell him not to proceed with the Managua project."

"…enthal. Got it. Will you—"

A loud crackling buzz came from the phone for a second before it went dark.

"Hello? Hello? Amanda?" He held the phone out to arm's length. It didn't react to the power button, shaking, or evil stares. Dead battery. "Damn!"

The mere thought of struggling to stuff it back in the too-small pocket made him angry. He took a deep breath, held it for a moment, and let the air hiss out between his teeth. The phone slipped into the coat without protest.

His dress shoes clicked over the sidewalk, falling silent once he reached the carpet leading up to the doors of The Tower. He frowned at the lack of a doorman and gripped ornate bronze handles with tiny gargoyles perched atop. Sudden wind picked up. The air, thick with humidity, made him think a September rain shower approached—or had recently stopped. A momentary vision of crimson droplets on the windshield stunned him for a second.

The lobby, predominantly dark marble and red, contained several columns ringed with curved benches. A table with a selection of magazines stood against the left wall next to a spread of complimentary coffee. Despite the lack of visible food, he smelled eggs. He frowned, sniffing. Spoiled eggs. Since his $6 latte sat on the floor of his car, he approached the table and helped himself to a cup, but stopped, grumbling.

"Decaf? Really? Is that all you people have out, damn decaf?" He threw the empty cup to the side. "And what the hell is that awful stench?"

He spun on his heel and walked to the unmanned desk, appraising the wood-paneling and crimson curtains by the windows. A warped version of Alex Grant looked up at him with mocking eyes from an inch-tall band of curved brass along the edge of the counter. The single flat-panel monitor cast a pale white blur on the wall. Alex fussed at his coat. He looked left, then right, adjusted his cufflinks… after a minute, he cleared his throat.

"Hello?"

The echo of his voice made him feel even more alone.

"Look, I know I'm late, but shouldn't there be someone at the desk?" Alex leaned around the counter to peer into an empty hallway labeled 'employees only.' Patience lasted only another minute and a half. "I can guess why the rent is so low here. Hello?" He slammed both hands on the counter and yelled, "Is anyone in there? You have a *customer* waiting."

He seethed, pacing.

"This is ridiculous," he muttered. "All the places I could possibly pick, and I have to choose the one run by incompetents. No wonder they're charging suburb rates for Midtown. If they treat *new* tenants like this, getting maintenance must take an act of Congress." He pounded on the counter again. "Come on. Last chance or I'm walking out!"

Silence.

"Fine." He started to whirl away from the counter when his gaze settled on a silver push button bell. "Oh, I get it. You're one of *those* people." He leaned forward, hovering his palm over the thing before driving it down in a contemptuous slap.

Ding.

The curtain over the employee-only hallway parted within a fraction of a second. A young man in a maroon uniform, flat-topped fez tilted a touch to the left, stepped through and flicked the curtain closed behind him in one fluid motion. His moustache, thin and black, looked like the attempt of a sixteen-year-old to grow facial hair, though he had to be at least thirty.

"Ahh, Mr. Grant. Right on time." The attendant produced a white keycard in his hand as if by magic trick, then offered it. "All the arrangements are made. Your new furnished apartment is on the twenty-fifth floor."

"Right on time? How can I be 'right on time?' Mario and Luigi ran me off the goddamned road on my way here and…" He gestured at the front. "It was sunny out, now it's… hell if I know what time it is. It was sunny, now it's dark."

"It rained, Mr. Grant. It's an unusual dark. Trust me, you have arrived here precisely when you were meant to." The man unfolded his arms, extending his left in the direction of the elevators.

The one in the middle opened with a chime.

Alex looked at it. Shiny, silver, new, and empty. *This jackass is messing with me. He's got some kind of button back there, I bet. I'll remember that at Christmas.* He heaved a breath and went for the elevator. Once inside, it occurred to him he left his briefcase in the car. *Screw it, I'll get it later.* He glanced at the lobby windows. The Mercedes was gone. He tried to jump out of the elevator, but the doors shut him in. Screaming at it to stop, he slapped at the steel and ground his hand into the buttons. The elevator ignored him.

"God dammit!"

He gazed up at the blinding mass of white and chrome. *This is the day from Hell. One more pain in my ass I don't need.* He pulled out his phone. One of his underlings could deal with the police report. *What kind of idiot steals a Mercedes, anyway? All the parts are marked.* The overhead lights intensified to blinding. The roar of a giant truck horn and squealing tires flooded in.

He screamed.

When the chaos stopped, Alex Grant found himself curled in a ball on the floor—arms crossed over his face as if they might stop the metal beast. A cold breeze tossed a bundle of plastic scraps into the elevator. He remained motionless for a moment before lowering his arms. All the rage drained from him as he stood and stared at the twenty-fifth floor.

No walls.

A wide-open space punctuated by support columns at regular intervals stretched from one end of the building to the other. Bare wood frames gave hints where individual apartments would eventually be. Piles of drywall, tools, and spindles of wire littered the area. He tentatively stepped out of the elevator to look around. Plaster crunched into the concrete floor. He gazed left and right at fluttering sheets of translucent plastic.

"This? This is my apartment?" Alex growled. "The idiots haven't even built it yet."

A discarded paper coffee cup bearing the familiar blue and white pattern used by every convenience store in the city rolled by. He let go of the doors, squinting at the incompleteness. The wail of a distant siren lifted and fell, chased into silence by a smattering of faraway horns. Between the city sounds and wind, the lack of exterior walls made him feel as if he stood outside. Each step crunched louder and louder. Plastic crinkled in the breeze. A quiet voice muttered in Spanish from ahead, past a large stack of fiberglass insulation.

"This isn't funny," he mumbled, turning to look behind him at the open elevator. The number 25 occupied a steel plate to the left of it. "What the hell kind of scam are they running?" He faced the whispering. "Hello? *No cómico.*"

The Spanish mumbling continued without interruption. Alex picked out enough to grasp a complaint about pensions. He chuckled, remembering a banking trick that caused some city money to vanish last year. It had been so easy. Once the initial month passed, his anxiety evaporated. When he realized how incompetent the auditors were, the rest proved simple.

A board slammed into the ground.

Alex jumped and took two steps back before a metallic clatter came from behind him. He whirled, catching a fleeting glimpse of a steel reinforcing strip falling over. *Damn wind.* Grumbling, he relaxed and walked ahead, ducking a hanging strip of pink insulation. A bright yellow portable radio sat on a huge blue plastic drum, tuned to a Spanish station with the volume down. Abandoned sandwiches littered the area, wrapping paper drifting in the wind.

A blur of motion glided across the periphery of his vision.

He whirled toward it, the hairs on the back of his neck standing.

Nothing there.

Heaviness filled in the dead space behind him. Someone—or something—crept closer. Terror beckoned to the primitive man lurking well below the veneer of reason, gripping the portion of psyche programmed to react like a rabbit to a wildcat.

He ran. Thin plastic hoses all over the floor caught between his feet, clattering as it tangled his legs. Wind ripped past him, an intangible force trying to drag him to the edge to oblivion. Rushing air closed in from all sides. He staggered in an effort not to fall. Grabbing and pulling on anything he could—wall studs, cables, insulation—he sprinted for salvation of a cube of gleaming steel.

Thunder rolled on his heels, as if the Earth buckled under the weight of his pursuer. He clawed his way past a sheet of hanging plastic and collided with a metal support beam. Refusing to feel pain or look behind him, he pushed away from the metal and kept going. Only the roaring presence at his heels and the open elevator twenty yards ahead of him mattered. His six-hundred-dollar shoe smashed into a toolbox, tripping him to all fours. *Everything* closed in on him—the entire open story felt smaller than a closet. Whispering and scratching drew closer.

Alex wailed in terror. His hands burned from scraping the ground, his fancy shoes slipped over the grit. *It* got closer. Boards clattered to the ground, metal scraps clanged about, plastic ripped, and the howling rush of air tore at his soul.

Abandoning dignity, he scrambled forward in a crawl. The gurgle emanating from his throat built into an undisguised cry of panic when the elevator doors started to close. He leapt to his feet, diving in a desperate lurch—and got his hand between the doors. They nearly crushed his wrist, but reversed open. He jumped in, spinning to flatten himself against the rear wall, arms raised in a defensive cower—and stared at an empty floor.

Sound ceased.

No monster.

"What in the...?" He lowered his arms. *Alright, who's messing with me?*

For the two seconds it took the doors to close, he stared.

"Sweet mother of Christ..." His panting breaths echoed in the small chamber, drowning out the thudding of his heart. "My imagination." Alex looked down at the scuff on his shoe. "This is what happens when I don't get my coffee."

Wham.

Something huge and heavy smashed into the elevator, hard enough to knock him to the ground. Screaming, he crawled to the control board and pounded a fist on the L button.

Wham.

"Oh, God!" Alex screamed, pressing himself against the innermost wall. His mind conjured up all manner of promises if some higher power got this elevator moving again: actual bonuses for his staff, tipping the parking garage guy from now on, not being so cold to his wife. *I'll even go with her to the land of the primitives next time.* Alex stopped short. Someone, at this very moment, might be stalking his wife. *Please, God. Don't let them hurt her, make Rick forget.*

Lights flickered. The elevator moved. His rapid wheezing breaths echoed in the confined space. He huddled on the floor in a ball.

His watch still read 7:14 and ten seconds.

ON THE LONG RIDE DOWN, ALEX GATHERED HIMSELF. ASIDE FROM DISHEVELED hair and chafed palms, he looked to be his old self.

The clerk looked up as the elevator doors opened, a faint curl to make the Mona Lisa proud, and leaned his weight on the counter. "Can I help you, Mr. Grant?"

Alex stormed over, hand cocked, finger pointing. Heat flooded his cheeks. His finger shook. He couldn't think of what to scream about first. *They blew it. To Hell with this place, cheap or not.* Twisting on his heel, he stormed past the heavy brass-framed doors onto the sidewalk, all the way to the curb to where his Mercedes wasn't.

"All the options. Only had it for a month."

He bowed his head and stared past the scuffmarks on his shoes at the street, gesturing at the lack of car before him as if to tell the world someone stole his car. No amount of being angry would make it reappear.

"Hah!" he barked at the clouds. "Well, that's just grand." Spinning in place, he held his arms out to the side. "My car is gone! My hundred-thousand-dollar car is missing."

Echoes of his rant dissolved into silence. Not a single other soul walked the street.

He pursed his lips at the absence of traffic and pedestrians. Hands-in-pockets, he pivoted to challenge The Tower with a stare. Leaning back, he tried to gaze up to the top, where four stylized eagle heads pointed in the cardinal directions. The entire structure seemed intact from the outside. Not one level had only plastic sheeting for walls. He looked back to the empty parking space, and then to the entrance. He took out his phone again, intent on reporting his car stolen, but the phone ignored him, its battery as dead as a rock.

Alex stormed into the lobby, flinging the heavy doors open as if reenacting Nero's return. The attendant waited for him to reach the counter before looking up, smiling as if he'd had every expectation he'd be back.

Anger rushed to his cheeks. "I need to use your phone."

The clerk offered a pleasant nod, then lifted an ancient-looking black corded phone up onto the counter. "Dial nine for an outside line."

Alex swiped the handset and flicked his arm out hard enough to snap his sleeve. He held the earpiece to the side of his head, surprised at the presence of a dial tone. He dialed his secretary. Busy. Simons, rang to voice mail. The clerk smiled again. Alex dialed the police.

"911, what's your emergency?"

"My car has been stolen. I parked it—"

"Is anyone injured?"

Alex examined the back of his hand. A twinge of pain made him expect to see blood, but he appeared unhurt. "No."

"This is the emergency services line, to report a—"

He slammed the phone down, glaring at the clerk. "I need a different apartment. There's a problem with the twenty-fifth floor." His voice quivered in rage, but remained mostly calm.

"Oh, I'm sorry." The attendant took the room key back. "I had received a complaint the twenty-fifth was a bit drafty. Here, sir. Please accept this upgrade with our apologies. Same rent."

Upon a white card, the number 66 appeared in calligraphic script above a plain font that read, "Floor 6."

"Cute." Alex turned the keycard over in his hand.

"You're not superstitious, are you Mr. Grant? I can give you a different one if it's a problem."

"No. I don't believe in that sort of thing." He continued to rotate the keycard around his fingers. "What, exactly, am I going to find on the sixth floor?"

"Your new home," said the clerk. His smile deepened only enough to be perceptible.

He wagged the card at the young man, debating the effectiveness of screaming. The clerk's placid smile didn't crack. Alex clutched the keycard in a fist and returned to the elevator, then traced his finger around the rows of buttons in search of the one for the sixth floor. It looked like the most used of the lot, the engraved 6 barely visible at the center of a worn depression in the steel.

He frowned at his reflection on the door while waiting for the elevator to stop.

Stuck in traffic, stuck in an elevator.

A brief flash of weightlessness accompanied the halt. Alex held his breath, dreading what he'd see on the other side when the doors opened.

An abnormally loud *ding* made him jump. The doors slid open, revealing an ordinary hallway with white walls and forest green carpet. Small brass light fixtures bearing flower-shaped glass glowed in pairs at regular intervals. He put a hand on the edge of the door to keep it from closing, studying the innocent corridor for a moment before risking setting foot out from the safety of the elevator.

A small oval table, dark mahogany wood polished to a mirror shine, sat against the left wall a short distance in front of him, flanked by chairs. He moved forward, studying the lights, the pattern in the carpet pile, the flat, featureless white ceiling. Not a sound disturbed the air. The overbearing silence allowed the noise of crushing rug with each step. The elevator remained open, taunting him. Ahead, the corridor stretched off to a narrow point—an unbelievable distance given the size of the building from the outside. Every so often, the pattern in the wallpaper appeared to take on the shape of blurry, leering gargoyles. Whenever he looked directly at them, it seemed to be a trick of his eyes.

He squinted at the endless doors and shot a questioning glance at the elevator.

Ding.

He leapt against the wall, clutching his chest, staring death at the closing elevator doors. Feeling foolish for jumping at such a mundane sound, he scowled, stood up straight, fixed his coat, and proceeded down the hall, frowning at the floor.

"The brochure said they had *blue* carpet."

After passing a door marked 30, he turned left and went down an offshoot past five other apartments until he took a right into a different passageway. The same green carpet and the same flower-glass light fixtures waited for him. Only the numbers on the doors changed. Were it not for the numbers, any point in this place would be exact copy of any other. *Must be fun to stumble home drunk here.* He sidled up to the door marked 66, emitting a faint chuckle.

"Room sixty-six on the sixth floor." He shook his head and inserted the keycard. "This has to be Gene's doing."

A little green light flashed. The lock emitted a *click.* He pushed the door, which opened giving off a long, laborious creak. Alex remained in the hall, staring into an apartment smaller than the advertisement led him to believe. The modest living room was already furnished with a sectional, a coffee table, and a flat-screen television mounted on the wall. Charcoal-colored blinds had been drawn closed over the large window on the left.

Beyond the sofa, archways separated a small dining area, which ended at tall windows overlooking the city. A passage with a curved ceiling opened to the right.

He cautiously entered and draped his coat over the back of the couch before wandering to the dining area. The first left in the little hallway connected to the kitchen. A low, steady hum came from a silver fridge with French doors. Alex made an appraising face at the green faux-marble countertop and large sink. The corridor continued to two bedrooms and a bathroom. A hanging piece of art not far from the kitchen caught his eye. Six panels of curved bronze, each a six-inch square embossed with the shape of an animal's face, perched in a diamond orientation on struts of copper tubing.

"Amazing," he muttered, smirking at it. "Some schlub with a welding torch gets a hold of scrap metal and it's suddenly art."

Heaving a sigh, he took three steps down the corridor before a growl broke the silence behind him. He peered over his shoulder—at a full-sized black panther standing in the kitchen, staring at him, tail swishing.

"Gah!" he cried, whirling into a sprint.

Alex leapt through the door into the master bedroom, slammed it, then leaned his back against it. *I'm losing it. I must have hit my head harder than I thought.* Wood crunched under a heavy weight smashing into the door. Claws pierced an inch from his ear.

"Aaaaah!" he yelled, spinning to face the door and bracing it with both hands.

The panther ripped its claws back out, leaving four holes. Spine-tingling screeches vibrated the door as the panther clawed at it. More splinters fluttered to the carpet as the claws pierced again. Deep snarling emanated from the other side.

"Dammit… dammit," he muttered, trying to shift his foot to the base so he could move his hands long enough to reach for the lock.

Growling, raking, and crunching continued. Alex screamed, closing his eyes from sheer terror while fumbling to find the little deadbolt. As soon as it clicked, the assault on the door ceased as if on a switch. Only a low, throaty rumble lingered outside. After a few erratic breaths, Alex peeked through one of the claw holes.

The panther perched in a sphinx pose nearby, pale green eyes staring right at him, tail swiping side to side. A voice, deep and silky, spoke in his brain. *Come on, Alex. You can't hide in there forever. Open the door. I love the taste of art critics.*

He closed his eyes, whirling to again put his back to the door. "What the hell is wrong with me? Why does a damn panther sound like Barry White?"

"Maybe he really likes you?" purred his wife.

Eyes open.

Rachel Grant reclined on the bed, her back against the wall, her long pale legs crossed at the ankle. She held a glass of champagne in one hand, pink silk gloves up to her biceps, her only clothing. Her long blonde hair cascaded over her shoulders, almost to the mattress. She smiled. A deep shade of chipmunk brown flowed up from the roots, flowing to the ends.

"I'm not really a blonde, sweetie." Rachel sipped her drink. "But what's a little white lie between husband and wife?"

Trails of sweat slid down his cheeks. He pointed back over his shoulder with a thumb. "T-there's a damn panther in the hallway. How did—?"

Her stomach undulated. Alex's cheek twitched. Her stomach inflated as if eight months of pregnancy occurred in the span of twenty seconds. He lowered his arm, pressing both hands into the door behind him.

"I brought something for you from Nicaragua, sweetie." She winked, licking her upper lip.

Blood oozed out of her navel seconds before her ballooning stomach burst open. Specks of crimson spattered her porcelain face, spattering all over her chest. Twinkie-sized rubber sausages of white powder welled up and out of the gore, sliding off her to either side. The geyser of heroin continued erupting, far, far beyond what could have possibly fit inside her.

"Oh, God," he croaked. "I told him not to do that."

Rachel bit her fingertip and tugged the glove off her right arm using her teeth. She reached into the gory mass, held up one blood-covered balloon, and squeezed it until it ruptured. White dust puffed into the air. She dumped it out on her chest, inches from the gaping hole, and held up a handful of it.

"Come on, honey. It's uncut." She made cute bloody faces at him, gesturing at the still-emerging drugs. "Don't you love me anymore? I'm worth ten million bucks now."

One tear rolled down his cheek as he beheld his mangled wife. *What have I done?*

Alex howled, struggling against the doorknob for seconds before remembering he'd locked the deadbolt. He flicked the latch and flung the door open, forgetting all about the panther as he leapt out of the bedroom and slammed the door. His scream of horror became a shriek of terror—but he froze, wide-eyed at an empty hallway.

No cat.

"Leaving so soon?" asked Rachel, from behind the door.

Clutching his chest, he staggered to his coat and grabbed his phone. Remembering it dead, he hurled the useless thing onto the sofa. It bounced off the cushion and slid to the floor. The screen lit up. Alex blinked at it.

"Okay, whoever you are, this prank is going too damn far."

He rushed over to the phone, expecting it to be dead again, but it lit up when he touched the button. Head spinning, he staggered in a drunken spiral over to the window, leaning against the closed blinds while fumbling to enter the security code. The phone kept buzzing as he mistyped the pin. The third time, the entire apartment vibrated with it.

"Come on, come on, you piece of trash!" He shook it. It finally accepted the pin, one attempt before he smashed it in rage.

Office: busy signal.

Home: busy signal.

Rick: busy signal.

Rachel's Cell: ringing from the back bedroom.

"No!" He raised his hand to smash the phone, but paused. "No, that's in my head."

He clutched the phone in both hands, pressing it to his forehead. *What's wrong with me?* Blinds crinkled under his shoulder. "She wouldn't be alive, wouldn't be smiling with that junk coming out of her. I'm having a stress meltdown." He panted, eyeing the room and gave an anticipatory snarl. "The twenty-fifth floor was in my head. Like the panther. Like that *thing* on the bed."

Grinning maniacally, he held the phone out to arm's length and poked an imperious, stabbing finger at his wife's entry. Bulging eyes fixed on her one-by-one-inch portrait.

"Hi, this is Rachel, I'm in Nicaragua for two weeks. I'm probably out of signal at the moment. Please leave me a message and I'll get back to you if it's worth the $5 a minute." She giggled.

Alex pressed the phone against the sore spot on his head. "Rache, Listen to me... Check your carry-on bags *before* you go through customs. Do it somewhere you won't be watched. I'll explain later but be care—"

Beeeeep. "Message saved for *thirty* days."

He nearly crushed the phone in his grasp, but dialed again. Busy.

Scowling, he jammed his hand into the blinds and peeled them open.

Fog. Nothing but thick, grey fog. A heavy clattering *thud* hit the window on the outside, dragging across with the sound of skin on glass. Alex leapt back, letting the blinds snap closed. *Was that a body?* Curiosity overwhelmed him soon, so he pulled the blinds apart again. A charred-black hand tipped with onyx claws reached up from below and struck the glass. The *thud* reverberated over the apartment.

He yelled and staggered backward.

Rachel's giggle came from the bedroom. "You have *got* to try this, it's pure!"

"This is not happening." Alex jammed his finger at Rick's contact entry.

"Hey, man," said Rick before it even rang.

"Rick… Thank God. Look, call it off. Don't do anything to her. Abort."

"You alright, man? You sound delirious? What happened? I hear horns and sirens in the background."

Alex looked at the window. Dead silence. "There's no sirens."

"Backing out on these people is dangerous, man. You have the police banging on your door?"

"No, Rick." Alex crept back to the window, whispering. "Listen to me, Rick. I'm alone, there's no one here. I'll still pay them for their time, but do *not* tamper with her luggage."

"I can barely hear you over all that noise, man. You say you payin', but don' do it?"

"Correct. Dammit, call it off." Alex waited ten seconds. "Rick?"

No answer. He held the phone out to look. Dark screen.

Dead phone.

He paced, trying to decide if he should keep the thing or toss it. On his fourth circle around the living room, he hesitated by the back hallway. The strange piece of bronze art seemed different. One square had become plain, no longer containing an animal portrait.

He stood rigid, color and warmth draining from his face as the visage of a smiling monkey on the second panel receded into the metal as if melting. Something tugged on his pant leg. Alex hesitantly looked down. A cute tan-and-black monkey grinned at him, waved, and punched him in the crotch. Red-faced, he hit the ground, gasping. The little terror screeched, ran over him, and vanished into the kitchen. Cradling himself, Alex struggled to breathe, wondering how a little critter could hit that hard.

On all fours, he looked up in the direction it had run off in time to catch a fist-sized jar of mayonnaise in the forehead. It didn't break, but it knocked him senseless. The monkey sat in the fridge, throwing everything it could grab. Yogurt went overhead, splattering into the wall. The same brand his wife liked. An entire celery stalk hit him in the chest. The creature leaned out, baring its teeth in another smile, raw egg in each hand.

Alex pointed. "Don't you da—"

He dove to the side. The gooey missiles smashed into the floor. Shouting curses, he crawled behind the couch while glass shattered behind him. After a minute of silence, he grasped the top of the sectional and pulled himself up to peer over the back. Peering over the top, he scanned the apartment, finding no trace of the monkey until he glanced down at the cushion right in front of him. There sat the little furry horror. It swung a bag of flour over its head, smashing it into his nose. Alex landed flat on his back in a white cloud. The monkey made a noise startlingly close to human laughter.

"Monkey!" he roared, scrambling upright, then diving at it over the couch.

The creature ran, zooming under the coffee table and shoving it into his shins as he tried to chase. Alex spilled over forward, face bouncing off the thick glass surface with a ringing *clank* before he slumped to the floor. He lay still on his side, finding the beige carpet comfortable. Motion caught his eye. The monkey ambled up to him, its little weapon poised to project a stream of insult all over him.

"The hell you—"

It screeched and ran as he lunged for it, around the kitchen island counter, around the couch, up the drapes, over shelves, knocking books and kitsch to the floor. It seemed impossible to chase the thing while guarding his face from the unending assault of hurled objects. When he disregarded the passing pain of little things hitting him in the head and gained on the monkey, the furry terror dashed into the hallway. Alex stomped after it like an angry Gulliver, but couldn't corner as tightly as an agile monkey. He skidded out of control into the kitchen, landing on his chest and sliding across stone tile into the fridge.

Thud.

Alex held perfectly still.

The *patter* of little monkey feet approached. A small finger poked him in the side of the head.

He didn't move.

As soon as it leaned back in another attempt to deliver a liquid insult, Alex's thrust his arm out and grabbed it around the chest. Screeching and spraying, the monkey bit down on his hand as he wrestled it into the air.

"Hah! Got you, you little turd." Alex cackled, elbowing open the door to the microwave and throwing the little furball inside before slamming the door. "What do you think of *this?*"

He held his finger over the "minute plus" button. A cute little face pleaded at him from behind the glass. Alex's arm shook. He stared. He pointed at the monkey rather than the button, unable to find the cruelty to turn the microwave on.

"Damn."

Leaving it trapped but alive, he paced, rubbing innumerable bruises and sore spots. A chill ran down his back at a sudden worry. He rushed back to the hallway and stared at the bronze artwork, whimpering. The next embossed animal after the two blank tiles was a lion. After that, an elephant.

"Oh, crap."

Alex sprinted to the closet door and yanked it open. Blinding white light and a blaring horn knocked him back on his butt. Large letters spelled out *Mack* in steel between the glaring orbs. Fetal, he screamed and closed his eyes. Horn and light faded, leaving him drenched in sweat and hyperventilating. The monkey's plaintive tapping on the microwave door grew thunderous.

"Oh, no…" Alex uncurled and sat up. "No, no, no, no, no. You're just going to start throwing poop at me if I let you out of there."

"Dad!" *Thump.* "Dad, help!"

He froze. The little face in the microwave door now looked like his son. Alex clamped his hand over his mouth, shaking. Once emotion faded, he shook his head rapidly. "Michael is ten years old. He's too big to fit in that microwave. Whoever you are, I don't find this amusing at all."

A creak came from the hall, something heavy making the floor shift.

He glanced briefly at the corridor, finding it empty. When he looked at the microwave again, it appeared empty. A shadow moved in the hallway. Alex gulped, too frightened to move. The sinewy form of a male African lion stepped halfway into view and looked at him.

"Nice kitty," said Alex, in as soothing a tone as he could manage. He put an arm on the sofa and pulled himself standing, backing away. "Nice kitty. That's a good kitty."

He gingerly grasped his coat.

The lion roared.

Alex screamed, ran, and shoved the front door out of his way. Corridor flashed by, blurs of green from the doors on either side. His lungs burned. He couldn't remember which way to go in the baffling maze of identical passages. Growls and the rips of shredding carpet chased him. He sprinted, turning randomly, fear boosting his speed in short bursts whenever the creature crashed into something. Tables crunched. Vases shattered. Chairs banged against the wall. After an endless series of turns, he finally spotted the elevator. Shrieking, he skidded to a stop, backed up, and scrambled to the left, dashing into the elevator and pounding the call button.

The lion growled.

Alex whirled to look behind him. The lion padded around the corner by apartment 30, far enough away to not cause an immediate heart attack. It sauntered closer, unblinking amber eyes staring through him, mouth hanging open. He pressed himself against the doors, trying to get away. The instant the doors opened, he fell backward, howling from the suddenness of it.

The lion bolted forward. Screaming, he kicked at the buttons, not caring which one he hit as long as it took him to a different floor. The lion pounced, reaching one paw between the closing doors far enough to tear his pant leg before they shut. Alex cringed at the scraping of claws on steel as the beast scratched at the doors. He didn't bother trying to stand.

After a short ride, the elevator opened on the eleventh floor.

He reached up to push L. "I'm out."

The doors closed again. Clutching the handrail, he pulled himself upright, shaking, head pounding. *Ding... Ding... Ding...* the elevator called out each floor. Twelve... Thirteen... Fourteen...

"Up? What the hell? I want the lobby, dammit!"

He whacked the console. The elevator accelerated, the force of it crushing him to his knees. Eighteen, twenty, twenty-four...

"No! No!" he bashed the L button over and over. "Lobby!"

Forty, forty-one, forty-five...

Screaming, he tried kicking at the door. When that did nothing, he jammed his thumb into L button, twisting it like a knife in the gut of a mortal enemy.

"Lobby, you obstinate piece of garbage!"

Bracing to be launched straight out of the roof, Alex closed his eye and waited. Unexpectedly, the elevator slowed and stopped on the sixtieth floor. He waited a moment, then righted himself and tucked his coat over his left arm. The elevator crept down one floor. He squinted at the button. It moved down another floor.

Freefall.

Gravity lost meaning. He shrieked in terror, clinging to the handrail. The floor display above the door blurred, going too fast to be readable. When his back touched the ceiling, he braced for death. Images from his life flashed by, college, Rachel, the marriage, his son, his job.

Alex waited for the final impact, but crumpled to the floor far softer than he expected. Panicked breaths interrupted the silent stillness. Each breath lit a thread of pain in his chest. He pressed a hand over his heart and sat. The display above the doors flashed 88.

He gasped for breath. "If that didn't give me a damn heart attack, nothing will."

Trembling, he grasped the handrail and dragged himself to his feet, then stared at the quarter-sized silver disc with the engraved L. It defied him by existing. Like the microwave, he reached for it, but hesitated. As if sensing his intent, the elevator chimed without him pushing anything.

The doors slid open, allowing a cold wind to blast into the elevator, swirling his hair.

Open sky yawned before him above a gleaming silver platform stretching forward from the elevator. The distant end curved downward into rolling clouds, growing narrower. He stood still for a time, staring, mouth agape.

For no reason he could fathom, Alex Grant stepped out onto the polished metal surface. Behind him, the elevator house occupied a projection at the meeting point of four massive eagle heads. He stood atop the one facing south, compelled to approach the curve by the brow, the beak.

The distant horizon rolled with sickly beige clouds, gouts of inky smoke, and flashes of fire. A warm breeze carried the scent of sulfur past his nostrils, the same bad-egg smell from the lobby, only much stronger. All around, the city had given way to cracked and scorched basalt full of jagged ebon rock spires and hundreds of fast-moving creatures scurrying about, all with horns, wings, and long barbed tails. He let his arms fall limp at his sides. The jacket of his twelve-thousand-dollar suit slipped from his fingers, caught the wind, and drifted away in lazy swirls toward oblivion.

Alex's left eye twitched, the same tic he suffered whenever a deal didn't work out.

"I'm sorry, Rache. Please let Rick stop them in time."

Something huge pounded on the inside of the elevator doors behind him. The dull crunch of breaking glass followed, accompanied by a hydraulic whine. The elevator doors trembled under the assault, swelling outward. He looked away from the wail of crimping metal, no longer caring what happened to him, and gazed at a distant shaft of black smoke tinged with flames belching from a crack in the ground.

"Well, that explains why the rent was so cheap."

VIII

THE ROOMMATE

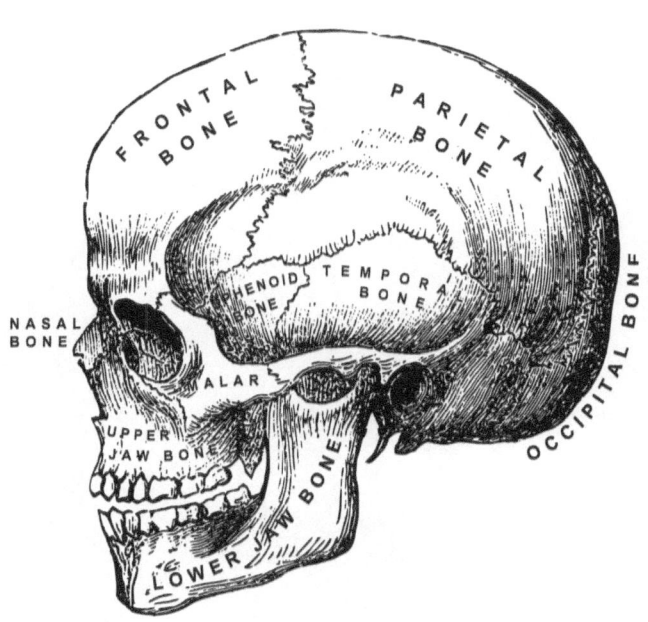

ABOUT THE ROOMMATE

During a discussion in a writer's chat group, the subject of writing blurbs and queries to literary agents came up. I mentioned the idea of 'hook' lines to open with, as in a sentence to hopefully get someone reading it to pause, have a 'wait… what?' moment, then want to keep reading.

A sample hook line I came up with out of the blue went something like 'Many people have skeletons in their closets, but Roy talks to his.' At the time, I didn't have any story behind it, merely a quirky line. Something about it stuck with me, though. And when I went on the bender of writing short stories, it came back to 'haunt' me. (Pun intended).

Unlike my novels, I tend not to outline short stories, so they're more a flowing process. At first, this one started off somewhat whimsical, but the tone changes a little bit as it goes on.

8

THE ROOMMATE

Anxiety held Roy in its grip. He paced back and forth across his living room, circling the coffee table. No amount of staring at the door made Tamara appear. It had taken him months to find the courage to invite her to the house, to let her into his inner sanctum, the only place in the world he truly felt safe. Everything had to be perfect. Hopefully, his roommate wouldn't make an ass of himself and stay out of sight the whole time. He pulled up the sleeve of his sweater and looked at his wrist, forgetting for the fifth time in as many minutes he didn't have a watch on. Back to pacing.

Minutes later, the shadow of her form darkened the frosted glass beside the front door and the bell rang.

He almost fainted.

Roy bit his knuckle. *Come on, man. You can do it. This is what you've been waiting for.*

Tamara rang the bell again, bouncing from the chill outside. "Roy?" Soft knocking followed. "Roy, are you in there?"

He covered the distance to the door in two huge steps, pulling it open before he could overthink the moment. "Hey, baby."

She evidently ignored his suggestion to 'dress casual.' Roy stared transfixed at her bare caramel legs stretching out from a silver fox fur coat. After stepping inside, she removed her coat to reveal a knee-weakening plum-colored shift dress, her high-heeled shoes the same shade. Tamara glanced around, whistling at the eggshell carpeting. Her expression mixed curiosity and annoyance.

"Wow, you keep a neat house for a guy. More of a place than I expected."

Roy numbly took her coat. "Thanks... Uhh, the house used to be my grandmother's."

"Is that her?" Tamara wandered over to a portrait near the front window. "She looks like Rosa Parks."

Roy let off a somber chuckle and put the coat on a hanger in the foyer closet. "Yeah, I guess. I'm still not really sure how to process losing her. I wish I'd invited you over a couple of months ago. You two would've gotten along well."

"She sounds like a wonderful person."

"Yeah." Roy glanced at the portrait and sighed. "She was. Took me in after the accident."

She made sad eyes at him. "I'm so sorry for you. Bad enough to lose her, but to be the one to find her. It's gotta be so hard. If there's anything I can help you with..."

He took her hand. "I appreciate that. Being with you is the only medicine I need."

"Is it now? Sure took you long enough to invite me over." She winked.

Roy eased the closet door shut, thinking about his grandmother. She always used to cook macaroni and cheese to cheer him up as a kid. "Umm, please, make yourself comfortable. I'll be right back." He started toward the kitchen.

She sniffed at the air, eyebrows drawing together. "Please tell me that's not mac and cheese I smell cooking."

Roy froze in his tracks. "Uhh, that's strange. Gran made it a lot for me as a kid. I'm uhh, definitely *not* making mac and cheese. Talking about her made me think about it."

"So weird." She waved dismissively. "Must be in my head. I don't smell it anymore. I swear we must have been separated at birth. Every time you think about something, it's like I do, too."

He half ran down the hallway to the kitchen. After checking a pot of simmering sauce and another of boiling water, he rushed to the living room. She'd taken a seat on the couch. Roy pondered taking the space next to her, but paced instead.

"I smell garlic." She grinned and leaned forward, her hands leaving dark grey lines in plush fabric.

"Tortellini and white clam sauce." He shot a worried glance at a small closet in the back corner of the living room before sitting on the edge of the couch. "It should be ready in a few minutes."

"What's wrong, sweetie?" She leaned close, draping an arm across his shoulders. "You're as nervous as you were on our first date."

He forced himself to smile, adoring her touch. "Tamara... I've been with you for almost six months now, and I gotta say, you're the most amazing woman I've ever met."

"Go on," she purred.

"There's something I have to tell you. I want to take our relationship to the next level, and I can't do that unless you accept everything about me."

She sat up, raising an eyebrow. "You're not like wanted or something, are you? I figured you were too clean cut to be true."

"No." He looked at her, smiling again. "I have a skeleton in my closet."

"Don't we all?" Tamara draped herself over his shoulders again. "So, what did you do?"

They kissed.

"I'm being literal, girl." He gestured at the closet. "In there."

A disbelieving frown spread over her lips. "What, you have your gramma in the closet? That's kind of creepy."

"No, Ed's not Gran."

"Ed?" she asked, laughing her way to her feet. "Y-you're serious. You didn't kill him, did you?" She crept to the door. "You sayin' you got a legit skeleton in here?"

"No, I didn't kill him. He's just kind of always been there." Roy exhaled. "Ever since the accident."

Tamara smirked at him and opened the door, then blinked, pointed, and screamed.

"Hi," said a man's voice from the closet.

She fainted.

A stark white skeleton ambled out into the living room and shrugged at Roy. "Well, that could've gone better, I suppose. Sorry. Only waved to her."

Roy buried his face in his hands, moaning.

"Well, what did you expect?" Ed the skeleton stepped over the unconscious woman and joined him on the couch. "Most people don't handle this sort of thing well." He crossed his bony legs, bobbing the upper foot. "Your grandmother wasn't too fond of me either."

Roy grumbled. He got up and hurried past Ed without looking at him.

After retrieving his girlfriend from the rug, he set her on the couch and sat between her and his roommate. Once again, he cradled his head.

"Roy?" asked Ed.

"Yeah?"

The skeleton pointed toward the kitchen. "Your tortellini is going to burn."

"Dammit." Roy ran into the kitchen.

The sauce bubbled, almost boiling over. He rushed the sauce onto a cold burner before grabbing the boiling pasta and hurrying to dump it into a strainer in the sink. A cloud of steam billowed up from the sink. He eyed the basement door and clenched his jaw at a twinge of unease. Roy had never been afraid of the cellar before, not until Gran died falling down the stairs. *This is not a good sign. Fearful he'd overcooked the pasta, he tasted one. Fine. Nearly perfect.* His mood improved. The instant he started portioning it out onto plates, Tamara's scream came from the living room.

He jumped at the sound of a body hitting the floor and managed to get the colander on the counter before his now-barefoot girlfriend ran into the kitchen. She scooted around behind him, clung, and pointed past his side at the corridor.

"There's a god damned skeleton in your living room." She trembled. "It's freakin' moving."

The shadow of bones appeared in the hallway, stretching across the hallway. Tamara screamed and buried her face in the back of Roy's powder blue sweater.

"Hey, girl. Calm down." He turned to face her and patted her on the back. "I've gotten used to him. He's harmless… Just my roommate."

"He's dead," she yelled, sobbing. "That's not normal. Skeletons don't talk. He doesn't even have… have—" She rubbed her throat, lost for words. "You know… things."

Ed stopped at the archway to the kitchen and offered a plaintive shrug. "Sorry, I wasn't trying to make a scene or anything."

Tamara whimpered, clinging.

"You know, the first time I saw him I was like… six or so. He scared the hell out of me then."

She looked up, risking a peek at the walking, talking, *skeleton* in the doorway. "Y-you've lived with this thing for twenty years?"

Roy gave Ed an apologetic look. "Yes, I've lived with *him* for a long time. He's really harmless. Sometimes, I think he's the only reason I'm sane. After the car accident…"

Tamara squeezed him.

Ed pointed at his teeth. "This is my innocent smile."

"You can't smile. You're just bones," she whispered.

"Ooh, I see why you like her," said the skeleton. "She gets the subtle humor."

"Baby, now you know why I was so nervous about inviting you over. I figured you'd react like this. I want to spend the rest of my life with you"—she looked up at him as if slapped—"and that means you'd have to find out about Ed sooner or later."

She stared.

Tamara continued staring ten minutes later as they sat at the dining room table, food in front of two out of three. Ed twiddled his thumbs. Neither Roy nor Tamara had touched a single tortellini. Such silence hung between them, the flame on a lone lavender tapered candle made noise.

"I'll pass on the food, Roy, I'm trying to watch my figure." Ed held up a hand.

She looked from him to Ed.

"Lactose intolerant? No, I suppose that's not funny either. At least you've stopped trembling." Ed pointed at his teeth again. "This is my happy smile."

"You know, Ed. Now that you've met her, do you think we could get a little space?" Roy nodded at the closet door. "This was supposed to be a romantic dinner for two."

"Oh, sure." The skeleton got up. "I don't mean to be in the way. It's hard enough getting anything done with a dog staring at you. I suppose I'm probably at least double that on the awkward scale."

Uncomfortable silence lingered for a few minutes after Ed vanished into the closet.

"Maybe triple," said Ed, from inside.

Roy pushed pasta around his plate. "I'm sorry. I should have mentioned him earlier. I've ruined the night."

"You know since we've been seeing each other... The past couple of weeks I've really started to feel like I knew you. Guessed the kind of music you wanted to listen to. Finishing your sentences... sometimes I swear I smell or taste things you're thinking about." She shrank forward, glancing at the closet. "A skeleton, though. This is really out of left field."

Roy tried to bore a hole in his plate with his eyes. "I really think we were meant for each other, baby. I promise you."

She bit her lip, twisting the fork in her hand. "It's a lot to take in."

"You're beautiful when you're terrified." He risked a grin.

"So... a skeleton." She stabbed a tortellini but didn't lift it off the plate. "A live skeleton."

Ed snickered in the closet.

"Well... he's not *live,* but... yeah, I guess." Roy ran a hand over his head. "I'm sorry."

Tamara bit her lip. "Ever thought of going on TV with him? You probably wouldn't have to work again."

Roy exhaled. "Can't do it. Ed's shy. He won't come out around strangers. A couple times, I was sure people would spot him and freak out. Cable dude. Electrical guy. The paramedics who tried to help Gran. Somehow, they didn't notice him. I guess they didn't believe their eyes and acted like nothing happened."

"I guess I should feel honored." She laughed nervously, then tried the food. "Little tepid, but it's good. You went to cooking school?"

"No, I read a lot of books about it. I have a hundred and fifty-seven cookbooks. I... tend to go a little overboard on research when I get into something. In high school, I got interested in pool. You know, eight ball? I read books, watched videos. I'd even wear these horrible white tiger-striped pants as a distraction."

Tamara blinked. "Uhh, that's interesting."

Over the course of the next hour, they finished eating while making idle chat about little of consequence other than her continuing to attempt to talk him into going to some 'family thing' she had been obligated to go to in Atlanta next month. Ed, thankfully, remained out of sight. Eventually, they migrated to the couch.

Tamara glanced past the large television at a series of small wooden carvings on the wall. Roy put on a romance movie suggested by Jimmy from the office. He'd borrowed the Blu-ray without even reading the movie's description. A man in a puffy shirt on the cover suggested a movie about pirates or the revolutionary war. With a bounce in his step, he returned to her side. He sat for a moment with his hands in his lap, eventually reaching an arm onto the backrest. Said arm later found its way around her shoulders, and she leaned into him. Tamara seemed comfortable, but distracted by the movie. Roy stared at her neck, admiring how every part of her was so *perfect.* His awkwardness faded. Soon, his thoughts consisted only of how turned on she made him. He shifted to let his erection sit more comfortably under his pants. She broke out in a light sweat and squirmed.

"Wow, this movie…" Tamara glanced at him, transfixed like a deer in the headlights.

Roy smiled. "I'm not sure it's the movie… You're so… damn… hot."

She put a hand on his thigh. His desire for her surged. The look on her face said she felt as light headed as he did. A few minutes later, neither paid much attention to what happened on the screen. The shock of seeing Ed had worn off, and she once again seemed like her usual self. They kissed and embraced to a backdrop of flashing swords, pounding waves, and cannon fire. Snippets of dialogue trickled into his consciousness, but all that mattered was the woman pressed against him, writhing.

The sound of Ed sobbing from the closet at a tragic on-screen death made her sit up, glaring at the knob. Roy offered an apologetic smile, but she fixed her dress back in place and stood.

"Sorry. I need a minute… Where's your bathroom?"

He pointed at the hallway to the kitchen and let his head fall back against the couch.

"Sorry, man," said Ed. "You know these movies always get me at those parts."

Roy rubbed his face, trying to get his breathing under control. "Yeah…"

TAMARA CREPT PAST THE SMALL ARCH AND PADDED DOWN THE HALL.

She found a bathroom halfway between the living room and the kitchen, on the right. After locking the door, she sat on a closed toilet and slid her bare feet back and forth over a fuzzy white bathmat. The incredulity of a living—or whatever—skeleton had slipped from her mind, enough to let her work up a sweat on the sofa. She shivered, unable to explain how she went from being freaked out and worried to wanting to rip his clothes off in a matter of seconds. *I guess I had an odd reaction to bein' scared out of my mind.*

How long would it take to be able to deal with a thing like Ed? Could she ever get to that point? A few minutes later, she stood, leaning on the sink and gazing at the half-open medicine cabinet. The face in the mirror looked as though she had been awake for two days without sleep. She took a wad of toilet paper and dabbed at her smeared lipstick.

"Ugh," she whispered. "I knew you were too perfect, Roy." She stood up straight, picking at her lip. "Can I handle this?" *No, you're gonna go straight out the door and forget this ever happened.*

While raking her fingers through her hair to set it back to some semblance of order, she noticed a dusty pill bottle in the medicine cabinet. Curious, she edged the sliding door open, tilting her head to read the label. *Risperidone.* The prescription was filled months ago and the bottle didn't look like it had been touched in almost as long, being nearly full. Another bottle deeper in, older by nine months and empty, said *Haloperidol on the label.* Both bottles had Roy's name on them.

Tamara took slow, measured breaths. "Those sound crazy serious." She locked eyes with her reflection. "Look, you've known him for eight months, dated him for six. He's been nothing but a sweetheart the whole time." *There's a goddamned skeleton in the house.* "Oh, come on. This has gotta be some kind of prank." She smiled. *What if he's setting me up to propose? I gotta find out what those pills are.*

She edged the cabinet closed as near as she could remember to where the door had been and made her way to the living room. Roy remained on the couch, throwing a worried look at the wall. He'd paused the movie on a blur of ocean water crashing against the side of a galleon. Tamara rounded the armrest and sat by her purse. She glanced at the closet, now quiet, and put her hands on her knees. A strange sense of worry crept up her back, sliding ghostly fingers into her mind.

"What's wrong?" Roy offered a hopeful lift of both eyebrows. "You look tense again."

The feeling faded as fast as it came, shifting to optimism.

"I'm only trying to make sense of this, Roy. What I saw tonight is impossible. I'm not sure if I believe it. If I told anyone, they'd think I was nuts."

"I don't think you're nuts." Roy offered a weak smile. "Neither does Ed. How about some wine?"

She fidgeted. Out of nowhere, she felt horny. Tamara bit her lip and kept her hands on her knees, trying to ignore the urge to touch herself. She stared at the picture of Gran, hoping the old woman's smile would chase away the inexplicable lust warring with her anxiety.

It didn't.

Roy got up and moved around behind the couch. "If it helps, think of him as a roommate. You've been the best part of my life for the past six months, and there's no reason any of what we have has to change."

"I know, Roy. It's... Lately, it's like I know what you're thinking half the time." She forced herself to smile, knuckles whitening on her knees.

Soon, the touch of his hand on her shoulders worked relaxation into her muscles and she let herself lean back. Her mind recoiled at the thought of what sat behind the closet door, but other parts of her body had different plans in spite of it. He massaged her neck and shoulders a little while longer and leaned over the seat to kiss her again.

"I'll get us some wine. Be right back."

As soon as he left the room, the mysterious lust evaporated to pure worry. Tamara gasped for air and hid her face behind her hands, staring at the closet door, terrified it might open. Dread morphed to curiosity. She edged off the couch and tiptoed over to the door. Total silence. Her shaking hand stilled only after she whitened her knuckles on the knob. A deep breath later, she jerked the door open—and stared at four old woman's coats, and bare floor.

No skeleton.

ROY JOGGED DOWN THE HALL TO THE KITCHEN, STILL THICK WITH THE SCENT OF garlic.

He headed over to the basement door in the corner. Whatever odd sense of fear he'd gotten from it earlier had faded. Dismissing it as nerves from having Tamara here, he flung it open and made his way down a rickety wooden staircase to the basement. A dusty shelf of random ancient things Gran gathered over the years sat two feet away from the last step. He reached to his left and flicked a light switch shrouded in cobweb. A naked bulb flickered to life, as if under protest. Its labored glow chased away the darkness, but threatened to go out at any second. He crossed to the other side of the room and retrieved one of three bottles of wine from a shelf by the wall.

The workbench next to it held dozens of plastic models in various states of completion, mostly fighter jets or ships. As a teen, he'd gotten into model building for a while. Invariably, he'd always make one tiny mistake and become unable to continue working on it, convinced he'd ruined it beyond repair. No matter what he did, *he* would know about the error.

Roy looked down at the wine bottle in his hand. "Sorry, Pop-pop. I know you savin' these for a special occasion, but... Tamara's special." He smiled, eyes closed, and daydreamed about growing old with the woman he loved.

Happy thoughts left him feeling confident. With a spring in his step, he made his way upstairs. When he strode into the living room carrying a bottle in one hand and two glasses in the other, Tamara jumped and dropped her iPhone. It bounced to a halt by his shoe. He set the wine on the coffee table and stooped to get it for her. Their hands met on the device. His smile fell at the contents of the screen. She'd been Googling *Risperidone.*

She glanced down at her purple toenails. "When were you going to tell me that you're on anti-psychotics?"

His heart felt like a bowling ball as he let go of the phone. She cradled it to her chest as he moved around the table and sat a cushion away. Tamara shuddered as if in response to the wave of guilt crashing over him.

"I'm not *on* them. I"—he rubbed his hands down his legs a few times —"They had nasty side effects. I'm fine. The doctor thought I might have been schizophrenic, but I feel *fine."*

She glanced at the closet. "You hallucinate things, don't you?"

Roy reached to take her hand. "Ed's not a hallucination. You saw him. He can't be a hallucination."

Tamara's defensive grip on the phone weakened as what he said sank in. "Maybe you should go back on your meds?"

A pale white skull leaned out of the closet; empty sockets stared at her. Roy's roommate seemed far less whimsical now. He looked the same, but something about him had gone from offbeat to sinister. She squeezed Roy's hand.

"You do see Ed, don't you?" he asked.

She offered a mute nod, trembling from the way the skeleton stared at her. Even without a face, it radiated malice.

"The doctors wanted me to believe I hallucinated him. They refused to accept he is real. If Ed existed only in my imagination, you wouldn't see him. I'm not really schizophrenic, so I don't need medication."

"You don't like the pills?" asked Tamara.

Ed shook his head in a slow, menacing gesture.

"Nah." Roy smiled. "They made me depressed and lonely. I took them for a while, Gran insisted even though the doctors were wrong.

Obviously, Ed is not a hallucination since you can see him. On those pills, I felt like shit for months. Sat in my room all day, no one to talk to. Until the pharmacy screwed something up a while ago and I ran out. I hadn't felt that good in... Gee, I dunno how long. Staying off the meds was Ed's suggestion. I didn't like feeling asleep all the time, like I was half awake or out of my head watching my life from across the room. You understand?"

"I-I guess so." She gazed longingly at her shoes under the coffee table.

"Please, calm down." He let go of her hand and poured the wine out into two glasses.

Information about *Risperidone* filled the little screen in her hands. She hit the side button, turning the screen off, and slid the iPhone back into her purse.

"Please let her stay. I love her," said Roy.

"What?" Tamara whirled, almost knocking the wine glass he offered her out of his hand.

"Uhh... I didn't say anything."

"You really didn't just say something?" Tamara blinked. *Does he love me?* She accepted the wine, clutching the glass in two hands. After a moment of him giving her a reassuring smile, she breathed. They clinked glasses.

Ed no longer glared at her from the closet.

"Since you're not running out the door screaming, I think I might have a surprise for you in a week or so..." He sipped at the same time she did.

I hope she likes the ring.

That time, she heard Roy's voice. Clear. Distinct. While he drank. She tried to gasp in mid sip and ended up choking on the wine. He eased her glass to the table, scooted closer, and patted her on the back. Once she recovered, he brushed tears from her cheeks. Despite knowing a frightening skeleton listened to them from the closet, she felt the need to be with Roy.

He held her. "I'm sorry, baby. This night was supposed to be so special. I... I should've told you about Ed sooner. I was terrified you'd leave me. I suppose it would have been easier for me to take it if you got freaked and left when I'd only known you for a week. If you left me now, it would kill me."

"He's not dangerous, is he? He lives in your closet?" *I'm seeing skeletons, I'm hearing Roy's voice in my head. Did he slip me something?*

"Dangerous? Ed?" Roy chuckled. "He used to read me Dr. Seuss when

I was six, right after Gran took me in. If it wasn't for him, I don't know if I could have coped with the crash."

Roy stared into space. She shivered at an inexplicable need heating up inside her. The look on his face reminded her of a terrified boy about to be told his parents bled to death in a car wreck. Tamara ran a hand over his short, curly hair. She managed a smile and leaned in to kiss him. He cradled her against him while they kissed.

"Oh, baby, this is so messed up," she rasped, shuddering as his hands ran down her side. "I don't know why I'm so hot for you right now. I should be scared out of my head."

"There's nothing messed up about you." He kissed the side of her neck.

Tamara shivered, no longer able to hold herself back.

Minutes later, she writhed, squirming in time with him as he worked the tiny purple dress past her hips and up over her head. He dropped it on the rug, then leaned back to pull his sweater off and toss it. She made a series of odd squeaking noises as he licked around her navel while tugging her panties down. While he unbuttoned his white shirt, she leaned in to kiss his bare chest. He groaned, shifting. Soon, they rolled in a naked embrace on the couch. All thoughts of Ed the Skeleton fled her mind. His touch, as he had done dozens of times at her place, sent her into the throes of ecstasy. She'd never felt emotion this intense with anyone else. The more she had him, the more she wanted him.

Tamara closed her eyes as he slid down to explore her with his tongue. She couldn't tell if his sexy talk happened for real or if she imagined the voice in her head.

Moaning and gasping, she reached over her head to hold on to the arm of the couch. "Oh, Roy… Do you really love me?"

"More than anything."

"Come up here and say that to my face," she cooed.

Roy slithered up and nibbled on her earlobe. "I love you more than anything."

She kissed all over his neck. *This girl is amazing.* His voice echoed in her head but his lips didn't move. Next to a moving skeleton, hearing him talk somehow straight into her mind didn't seem odd at all. She'd gone well past caring. Their sweat-covered bodies slid back and forth, skin on skin. He kissed her lips, neck, and breasts. She arched her back, holding on to his shoulders, and then he entered her. She cried out, clinging to him until passion boiled over. Tamara's body convulsed. No man had ever gotten her *there* so fast.

Minutes later, she stretched out on the sofa, limp and exhausted.

She lay with her arms above her head, lost in a near sleep of total contentment. His hand stroked her breast as he mumbled random silly things. He started comparing her beauty to natural wonders, but ran out of ideas and moved on to household objects. It was so silly it came off as cute. She giggled. Tamara had never felt as close to Roy as did in that moment. After she said he'd make a wonderful father, he'd talked about the pain of watching his parents die trapped in a burning car after he'd been ejected from it. The bliss of the moment chilled at a sudden flash of remembered screams.

Roy's memory, somehow in *her* head.

A dry touch raked over her nipple, scratching at her breast. The sense of Roy's presence on top of her gave way to something much lighter and much less soft. Her eyes snapped open to find Ed's skull hovering an inch from her lips. She gasped, grabbing the bony wrist to yank his hand away from her chest. Roy had vanished. Naked bones lay atop her body.

"Ed, what the hell?"

She tried to sit up, but he pushed her down.

"You're trying to kill me." Ed tilted his skull at her. "I can't let you do that."

"What?" She grabbed his other arm, holding him by both wrists. "You're already dead. I can't kill you."

Bony arms slid through her grip; slender, bony fingers closed like iron bands around her throat. "You want Roy to take those pills again, like his Gran did. I can't let you do that. I don't want to go away."

"Ed." She gasped, thrashing. "Please, no."

He squeezed. "I've been with Roy since his parents died. He saw them burn. I have to protect him. Without me, he'd be lost."

Tamara grunted, driving her knee up into his pelvis. Ed flipped over and landed seated on the floor. She jumped to her feet and tried to run, but he grabbed her by the ankle, tripping her flat on her chest.

"Roy!" She pulled herself forward, kicking blindly at the skeleton holding her leg. "Roy! Help!"

By sheer luck, she hammered her heel into Ed's skull, knocking him away. Shrieking, Tamara crawled up to a run and sprinted directly at the first opening she could find, not realizing she'd gone out the front door naked until she stood on the sidewalk. Lights came on in neighboring houses. Panic gave way to mortification. Tamara tried to cover herself with her hands, shaking and crying. Ed didn't come outside. The house looked empty. Even Roy had disappeared.

A porch across the street lit up. She bolted back into the house before the neighbor came out and slammed the door behind her. After two breaths, she ran to where her clothing lay scattered across the carpet. Barely able to see past her tears, she pulled her dress back on as fast as shaking hands would allow. Ed came out of nowhere and tried to grab her as she reached for her purse—and phone. Screaming again, she jumped back. Ed pivoted and lunged, growling.

Tamara dove to the ground by the coffee table as the skeleton closed its arms nothing and stumbled past her. The wine bottle sat inches in front of her face. She grabbed it, got to her feet, and swung the bottle at him like a club. He leaned out of the way, laughing. When he took a step toward her, she kicked the coffee table into his shins, tripping him in a clatter of bones. Tamara jumped over him, scooped her purse from the floor and ran down the hall to the bathroom, intending to secure herself inside and call the police.

She found the door closed and locked.

Tamara rattled at the knob, pounding on the door and shrieking. Roy yelled something as if far away. Hissing, Ed appeared at the alcove where the hall met the living room, casting a sinister shadow of bones over the floor. She scooted back, so frightened she didn't even want his shadow to touch her feet. He leaned forward in a menacing posture, pointing a twelve-inch carving knife at his teeth.

"This is me not smiling."

Tamara screamed and ran to the kitchen, Ed clattering after her. She hurried to the sink in search of a weapon. As soon as she reached the counter, Ed slashed at her. The knife whooshed over her head as she leapt aside. Ed swung too hard and almost flung himself to the floor. As he stumbled to keep his balance, she lunged for the sink and grabbed a large pot handle jutting up from the soapy water. As soon as Ed faced her, she rounded it at him, hammering the pan into his right arm. Suds and dishwater splashed everywhere.

The skeleton stumbled back, sliding on the soapy tiles. She swung at him again, but her bare feet slid out from under her in the puddle, tossing her over sideways and redirecting her attack from his head to the side of his knee. The strike swept the skeleton's legs out from under him. He lurched forward, losing his grip on the knife and grabbing at the counter for support. Tamara landed flat on her left side. Ed's feet scrabbled around in the puddle, unable to find traction. He frantically pulled the basin of drying dishes to the floor as he went down. Knives, forks, and ladles clanked to the tiles around them. Ed reached for the steak knife. Tamara jumped on his back, grabbing him by the shoulder blades and repeatedly bashing his face into the floor.

He rammed his elbow into her side twice, knocking the wind out of her, then stretched to grab the knife. His fingertips brushed the end of the handle. She roared, finding the strength to haul him away from the deadly weapon before diving on it herself. It vanished right out from under her hands. Tamara shrieked and leapt up, a glint of metal on the countertop caught her eye. Without a care for how the blade had gone from floor to counter, she lunged at it. Ed grabbed her ankle again, the puddle of soapy water making it easy for him to yank her off her feet. She managed to get a hand on the weapon before crashing to the floor, and kicking back into his ribcage. Ed flew backward into the fridge.

A dozen magnets fell on him.

Tamara reared up, raising the knife over her head in both hands.

Ed raised his hands in a pleading, defensive maneuver. She stabbed down, catching him in the left leg. Howling in pain, he punched her in the face, knocking her into a roll that stopped against the oven. Having a knife stuck through his femur didn't slow him down. He wobbled upright, using the counter for support. She crawled left, headed for the dropped pan.

"You had to go poking around the medicine cabinet, didn't you? Why couldn't we have been a nice little trio? I don't take up much space. All I need is the closet. I like the same kind of movies he does. I don't eat his food. Did he tell you Gran wanted to kill me, too?"

Tamara gathered her footing, backing up. "I would have found the meds, eventually. Roy wanted to propose. I would've said yes... Why are you trying to hurt me?"

"I don't want to kill you." Ed tugged at the knife, unable to wrench it out of his leg. He shambled at her. "I don't want you to kill me. All I want is for us to be happy. Gran was an accident."

"Stay away!" She raised the saucepan and limped toward a back door.

"Baby," hissed Ed, "this is all just a big misunderstanding. Think about what you're doing. Put the pan down, please. This isn't like you at all. It's stress. I need a doctor. I won't press charges, I swear. I know it was an accident. We'll tell them it was an accident, just like Gran."

She whirled, grabbing the little iron knob and throwing open the door

—to the basement. Tears ran down her face as soon as she realized she hadn't discovered a way out, and the skeleton had trapped her in a corner. Ed staggered closer, still clutching the knife impaling his leg. She closed her eyes and screamed.

"Baby…" A warm hand squeezed her shoulder. "Calm—"

Frantic, she attacked in a frenetic barrage of blind swings. Again and again she flailed the pan at the skeleton, clunking and clanking until the jarring impact of smacking a saucepan into the wall jolted her knuckles. A bony hand scraped across her chest, pulling away fast. A heavy thud made her look. Ed tumbled down the basement stairs, shouting and roaring.

With a manic laugh, she slammed the door and dragged a kitchen chair over to wedge under the knob. Shivering, half hanging out of her torn dress, she padded across the kitchen and grabbed the wall phone. No sooner had her hand touched it, than pounding came from the front of the house.

"Police! Mr. Evers, please open the door."

Tamara let the handset drop against the wall with a plastic *thunk*. Dial tone flooded the room. For a second, she stared at the dangling cord, wondering how the police knew she wanted to call them. At another heavy knock, she snapped out of her mental fog and walked down the corridor to the living room. The windows flashed red and blue, violet where the light mixed in the curtains. Shadows moved over the frosted windows on either side of the door.

Bang… Bang… "Mr. Evers, we got a call about a disturbance. If you do not answer, we will have to assume you are injured."

"Kick it in," said a woman. "I swear I heard a scream."

Tamara flexed her grip on the pot, edging closer step by step. She twisted the knob, pulling, squinting at the brightness outside. Blood dripped from her nose as she shivered, unable to think of what to say to the two police officers. At the sight of the pan in her grasp, they put their hands on their weapons.

"Easy, lady. Drop the pot," said the male cop.

"He's trying to kill me." Tamara released the saucepan, which slipped out of her hand and fell to the porch with a *clang*. "Please, help me!"

The female officer let go of her weapon, gathering Tamara to the side with a hand on the shoulder. "Ma'am, calm down and tell us what happened."

"My boyfriend, Roy. His roommate tried to stab me with a knife. Ed thought I was trying to kill him, but I only wanted Roy to take his meds.

He's schizophrenic and sees things. He's been off his pills for a while, and now he's gone. I can't find Roy anywhere!"

"Take a breath. Easy." The female cop stared at her. "What's this roommate look like?"

"Uhh, he's white." Tamara shivered.

"How old?"

She bit her lip and whined. "I… dunno. This is gonna sound crazy, but he's only a skeleton."

"A skeleton?" asked the male cop. "Like bones walking around?"

"Yes." She pulled her dress back into place and sniffled. "I told Roy he should take his meds again, and the skeleton came out of the closet and tried to kill me. It chased me around the house into the kitchen. I knocked it down into the basement. It's still down there. Please, don't let it get me." Her eyes bulged as she stared at the open doorway, trembling.

The cops exchanged a glance. Glock in hand, the male officer entered the house while his partner remained with her on the porch. Tamara held both hands over her face, shivering. A moment later, the male officer's voice came over the radio clipped to the woman's shoulder.

"Central, this is 1357 on scene at the domestic on River Street. Confirm one black male with a deep stab wound to the leg. He's lost a lot of blood and has multiple blunt-force injuries to the face and chest. Need medics out here ASAP."

"Copy that, 1357. Please stand by for medical transport," said a bored sounding woman.

Tamara glanced at the female cop. "Did Ed hurt Roy? Is Roy okay? Please, tell me what happened? You shouldn't leave your partner alone in there with that skeleton. He's dangerous." She looked away from the cop, past her shivering legs—at a bloody saucepan lying on the porch.

"WHERE'S ROY? PLEASE, WHY WON'T ANYONE TELL ME WHAT'S GOING ON?" Tamara shrieked, struggling against the straps holding her to the stretcher.

"Easy, ma'am."

She jumped, not having noticed the man in an EMT uniform until he spoke. "Where's Roy? Why am I tied down? What the hell is going on?" Tamara strained and thrashed in a futile effort to free herself.

"We're taking you to the hospital so you can see a doctor. He'll be able to answer all of your questions. I'm going to give you something to help you relax now."

"No!" she shouted, trying to lean away from the needle going for her arm. "No! I'm not crazy! There's a skeleton in that house trying to kill me."

Warmth flooded into her veins, riding up to her shoulder and into her neck. The roof swam into a smear of color as heaviness overcame her mind. A blur of blue uniform moved away a few seconds before two metal doors past her feet closed with a heavy *clunk*. The room wobbled and dimmed. Somewhere in the distance, indistinct voices spoke in bits of radio snippets.

"Hey," said a familiar voice.

She jumped, and turned her head to the left.

Ed the skeleton sat on the bench beside her stretcher, elbows on knees. He raised one hand, waving in greeting. "Looks like we're gonna be friends after all." He pointed at his teeth. "This is my happy smile."

THE TWO EMTs GLANCED AT THE PARTITION DOOR TO THE BACK AS A LONG, bloodcurdling scream rang out. When it stopped, they shifted around to face forward.

"Wow, Lynn, the doc is gonna have fun with this one."

"No kidding." The driver turned on the emergency lights. "You ain't kidding."

IX

A GHOST AMONG FIREFLIES

ABOUT A GHOST AMONG FIREFLIES

This is another story that came from a dream. Main difference here is, this dream only gave me a short glimpse of a scene. Unlike *The Tower* or the novel *Caller 107*, this dream felt like it lasted only a minute or two. The opening scene of this short in the abandoned room, the girl approaching the window, and the rain of fireflies in the air is all the dream contained.

It's a dream that recurred to me over and over for several years, three or four times a month. If it means anything, I don't know. It eventually stopped before I wrote anything down and before I tried to take writing seriously. When looking for short story ideas, I remembered having the dream and developed a story behind the imagery to explain everything. I hope I've conveyed it in words within the story, but the dream was haunting as heck. Imagine the feeling of walking through a place where you know hundreds of thousands of people died... that's the kind of mood I had waking up from the dream every time.

I took some inspiration here from Japanese anime as well as classic Sci Fi. The music Naris listens to while playing chicken with laser cannons is *You got the Touch* by Stan Bush. On a final note, when I first thought about writing this one, I was going to title it simply *Firefly*... but I waited too long and some other guy beat me to the title.

9

A GHOST AMONG FIREFLIES

Loneliness came on without warning riding the wave of a sudden chill. Powerful, overwhelming, inexplicable. Naris shivered. The scent of mold made her flee from the damp softness upon which she lay—a gargantuan bare mattress upon warped and twisted imitation wood.

She sat up and found herself surrounded by peeling grey paint flaking from grimy walls. Broken dolls, crushed toys, and smashed furniture packed the room from edge to edge. Two curtains wavered inward from a large window with a balcony extension, soundless as wraiths in a spectral dance. Plastic cartons crept along in the invading breeze, scratching at the floor as loud as her breaths that formed visible puffs.

Overcome by the smell, she reached up to cover her mouth, but at the sight of her hands, grimy, small, and pale, she froze, then looked down at her body. Naris gasped, stunned to see a tattered nightgown embroidered about the hem with faded rabbit heads. Bare legs, scrawny and dirty, stretched stark and pale against the mold-stained cushion. Her chest, flat. Her hips, gone. She didn't lay upon a massive bed—she'd become tiny. Confused, she faced the room and scooted forward until her feet touched the frozen floor.

A crowd of dolls scattered around the floor all stared at her. Two had tea at a makeshift table made from old shipping cartons. Four more littered the far end of the dingy bed, each caked with dirt and on the verge of disintegrating. Others perched here and there on old chairs and a desk, while two leaned sentinel against the wall on either side of the window. Innumerable disembodied doll parts lay throughout the rest of the space, twitching in the constant wind. She stood, gazing down at her feet and torn nightdress. Confused, she swiped a hand at hair longer than it should be, black as night instead of her usual light brown.

The strange feeling of having been here before beckoned her. As if by memory, she navigated a minefield of old toys, broken computer equipment, and the shattered remnants of once-furniture, all coated in creeping mold. She glanced at a desk to her left, her eyes at the level of its surface. An old, broken holo-terminal glimmered in the weak light from the window, reflected curtains the only image on the screen.

Naris approached the desk, staring at a picture set in a block of Lucite depicting a middle-aged man with greying hair wearing a white lab coat. For some reason, Naris wanted to call him Daddy, but he looked nothing like her father. An etching in the clear plastic below the picture read 'Volunrad Corporation Innovation Award – 2114.' *Over fifty years ago.*

She moved away from the desk toward the great window, flanked by strips of gossamer curtain lit blue from the outside. Naris looked down, placing her bare feet carefully around sharp pieces of broken electronics. Strong wind blew in the window, pressing her nightgown against her front, revealing the form of her little body. At the balcony edge, she leaned up on her toes to peer over a railing covered in fine brown silt at the ruins of a dead city stretching out below the balcony.

Great monoliths of metal rose on the far side of the street, dull metallic walls with thousands of gaping voids where windows no longer existed. Dense fog enveloped everything, thickening to an impenetrable curtain of gloom only a few streets away in both directions. She recognized this strange abandoned city painted in monochromatic green and filtered in shadow, but couldn't understand why. Baleful wind howled in the distance, but she didn't fear it. Nothing here could do her more harm.

Far below, the husks of old ground-cars sat in the road, standstill traffic that had died and rotted in place. Smoke peeled up from numerous holes in the buildings across the street where the wreckage of crashed aerotrans still smoldered.

Dense fog far off to the left cleared, exposing the edifice of a distant building facing the street. The grand structure appeared pristine, standing out of reach from the roiling mist. Upon it, a symbol: an enormous hollow gear, toothed inside and out, with three more inside it, each smaller than the last. An odd urge to go there called to her, but as soon as she decided to try, the smog thickened, devouring the strange building once more.

Pale and glowing in the moonlight, Naris seemed the only item of color in the world.

A faint chorus of chirpy voices drew her attention upward. Countless specks of emerald light gleamed like a snow of floating emeralds, filling the sky for as far as she could see. The glowing spots drifted and whorled without substance, swarming wherever the wind took them. The faint, echoing whispers of thousands grew louder, as if she stood near a park full of random conversations too distant to listen in on.

She smiled, up on tiptoe, reaching one hand out over the edge as high as she could. The swarm of brilliant green specks continued drifting down from the sky until they filled the air outside the window. Naris tried to stretch even taller, offering her hand to one of the fireflies.

A shimmering sphere of pure energy alighted on her fingertip and emitted a pixie's giggle. The amorphous mass radiated emotion—love. She stopped standing up on her toes and took a step back from the railing, smiling at the little creature on her hand.

The sense of reality changed; within the dream, she became more a spectator than a participant. After a moment, the little flickering sprite spiraled off in the wind to rejoin its brethren. She watched it drift for as long as it took to lose track of it in the swarm, then gazed higher, to the thick black clouds from whence they rained.

A rush of whispering voices filled the back of her mind, as though the city had come alive.

The little girl closed her eyes and made a wish—not to be alone.

NARIS SAT UP WITH A START; A THIN GREY BLANKET SLID AWAY FROM HER naked chest.

She looked down and loosed a sigh of relief as she regarded her adult body, then yawned, drawing her knees up and setting her forehead into them. Long light brown hair draped over her eyes, hanging halfway to her waist. She basked in the joy of being herself again, trying to understand how a dream had felt so real.

"Damn, I've been out here too long."

She swung her legs out into the hall, sitting on the edge of the heating pad lining the bottom of her bed: a coffin-shaped hole in the wall of a narrow passageway between the cockpit and the rest of the ship. Stretching made her yawn again. After, she rubbed sleep out of her eyes. To her right, the soft hum of electronics came from the cockpit. Farther away on her left beyond a doorway, a few slivers of gleaming steel shone from the darkness in a room some engineer had the gall to refer to as a lounge.

A similar berth, never used, gaped at her from the facing wall in front of her. Loneliness knotted in her gut at the sight. *Maybe that's why I keep dreaming about being stuck alone on a dead planet. Why do I see myself as a child though?*

"I was just about to wake you," said a disembodied male voice, her ship's AI.

"Thanks, Ein."

She sat still for a few minutes, gritting her teeth against the chilly air. The floor froze her feet, but her legs no longer bore a coating of dark grime, no longer those of a little girl. "Shit, maybe I should retire. I think I'm getting delirium."

"You have not yet exhibited any symptoms of psychological maladies that I am able to discern, Naris. At twenty-six Earth years, you are in perfect health and do not exhibit any of the markers for mania or delirium. However, while you were sleeping, I did notice unusual levels of brain activity in portions of the frontal lobe not normally associated with nocturnal hallucinations."

"They're called 'dreams' you know." She stood, stretched, and scratched her stomach. "Thanks. Always good to hear an AI tell me they think I'm sane."

"Are you attempting to be humorous?"

Twist left, stretch. "I'm not really sure." Twist right.

She went toward the lounge. Lights glimmered on in sequence as she passed through the bulkhead door. A tiny silver table ringed with a C-shaped bench, a small food synthesizer, and a lone multifunction tube near a pair of locker doors greeted her.

Naris frowned at the hatch on the other side, leading to the cargo bay. *Staring at that door won't put payload in the hold, or credits in the bank.*

The tube rotated open as she approached. She squeezed in, stepping up on a raised steel disc with a drain at its center. Once the clear partition closed, a rainfall of warm water fell on her from above. She grumbled.

"Ein, can you turn up the pressure in here? And how 'bout some soap?"

A nozzle on the wall emitted a tiny electronic growl as it extended to point at her. A second later, a spurt of pale blue slime hit her on the chest.

She frowned at it. "Gee… thanks. Don't be so extravagant."

"I'm sorry, Naris. When you engage in personal hygiene maintenance daily, the cleaning agent reserves deplete more rapidly than the design was allocated for."

She rubbed the soap, a squiggle the size of what one might use as toothpaste, over her body. "What was the design?"

"Two-person crew, each individual showering once approximately every seven to ten days."

"Ugh. Seven days between showers?" She shivered at the thought. "That's not happening. I'll have to get a bigger dispenser installed."

"Most privateers aren't too worried about personal hygiene as much as they are getting their payload where it needs to be. A larger reserve is, however, an option. Bear in mind it may reduce your allocation of cargo space."

"Ein, have you ever seen a logo with four gears?"

The water cut out, replaced by high-velocity warm air that blasted her hair straight up.

"Can you please be a little more specific?"

"One big gear circle with three little ones inside it."

"Searching."

She poked her elbow at the console; the tube opened. Naris ignored the cold-shift in the air outside as she went to the food machine and tried to dial up some eggs. A second after she pressed the button, a tray of reconstituted—something—appeared on a plate. Her tolerance for cold ended the instant her ass met the frigid steel bench.

"Gah!" she yelled, jumping up and holding her backside. "Damn, that's cold."

"Beyond recorded history, humans invented objects designated as: clothing. Such objects often solve problems caused by frigid steel benches. You do have ample quantities of said objects in your storage spaces. I am unable to calculate why you seldom make use of them."

Naris gave the middle finger in several directions, never quite sure where to aim a bird flipped at her starship's AI. "We're going to be jumping as soon as I figure out where to go. No point getting dressed only to have to strip again. Besides, if I wear it, I gotta wash it. And we're apparently low on soap. And naked is 'comfortable.'"

"The bench would state otherwise."

She again waved a middle finger around.

"Oh, I am not criticizing you. I have no opinion as I do not possess a rear end vulnerable to contact with a cold bench."

She eased herself down, sitting rigid until her body heat made the surface tolerable. Whatever the food synth gave her smelled like eggs, tasted like bacon, and had the consistency of cottage cheese. Naris ate it only because it existed, and because pushing the button again might commit an even worse atrocity against cuisine. *Next time I get paid, I'm buying a Platinum Chef. I can't take this crap anymore.*

"Can't you fix that damn thing?"

"Did you forget that you disconnected it from the hardline? I cannot even see the food synthesizer as part of the internal network anymore."

Naris squinted at the ceiling, half-growling. "You made liver quiche. The ship smelled like egg farts for two weeks."

"You wanted something different."

"You told me it was chocolate mousse!" she shouted, before hunching over and attacking the slime-elet. *Omelet my ass.*

Minutes later, she hovered by the trash panel licking the empty plate, pondering the material. Tomorrow, the atoms assembled into something resembling polystyrene foam could be food. For a brief moment, she pondered saving time and eating it now, but tossed it in the hole. The plate vanished in a flare of blue sparks and static electricity that made her hair fluff up. With a sigh, she padded back down the narrow neck of the ship to the cockpit.

The large, soft pilot's chair had built in heaters, which she adored. Coffee-brown imitation leather almost put her back to sleep as she reclined in it with one heel on the dashboard, legs crossed. She leaned back, tapping one foot on nothing while gazing off into the endless distance of space.

"Any luck with the gears?"

"Actually, yes," said Ein, his voice emanating from everywhere at once. "It is the registered trademark of Volunrad Corporation."

From the dream... "Oh, lovely."

"Do they have any offices in bombed out wastelands?"

"I need more information than that to search."

Naris leaned over and grabbed a pink rubber ball from a cupholder, which she tossed up and caught repeatedly. "City, all the buildings made out of this same greenish metal. Cars and shit in the road, like everyone in the place dropped dead all at once."

"One moment. You know there is a rather lucrative posting to move some Sel'Nithiri crystal off Hallos. You could get it to Farpoint Station in under a week."

"Yeah." She threw and caught the ball. "And have every mercenary, bounty hunter, and CPO from here to Paleon up my ass sideways the whole trip. No thanks." Toss, catch. "If I'm gonna get put in a cage, it's gonna be for six months or less. Nothing that major. Nith'll get me ten years, minimum."

"Consortium Peace Officers can't outrun me."

"You wanna run the Nith, you run the Nith. Leave me in a cantina and pick me up when you're done."

"I never knew you to be so risk-averse."

"A couple of idiots who think they can make quick creds pinching my cargo is one thing. I'm not moving stuff that'll attract every ship with a weapon on it for kiloparsecs. Besides, I want to know what this place is that I keep dreaming about."

"The only thing I've been able to find so far in the Consortium's databases points to an uninhabited planet charted as Acheron-18."

"It can't be uninhabited, Ein. There were buildings. A whole city." She held her arms out.

"It is uninhabited now and has been at least for the past forty years. The record I'm accessing indicates Volunrad abandoned it for unspecified reasons."

Naris squinted at a drifting cloud of nebula gas. *Forty years? She couldn't have been older than eight.*

"They listed it as a D5."

She blinked. "D5? Crap. Are you sure?"

"As sure as this data can be. Not even CPO forces have authorization to land there due to the theoretical risk of transporting unknown harmful substances off the planet. Only one city was built on the entire surface, despite it having once been an Earth-like atmosphere."

"Once been?"

"Oh, I imagine it still technically is. However, according to this, there is such a high degree of pollution in the air it is no longer considered habitable. In fact, they classified it as toxic. Even a few days' exposure is supposedly fatal."

"Sounds perfect. Plot it for jump."

"Naris, this is a toxic graveyard. There's nothing there but some old buildings and who-knows-what kind of contamination."

"I have to go."

"You realize it is only a dream?"

"Having a dream twice is a coincidence. Every night for four months is… something else." She withdrew her feet from the console and sat up. "Besides, it's… I don't know. It feels like more than a dream. Almost as if she's calling me. I have to go. Eden needs my help."

"Who, or what is Eden?"

"I—" *Where did that come from?*

A man in a black suit appeared as a twelve-inch tall hologram to her left. "Miss… Naris?"

She turned crimson, one arm over her chest, the other covering her groin. "Who the hell are you?"

"Relax. He sees you in a flight suit. You are welcome, by the way."

"Little warning next time," she whispered.

"I represent Volunrad Corporation. We noticed you accessed certain records recently in reference to Acheron-18."

"Public domain…" She squinted at the wall. "Right? It's on the open C-net."

"Indeed," said Ein.

"Miss Naris—"

"It's not *miss* Naris, it's just Naris. I don't use a last name."

"Very well, Naris. We couldn't help but notice you possess a privateer's registration as well as your own ship, and are not currently retained on any active contracts."

She pursed her lips. "What's it to you?"

"There is data on Acheron-18 we are highly interested in."

"Sucks to be you then." She examined her fingernails. "That place is a toxic dump."

The man flashed a placating smile. "Please, Naris, subterfuge is not your strong suit. Volunrad Corporation is prepared to offer you the sum of forty million Consortium Marks for that information. Unfortunately, obtaining it would require venturing to the surface and locating a functional terminal within our old office complex."

Her heart pounded in her head; her chest tightened. The cockpit felt colder all of a sudden. That would be enough money to retire, to stop being chased across the known universe by pirates and to get a dog, a cat (or six), or maybe a lover (or lifemate), and a home. She squinted at the sunglasses peering back at her. A faint diagonal image shift banded down the screen, noise in the long-distance comm. After the fourth time the distortion sank to the bottom of the display, she reached forward.

"I'll think about it." She cut the comm.

"Think about it?" asked Ein. "Forty million credits could set you up for the rest of your life, short as it may be given your predilection to danger."

Naris spun the chair to face the cockpit door and got up. "I gotta think. Something's not right. D5 rating or not, that's too much money for data." Daydreaming about retiring was one thing, but having it in reach, something else. What if she missed being out here? It didn't matter. No one legitimately offered money like that for data. Taking the job would absolutely end with her dead. They had no intention of paying.

"But, you want to go there anyway if I know you. I have the route plotted."

"Like I said, I'll think about it. I got a bad feeling is all. No one offers that much money for simple data unless there's a big catch or they're planning to kill me to keep their secrets."

She jogged down the tiny hallway, once more entering the shower tube and facing back the way she came as the cylinder rotated closed and sealed. Warm peach-colored gel flooded in over her feet, rising up past her knees in seconds.

"This one isn't about money."

The gel stopped at her neck.

"Are you sure about this, Naris?"

"You almost sound worried. I didn't think AIs got worried. And yes, I'm sure."

Pumps whirred, and the slime surged upward to fill the tube entirely. Naris expelled all the air from her lungs, sending a cascade of silver bubbles past her face. After a moment to psych herself up, she drew in a great breath of liquid, bracing her palms against the wall to handle the involuntary convulsions that came with the feeling of aspirating fluid.

Only a few years ago, the thought of breathing liquid would've made her break out in a cold sweat. The first time she jumped, she'd been seventeen. Her former crew had to manhandle her into the tank. She screamed and begged like an unwanted orphan being drowned. They said everyone reacted like that, at least anyone not suicidal. Without the cushioning of the gel in her lungs, the G forces of a jump would kill her. Much to her surprise, no one teased her about acting like a terrified scream queen. Her lungs full of liquid, she emitted a silent laugh at the thought.

Ein's voice seemed deeper, louder, and blurry while submerged.

"Coordinates are plotted. Initiating transition to jump space in twenty seconds. Initiating crew stasis in ten seconds. You may abort jump at any time within the next eight seconds by a thumbs-down gesture."

Naris waited. Sleepiness, sedatives administered by thousands of nanobots in the liquid, knocked her out. As far as she could tell, her head nodded forward and snapped right back up. The warm gel drained. She didn't try to stand while coated in such slippery liquid and sank to the floor. When the last of the substance exited the vents, the shower water started. She'd likely showered in that same water, drank it, and cooked with it countless times. The ship had damn good filters—not once had it ever carried a hint of pee flavoring. Eventually, she'd need to install new membranes and do a water change, but she had at least six months left.

She leaned her head between her knees and expelled as much of the goopy stuff from her lungs as she could without being upside down.

"Love these dual-purpose tubes." She pulled herself upright. "Don't have to fall all over myself going from the jump tubes to the shower."

After the cylinder opened, a distant buzzing broke the silence, coming from the cockpit. She bent forward, coughing and clearing the last of the liquid into the drain. It had been years since getting rid of the gel bothered her. The first time had been almost as frightening as going in, like all the worst parts of vomiting plus suffocating. These days, she found it less annoying than a chest cold. The left locker door snapped open with a hiss, revealing a red and black enviro-suit. The one-piece garment had attached boots and gloves as well as light-armor panels in the forearms, shins, and chest. She took it and sat on the bench, her back to the table.

"Thanks, Ein. How was the jump?"

"We emerged from hyperspace ninety-one seconds ago at a safe distance from the planet. I am reading a defense grid in high orbit composed of armed satellites. Standard Consortium procedure for a quarantined world. They are broadcasting a repeating automated message warning us to stay away."

Naris put her feet in the legs of the suit and stood up into it, shrugging it over her shoulders before zipping it and fidgeting to get the armor panels to sit comfortably. "Armed satellites?" She cracked her knuckles. "Guess we are going to have an interesting landing. Can we go for the poles?"

"I'm afraid not, Naris. The satellites are not a simple orbiting band. They are arranged in a grid pattern around the entire world."

"Serious shit. Now I really want to see what the hell is down there."

She nabbed the helmet from the locker and walked to the cockpit, snugging her gloves tight before falling into the pilot's seat and gazing at the viewscreen.

Amid the vast blackness ahead, a dull green orb seemed to stare back at her like a sentient being, daring her to challenge it. Dark shapes swirled among striations of green within the atmosphere. An uncountable number of silver dots fringed with red-white luminance blinked, looking like a giant net trapping the planet. Even though they appeared close, there had to be thousands of miles between each satellite. Scrolling text indicated the world's composition as primarily Earth-like, however it contained elevated levels of pollution and high concentrations of metal particulates. A few finger taps caused an amber dot to superimpose on the surface.

"That's the city. Gimme maneuvering configuration, Ein. And I'll need some tunes."

Mechanical whirring rumbled the hull as the ship's winglets extended. The two primary engine pods extended farther away from the main hull for greater maneuvering control at high speed. The noise ended with a pronounced *thunk*. After a moment of silence, the cockpit flooded with ancient rock music: a power-ballad with an inspirational 'you can do it' feel.

"Are you absolutely sure about this?"

"Yes, Ein. I have the touch. I have the power." Helmet on, visor down, hands tightened on the control sticks, she grinned. "Manual control, please... and if you could throw out a little interference, that would be awesome."

"No one over the age of ten should use the word 'awesome' unless they're watching a planet break in half." Ein played an artificial sigh over the speakers. "Very well. I'm engaging a transponder distortion that will make their targeting systems believe we are approximately a hundred meters to the right and down sixty-two degrees."

Naris glanced at the holographic starmap. A dotted red line indicated the demarcation point where the satellites would open fire. She poked a finger on the line and again inside the range of the satellites, about three hundred miles of space. "Calculate a jump from A to B. I want a micro hop."

"I rescind my previous diagnosis you are not suffering the onset of dementia."

"Do it, Ein. I'll blow all the air out of my lungs. It's so short we won't even tear the dimensional boundary all the way. More like that old weight in a blanket space time shit."

Silence.

"Ein."

"There's a fifty-nine percent chance of injury sufficient to render you incapacitated."

"Fine. Give me a little pool of breathable slime. I'll hold my breath."

Naris hopped out of the pilot seat and ran to the shower/stasis tube. By the time she got there, about a foot of the substance had collected in the bottom. She removed her helmet and took a rapid series of great breaths. On her hands and knees, she stuck her face in the gel and inhaled, coughing and gagging on it until she breathed the liquid.

"I'm going to tease you about this incessantly if there's nothing down there," said Ein.

Naris flipped a middle finger around at random. She drew in a huge breath of ooze, held it, and rushed back to the cockpit, jumping into the seat when she arrived.

Amber lighting throughout the console washed to green. She jammed forward on the throttle, ignoring the automatic pilot restraint system that leapt over her hips and chest, pulling her snug to the seat. Mentally belting the lyrics in time with the music, she lined the ship up with an arc trajectory plot ending at the planet's only city. Warning lights flashed, the last-ditch attempt by the defense system to dissuade her nonlethally. As a little icon of her ship passed the demarcation point, energy beams lit up the dark.

Rolling, diving, and spinning, Naris evaded the unending hail of particle bolts for four seconds. Her ship shuddered with each tight turn and erratic change in speed as it plunged toward the external 'shell' of satellites. One bolt came close enough to make her cringe from the intense light flooding the cockpit.

The windscreen exploded with a shimmering starburst of concentric circles formed of fractals and blackness. A great crushing wave slammed into her, pressing her into the seat and forcing gel out of her mouth and nose despite her best effort to hold it in. The lightshow in the windscreen faded in three seconds. Naris slumped to the side and gurgled the substance out of her lungs. Every bone in her body throbbed in time with her gagging.

She righted herself and thrust both fists in the air, cheering between coughs, "Wooo! We made it."

Ein cut the music. "Naris, that was an astonishingly bad idea, even for you."

"Prep for atmospheric entry." Naris bent forward, head between her knees, and spat up the rest of the slime.

The whirring of small electric motors and hydraulics vibrated the seat. All the narrow winglets, airfoils, and antennas retracted behind various protective cowlings. The engine pods moved close against the hull. Segmented metal plates extended over the windscreen, which went from real-time camera to a computer-generated estimation of the outside. She angled the nose up, triggering the re-entry thrusters to fire forward and down. A faint rumble shook the airframe.

"I can't explain why I want to come here." She fell quiet, her gaze lost amid the digital rendering of a planet's horizon. "I just… have to."

Fire and chaos surrounded them for a few minutes, giving way to calm as the ship completed entry of Acheron-18's atmosphere. They plummeted like a boulder for a few minutes until re-entry heat lessened enough for the airfoils to deploy. G-forces pressed her into the seat when the wings caught lift, slowing the ship's descent.

Naris rolled the ship level as soon as the controls responded again. The computer-generated image of the environment faded to black. Hydraulics whined from the armored canopy cover opening, revealing the outside world, a planetscape of billowing emerald clouds interspersed with darker trails and whorls of lime. Flickers of lightning danced back and forth in a mesmerizing display.

The AI remained silent for the next twenty minutes as she flew a path defined by a dotted line on her viewscreen. Her ship's nose devoured the navigation assist like some hungry creature chasing a series of floating treats. If not for the virtual 'road,' she'd have no indication of terrain other than billowing fog.

Staring at nothingness let her mind wander. A sense of pervasive melancholy came on at being alone. She never thought she'd miss the guys, but an unexpected inheritance gave her the chance to prove herself worthy of something more than being the 'backup pilot.' Ein (and the ship that housed him) used to belong to her uncle, a man who also liked to take risks and do stupid things on whims. Of course, his doing stupid things on whims is exactly how Naris ended up inheriting his ship.

Naris clenched her fists at the mere thought of her former captain, Sarkov, spouting off about how a 'girl had no place flying in combat.' She squeezed the sticks in anger until her gloves creaked. Somehow, despite his constant condescending attitude toward her, she missed him. Sixty something percent of pilots in the CPO were women. Sarkov had a lot of nerve to think she didn't belong flying because she had boobs.

"There are no traces of civilization on this planet beyond that one city." Ein's voice shattered the tranquil silence. "The good news is that whatever went wrong with this atmosphere isn't harming the hull."

"Well, at least there's that. Can the suit handle it?"

"By my calculations, it should. However, the level of toxicity in the air may overwhelm the molecular filter after about two hours."

"That's fine; I'm not planning on staying long."

A tug at the stick swung the ship into a wide, descending left turn. Instruments showed altitude at 42,200 feet and dropping. Still, nothing but green mist filled the window. The number continued to tick down. She eventually leveled off at 4,000 feet once hints of a black, rocky surface came out of the mist, bleeding off some airspeed in case she had to dodge a sudden spire. Soon, the horizon darkened where the trail of dots plunged into the ground, at the spot the computer estimated the city to be.

Indistinct rectangular forms emerged from the haze, blackish smears that gradually took on the shape of buildings. More and more forms faded in amid the sparkling hint of metal-coated streets and smaller structures in the shadows of the great towers. As in her dream, the landscape resembled the work of an artist using only varying shades of cold metallic green. Black plumes wisped into the air from holes in some of the taller buildings. Naris squinted, wondering how forty-year-old crash sites could still be burning.

The city she had seen every night for weeks unfurled beyond the mist below. The design reminded her of New Avalon, the capital city of Dathiel IV, her homeworld, only without the surrounding suburbs—and a lot more pollution. At least, if there had been suburbs here, the fog swallowed them.

Naris descended to 300 feet and slowed to less than a hundred miles per hour. Soon, she guided the craft down the largest street she could find. Ein adjusted the position of the wings, narrowing the ship's profile in an effort to avoid brushing buildings.

A poke at the console extended the landing pads, but she continued drifting—now less than forty feet off the ground—down the street. Taken by a sudden sense of déjà vu, she pulled back on the stick and brought the ship to a dead hover. After a quick glance at the shapes of the surrounding towers, she twisted the two sticks in opposite directions, firing maneuvering thrusters on both the upper and lower hull. The combined effect didn't move the ship; however, the downblast shoved ruined ground-cars out of the way like empty drink canisters. Glimmering metallic dust formed a cloud rolling out and away as she landed in the clearing of empty street she'd made.

Naris went to stand, but couldn't get out of the chair. A few tugs at the harness failed to open it, and she sighed.

"Come on, Ein. Let me out."

"Naris, I am unable to parse the nature of some of these toxins. For your own safety, I am of the opinion that we should not break hull integrity here. Please consider changing your mind and let us leave this place."

Naris struggled, feeling like a toddler trapped in a car seat. "Ein. I'm not a five-year-old. Let me outta this damn chair. This isn't funny."

A minute passed of fingertip drumming on the console.

"Look, Ein. I'll go out through the cargo hold. When we come back, you can take us up and I'll blow atmosphere in space before I come back in. Nothing will contaminate."

Silence.

"Ein." She tapped her foot.

"Fine." The pilot harness retracted into the chair. "What do you mean, when *we* return?"

Naris made a face no one could see. "I have a weird feeling I won't be alone when I come back. I can't explain it."

After taking her H9-B rifle from the locker, she climbed a narrow ladder-chute to the secondary deck. Ein sealed the cargo bay airlock above her as she approached the rear ramp door. A hissing sound indicated he had decided to reclaim the air. Her suit fluffed out in the vacuum.

Naris looked up. "I'm not sure that's a good idea."

Lights flashed around the door, and the ramp descended. As soon as the seal broke, a blast of planetary atmosphere rushed in the gap, knocking her flat and sending her sliding back into an empty cargo container. Stunned from the hit to the head, she curled fetal and waited for the gale to stop. The storm passed in seconds and she pulled herself to her feet, shaking her head at the olive-toned dust all over everything.

"Slick, Ein. We sucked up a bunch of silt. With any luck, it'll get blown out with the rest of the atmosphere if we purge once we're back in space. I don't much fancy flying a broom around here with the door open."

Naris jogged down the ramp, gazing up and around at dead monoliths.

She shivered at the sight. Wrecked cars littered the street as if a city full of people experienced only minutes of panic before everyone ceased existing. An ancient disaster scattered debris as far as she could see. The eeriness came from how familiar it all seemed. Rifle up, she walked out of the bare patch of road her landing cleared, finding the three-inch thick layer of silt soft and snowy.

Past the initial tangle of metal she made of the traffic, the vehicles sat in the road as if apocalypse had claimed rush hour. She imagined traffic merely stopping in place and time fast-forwarding forty years with nothing moving. Bumper to bumper ground-cars, doors closed, filled the streets to the limit of her vision. She leaned up to one, peering in untouched windows at pristine seats. A patch of color, coral, caught her eye. On the floor by the driver's controls sat a pile of clothing.

The next car had a stack of clothes as well, and the one after that. She cringed and rubbed her arms when she found a cybernetic eye and a length of wire in a passenger seat, grateful for having an e-suit between her and whatever was in the air here. She didn't want to know what happened to the citizens. Fair bet the entire population of a city didn't spontaneously strip naked and run off into the hills. The thought these people likely disintegrated where they sat made her stop and glance back at the ship. *Maybe I should listen to Ein.*

Futility welled up out of nowhere. Did she come all this way to find nothing more than a ghost? She twisted around, gazing at the abandonment, and sighed, pondering the forty-million-credit offer Volunrad had made. The empty clothing haunted her. *They want whatever technology did this.* Images of some theoretical energy weapon capable of destroying human tissue but nothing else teased at her brain. *There were no bones in the cars. Did they use multiple weapons?*

An unbidden urge pulled her forward. Something called to her from deep within the city. Naris shivered. Despite her terror, she couldn't turn her back on Eden. *Who the hell is Eden? Why do I care so much?* Primal urgency screamed at her to run, but a deep-seated beckoning urge pulled her onward.

Naris walked at a brisk pace, as if she hurried over familiar terrain she'd traversed a thousand times before. A car creaked as she climbed it to cross the street. On the sidewalk, she leaned back to stare up at a towering structure covered with symmetric rows of balconies—a residence building. An engraving by the door stated only for 'Grade 4' and higher employees of Volunrad Corporation were authorized to live in this building. She crept up to the main entrance and pulled one of the heavy metal-framed doors aside. A giant oval in the middle no longer contained glass.

I've been here...

Bones littered the floor inside. She brought her rifle up, gasping at the unexpected sight. A river of death flowed from three elevators and both stairways toward the front door. Skeletons, or at least eroded fragments that used to be skeletons, spread out like fallen dominos.

"Oh, my," said Ein. Little speakers in her helmet cut out with a faint chirp. "The arrangement of the bodies looks like they were attempting to flee from something."

Naris exhaled, gazing along the trail of dead people. "They never made it to the front door."

Her boots crunched over the fallen as she shoved her way to the stairs. The dark elevators seemed like a futile option. The cascade of corpses flooded the stairwell, but only as high up as the tenth story. Naris let her strange intuition and inexplicable sense of familiarity with this place guide her.

"I'm not reading any thermal signals in this city," said Ein.

I've been dreaming the last days of a ghost for weeks. A lump formed in her throat. Is that child already dead?

Despite the knot in her gut, she continued. On the landing of the forty-second floor, a child's footprint in the dust made her stop.

She crouched, staring at it, feeling a chill up her spine. *That print is recent.* Eyes closed, she pictured the small body from her dreams. Her eyes watered. Naris swallowed, her mind racing with a scenario of a child wandering this place alone until the food ran out.

Thunk.

Naris jumped. The sound came from the hallway among the apartments. She pressed one hand over her heart, waiting for the fog on the inside of her visor to clear. Once her breathing returned to normal, she nudged the door open with the tip of her H9-B. A once-luxurious corridor stretched out in front of her, lined with eight doors per side and a right turn at the halfway point.

It has to be the wind banging something around... or maybe some kind of cat? The urge tugged at her, pulling her forward. *What is wrong with me?* She shook her head. *I'm imagining shit. There's nothing here.*

"Ein, is there anything alive on this planet?"

She kicked the door open and went down the hallway, shivering at child-sized handprints on the wall and another footprint in the dust. *This is what you get for watching too many ghost investigations.* The tip of her rifle wobbled from nerves. Her mind raced in search of a calm, rational explanation for what she saw. Amid her mental wandering, she advanced on autopilot until she came to a halt by a half-open door. The familiar stink of wetness and mildew greeted her despite a sealed environmental suit.

It's in my head.

"If there is anything alive here," said Ein, making her jump and grab her chest, "the archives don't have much mention of it. I am rooting around the city's network. A few of the stationary cameras have captured fleeting humanoid shapes, but the gait and size imply nonhuman."

"*Greaaat.* Give me a holler if anything moves out there."

The weather-blackened room stalled her breathing. Bare, grungy mattress on the left, broken dolls everywhere, and the same smashed furniture she had seen three or four times a week for a month. She'd entered the apartment right out of her dreams. Dumbfounded awe opened her mouth. *How is this possible? I'm not psychic. I'm no seer... am I?*

"Ein. You said my brain was going nuts when I dreamed?"

"That is correct. Some of the activity occurred in parts of the brain which have been associated with psionic activity... but I didn't think anything of it because your profile is negative."

"Yeah." She stared at the dolls. "You're more psionic than I am."

"I'm an AI, Naris. I can't be—" Ein simulated the sound of clearing his throat. "Oh."

"What are the odds of developing mental abilities later in life?"

"It's not been noted before."

Naris found herself walking across the room, as though she'd been there a thousand times before. Her body knew where to step without thinking. Her adult-sized boots didn't fit as neatly in the gaps among the trash as a small girl's feet did, but she reached the desk with a minimum of stumbling. The terminal had broken years ago, cracked and covered in dust, weathered from the effects of absent windows. Long, diaphanous curtains wafted in on a breeze she could not feel. Her suit protected her from the bone-chilling cold she knew would be here. She picked up the old award, staring at the grey-haired man. The image gave her no sense of looking at 'Dad' this time, so she set it back on the desk.

Thud.

A metallic bang came from the entire room. Naris jumped at the noise and spun, aiming at the door. Nothing there. She stood alone with the dolls. A red-haired cherub-faced thing propped up at the tea party seemed to look into her soul. For a minute, she remained frozen in statue stillness, ready to shoot anything that moved. When her fear ebbed, she wandered over and sat on the mattress for reasons she couldn't fathom. After a while, she picked up a tattered stuffed rabbit on a whim. Despite knowing she had never been here before, the dingy toy felt like an old security blanket. Clutching it made the place less creepy.

Mr. Rabbit kept me company after everyone went away. Wait... no. That's not me.

Wind teased at the curtains by the window. Naris surveyed the floor; all the junk sat where she remembered. The room felt familiar and safe, as though she had lived in it for a long time. Little footprints crisscrossed the place, slightly cleaner spots on the dusty floor. She felt heartsick at the thought of what it must have been like for the child she kept seeing in dreams.

"I'm here, Eden." Naris looked around again, and chuckled to herself for talking to a ghost.

Naris clung to the plush toy, stood, and sighed. As in the dream, she tiptoed past the broken chairs and debris toward the balcony. The scenery she experienced so often spread out before her. Down and to the right, her starship taking up all four lanes of the road was the only thing out of place. That, and the lack of emerald fireflies falling like snow.

She gazed up. *Are they real?* Perhaps a figment her dream produced, a metaphor for something. Maybe living alone on a ship made her so lonely she imagined all of this—but how could she imagine so many correct details of a place she'd never been before? She brushed silt from the railing and leaned on it, as if watching a parade pass below. It felt wrong to be this tall, for the railing not to be at chest level. Volunrad offered to pay a lot of money for some data in this city. Question being, where did it hide and could she find it in an hour? Not to mention, *what* was it? If the data related to a weapon capable of wiping out everyone in a whole city without damaging any of the buildings or vehicles... it should stay right here.

An urge came over her to back away. Naris looked up. Her eyes widened at a sudden shimmer of lime-hued light in the mist. Thousands of glimmering lights appeared, gliding on the wind—just like the dream. With them also came the milieu of voices. A man murmured, a high-pitched giggle followed, thousands of voices whispered, sounding curious. Some glowing spots swirled in close, feeling her out. Awestruck, she reached a hand up just like the child in the dream.

"I wouldn't do that. They might burn you."

The tiny voice from behind startled her so much she nearly flung herself over the railing to a quick death forty-two stories down. Fortunately, instead of leaping, her legs gave out, and she wound up on her butt, leaning on the balcony wall.

"Can I have my rabbit, please?"

Naris turned toward the room.

A little girl with long black hair stood in the doorway, wearing a thin, tattered nightgown seemingly ready to disintegrate. The child looked pale as death and thin, but not malnourished. She raised one hand, in expectation of her stuffed animal. Fresh footprints led from where she stood to an open cabinet door in the desk—a hiding place.

Naris squinted; the eerie glow of the white fabric around the child lifted her out of reality. *Am I dreaming? Is that a ghost?* She offered the toy. When the child's hand tightened around it, Naris seized her wrist.

Solid.

She let go as fast as if the girl's arm burned her and recoiled into the wall. "You're real."

"Shall I point out that you also exist?" The girl hugged the rabbit, swaying back and forth.

"You're not wearing a suit, no shoes... not even a rebreather." Naris eyed the glowing status readout on her visor's HUD. "It's forty-nine degrees. How—?"

The girl shrugged, backing up. "Come inside before they touch you. They don't like people." She stepped with care across the room on her way to the mattress. "Everyone else who came here died because of them."

Naris jumped up, grabbing the metal ruin of a smashed patio door to pull herself into the apartment. Two steps in, she froze. A lone firefly perched on her shoulder, an orb of light about an inch across. It seemed to radiate curiosity. Despite the girl's warning, Naris thought it beautiful, and smiled at the creature. It emitted a chime reminiscent of crystals in the wind as it levitated, circled around her helmet, and cruised off out the window.

The child crept to the mattress, where she spun about to face her and sat on the edge, cradling the stuffed rabbit.

Haunting, sad blue eyes peered up at her. "My name is Eden. I'm seven."

Naris couldn't pull her gaze away from the girl. *There's no way. Someone had to drop this kid here somehow after the disaster.* "How are you still—"

Alive? So small? She took a knee, putting a hand on the girl's shoulder. Through thick gloves, the child felt solid, but hard-bodied—athletic, a feral thing on the edge of survival. "I don't understand how you're alive without a mask. This city was abandoned over forty years ago."

Half of Eden's face hid behind the rotting rabbit head. "I dunno. Daddy left me here when the bad came. He said someone would find and help me soon. I don't want to be lonely anymore."

A lump in Naris's throat stalled any words. The oddity of the situation impeded thought. She could only stare at the frightened little girl pleading up at her with a mournful expression.

"I'm glad you came." Eden relaxed, seeming less gloomy. "I have been calling you."

Ein's voice crackled over the speakers. "Be careful, Naris. The child may have mental abilities… Something is blocking my sensor reach. Thermal indicates you are alone, but I see her on the video feed. Also, I believe you should get out of there as fast as humanly possible. Some of the city's communication systems contain mention of an accident with 'Project SP-92.'"

Naris set the H9-B down on the mattress and clasped the girl by both shoulders. "How?"

Eden lowered the stuffed animal away from her face, staring up at her with a matter-of-fact expression. "The fireflies carried my dream to you." She stroked the bunny. "Please take me with you. I don't like it here. There's nothing but sadness. I'm lonely."

Naris slung the rifle over her shoulder and picked the girl up. "Do you have any more clothes?"

"No, everything else fell apart."

The nightgown looked well worn, so threadbare it might tear apart in a stiff breeze. *I can't believe this kid is both still alive and still so young. If she's from this city, she should be old enough to be my mother… by a healthy margin of error.*

Eden's eyes sparkled with gratitude. "Thank you for coming."

Naris ran a hand over the girl's head, tidying her hair. "Do you know anything about a 'Project SP-92'?" *What the hell am I doing asking a little girl that?*

"Yes. It is why this place died." Eden stared at the floor, swaying side to side. "I can't let anyone take the bad away from here." She remained quiet for a moment. "Are you going to take the bad?"

Naris paced to the balcony, gazing out over the devastation, wondering if any of the dead even had time to scream. She considered for a moment, and wandered back to squat in front of the girl, whose expression grew earnest.

"No, Eden." Naris brushed a hand over the girl's hair. "I... I came here for you."

The child stood and rested her cheek against Naris' shoulder. The unexpected gesture choked her up. *If I'm still dreaming, this is a good one. Everything is wrong with this situation... why do I feel like this? This girl shouldn't be alive in this situation. Have I gone insane?*

"Naris?"

"Yes?" She froze. "How do you know my name?"

The girl leaned out of the hug to make eye contact. "How did you know I was here?"

"I... don't know. I just knew."

Eden's expression lit up. "I called you. When I sleep, my dreams fly out in the stars."

Naris saw nothing but innocence in the little face smiling at her. "You... called me from so far away?" She muted her helmet's speaker so the child couldn't hear. "Ein, am I awake?"

"If you are dreaming, which I find unlikely given I am cognizant of your extra-vehicular excursion, your subconscious mind would create the illusion of me giving the answer you want to hear. Asking me if you are dreaming is functionally irrelevant. If you wish to enjoy the dream, you will perceive me as saying you are awake. If your mind objects to the dream and seeks escape, I will tell you that you dream."

That's Ein. I'm awake.

"I have been alone for a long time. You heard me." Eden hugged her again. "But there is something."

"What..." Naris suppressed the urge to shiver at the eeriness of the little girl who couldn't possibly exist.

"Before we leave, I must show you an important place. Daddy said I had to bring the first person I trusted there, or something very bad will happen."

"You trust me?" Naris tilted her head.

"Yes. The firefly sat on your shoulder, and it didn't bite you."

"I'm wearing a suit. It couldn't bite me."

Eden stared creepily up at her. "The suit wouldn't matter."

Ooo-kay. Naris picked the girl up. "How far away is it?"

Eden grinned like a kid playing a game. "Not far. You'll have enough air."

"All right." Naris carried her to the door. "Are you sure you don't have anything else to wear?"

"No. Only this."

A strange motherly feeling welled up within her, and she fussed at the girl for a moment before carrying her out into the hall. Her mind tripped over a logic bump. This child couldn't still be alive, not after so long, not with the toxins in the air. *Maybe the weapon was biological.* Naris pondered running like hell, but another look at the girl's huge blue eyes smothered her panic under a blanket of guilt.

"Eden, who was your father?"

"A doctor, but not the kind that fixes people. The kind that breaks people."

"Breaks people?"

Eden pouted. "Yes, he worked in a science room and helped make the bad."

Naris shoved the stairwell door aside with her boot. *Well, that makes some more sense. The 'bad' is probably that project weapon. I bet it's biological; maybe he gave his daughter something to make her immune to it. Still doesn't explain how she's still a little girl after so many years.*

She ran down the stairs as fast as she trusted her footing in the silt. Near the bottom, she encountered a strange dark cloud that hadn't been there before. It collected on her suit and coated Eden for a second before peeling away as she emerged from the other side. The mist behaved as a singular mass that refused to separate.

"What the...?"

"Nanobots," said Ein. "I am reading mild electrical activity within that suspension."

"What are they doing?" Naris hurried away from the cloud, which seemed to have decided to ignore her.

"I am unable to determine."

"There's some scary things ahead, close your eyes, honey."

"I know. I have seen the dead people. They are not in their bones anymore. They are fireflies now. They protect me."

Confusion didn't dwell long in her mind, for the child asked a frightening question when they made it halfway into the lobby.

"Naris? Why are the bones getting up?"

She whirled. The cloud from the stairwell emerged from the doors, split in half, and descended upon the dead both behind and in front of them. The seep of dark vapor appeared to absorb into the skeletons, blackening the remains. One by one, individual bones slid together, assembling into whole skeletons and climbing to their feet. A wall of restless dead cut off the front door, glistening ebon figures stalking closer, arms raised.

Naris screamed, though Eden tilted her head.

"They are not the dead ones. They are the bad."

Ein chuckled. "I am assuming the child means the SP-92 project weapon when she says 'bad.'"

"Thanks. Never woulda' got that if not for you saying something." Naris growled.

"The nanobots appear to be manipulating human remains with electromagnetic—"

"Stow it," yelled Naris. "Wiki me later when I'm not staring at an army of undead!"

She slid the H9-B down her arm on its strap into a firing position and opened up on the crowd of bones. A blast of red laser ignited two of the skeletons. Rings of embers spread outward from where the laser hit them, their bodies disintegrating into smoke as if made of compressed slow-burning powder. She fired as fast as the weapon's core could cycle, spraying wildly into the swarm. Burning bones collapsed to the side, creating a hole in the throng of dead. Naris jumped for it without hesitating, barely stifling the urge to scream as hardened fingers raked over her arms and legs.

"Do not let them breach your suit," said Ein. "By my calculations, they would only need a small point of entry to access your flesh."

Naris lost herself to a moment of terror and swatted the grabbing hands, using the rifle as a club.

Bony arms flew past her helmet as she sprinted to the back of the lobby by the elevators. Her ill-planned search for refuge ended with a louder scream when six more skeletons clawed their way out from a set of double doors. One hit her from the side, knocking her on her chest. The rifle went one way, the child the other. Bone clattered on her helmet as she dragged herself forward, swatting at the grasping limbs. A skeleton grabbed her shoulder, flipping her onto her back, its hand hovering over her faceplate.

Bony fingertips turned silver, exuding metal that formed into sharp spiky claws. The bizarre sight started to trigger panic, but out of nowhere, total calm washed over her. Eden, back to the wall a short distance away, stared at her.

Naris grabbed the skeletal wrist and squeezed, spongy bone crumbled to splinters in her grasp, severing the hand before it could tear her suit. Bladed finger bones clattered to the floor beside her arm. She kicked at another skeleton trying to grab her ankle and crawled away. After gathering her legs under her, she jumped ahead, twisting to the rear. The rifle had vanished. Eden still lurked by the wall, as calm as if watching a video. A dozen blackened figures shuffled past the girl without notice of her presence, the child's eyes wide sapphires in a porcelain setting.

They crowded Naris against chrome doors, once automatic, that refused to budge. Kicking at them did little, pounding even less. The walking horrors trapped her in a dead-end corridor. Her breath blew back into her eyes off the visor as she panted, unable to believe the sight of the creatures drawing closer. No warning lights flashed in her vision, the suit hadn't cracked or torn. She lunged to the left, seizing a small aluminum bench, which she hurled into the oncoming horrors. Two bore the brunt of it, shattering in half at the spine, broken fragments of bone collapsing to the floor, empty eye sockets still staring at her.

Naris grabbed for the pistol on her hip, too freaked out to realize she had to open the retaining strap.

Eden crept away from the wall, scurrying behind the skeletons to the H9-B. She squatted by it, both hands on the weapon as long as her height, and shouted, "Hey!"

Naris stared between the skeletons' legs at the little girl waving. The waif appeared neither scared nor excited—eerily calm. As soon as their eyes met, the child shoved the rifle forward and ran back to her place on the wall. The weapon skittered past the group of walking bones, halting under Naris's boot. She stooped to grab it, spinning the rifle into firing position as a bony hand grasped her helmet.

That one burned first. Rapid blasts ignited the crowd, packed in tighter due to the narrow corridor. Bright laser blasts scorched through two or three skeletons each shot. Fire spread among them. In seconds, only smoldering ash remained of the returned fallen. Eden smiled until she glanced at the front doors, then looked worried.

She ran to Naris's side. "More are coming. In here." The child pulled a vent cover open and ducked into a square metal-walled passage. "We can get out through the kitchen."

Naris hesitated at the claustrophobic exit, but heavy crunching footsteps in the lobby changed her mind.

———————

OUT OF BREATH SOME BLOCKS LATER, NARIS STAGGERED TO THE SIDE OF THE road.

She set Eden down on a sidewalk bench, then leaned against it to rest. A cartoon man in a business suit smiled at them from an advertisement for public transportation. She collapsed next to the girl, who swung her feet as if she calmly waited for a bus on an ordinary day. Naris gasped for air. A yellow light in the lower left corner of her visor warned about the air processing system reaching saturation. She used oxygen too fast, over-stressing the filter membranes in the rebreather. Leaning forward, she grasped the helmet, which felt more confining than protecting. *I need to get out of this suit.* She shuddered. *No, don't. You'll die.*

"Ein, is it still fatal to breathe this atmosphere?" Naris shot a wary look at Eden.

"It wouldn't cause you to drop dead immediately," said the AI. "However, after ten minutes, your risk factors for seventeen different forms of cancer go up to about forty percent. There is also the issue of heavy metal poisoning... and those nanobot clouds."

Naris swallowed hard. "Right. Helmet stays on."

Eden leaned forward, looking from side to side. "They are not coming."

"How..." Dry breathy rasps filled her helmet. "How come those things never went after you before? Why didn't they go after you now?"

"Daddy was a scientist." The girl shrugged. "He said I would be safe until someone came here to save me. I miss him, but his invention made him sad because it killed everyone." Taken by sudden gloom, she stood and paced away from the bench. "He said it would not be right for him to stay alive after what he did."

"If I may translate," said Ein. "This nano-weapon is likely capable of selective targeting. As the daughter of one of the designers, she is more than likely part of an exclusion list... as would be any Volunrad employee."

"Heh. Employees?" Naris glanced at the street. "Then who's in all these cars?"

"Perhaps they excluded only the executives, then? I do not have access to sufficient data to perform the requested analytical operation."

Naris, finally getting her breathing to a normal rhythm, stared at the shoeless waif ankle-deep in toxic dust. The fireflies had stopped falling at some point before they left the building. Perhaps the tiny creatures were an illusion created by altitude. But how then could they have killed people like the child claimed?

"It's cold enough to cause frostbite at night. The air is deadly." Naris ruffled the girl's hair. "How are you here?"

"I dunno." Eden shifted, glancing down the street and shielding her eyes from the sun with one hand. The building with the gears emerged from the cloudy fog in the distance whenever the wind gusted. "We need to go there."

"Oh, that sounds like an ambush," said Ein. "The only problem is it makes little sense to trap a lone individual. Oh, Naris, I should warn you. I'm picking up motion."

"Where?"

"All around the ship."

Eden twisted her toe into the dirt. "Daddy stayed and let the bad get him. He said he deserved it. I'm s'posed to wait for someone nice and show them something."

The overwhelming urge to scoop the girl up and hug her pulled Naris to her feet, but before she could do much more than stand, glass shattered to the left. A large figure bounded across the ground floor of a building on the far side of the road. It appeared humanoid in shape, save for how it moved on four legs. Patches of thick ebon fur covered its back and arms, however, armored black skin covered the majority of its body. Patterned lines crisscrossed it, like the hide of an alligator stained with India ink.

It leapt out a broken window, landed on the street, and reared up on two backward-jointed legs to a height about half again human. Four glowing yellow eyes locked onto Naris. A vertical mouth split the center of its head open as the creature roared. Filaments of viscous slime fluttered in the force of its breath from rows of needle-like transparent teeth. It started to charge at her, but a three-pulse burst from the H9-B put it down in a spray of foaming dark blood.

Unlike the dried-out skeletons, this creature didn't flash burn.

"Aliens too?" Naris leaned the rifle back on her shoulder. "No problem. Aliens I can handle. Undead... no, I didn't see that."

"They weren't dead." Eden shook her head.

"Nanobots," said Ein. "Nothing magical about them."

Naris watched the building where the creature came from, waiting for more. "Right…"

Eden pulled on her arm. "Naris?"

"Yeah?"

"We should probably run now. These monsters don't like me. I have to hide from them."

Naris raised an eyebrow. "My system turned green again, I should be okay."

Eden pointed. "No."

She looked at the small finger for a second before twisting to peer in the direction the child indicated. Her arm fell limp at her side. Dozens of the beasts clambered out from windows, alleys, and abandoned cars. The city bled black. Naris glanced at the rifle.

"You can't shoot them all. We are close." Eden ran to her, arms up.

Plasma globs sailed in from far off down the road. A few of the creatures in the rear exploded in dazzling showers of blood and loose photons. Ein tried to help using the anti-missile turret, the smallest weapon he could safely fire without incinerating her too. Granted, having her ship's weapons pointed in her general direction scared her more than a bunch of bones walking around.

"Ein! Careful!" Naris grabbed Eden and went to balance her on one hip again, but the child crawled around behind her like a living backpack.

"Go! Go!" A small arm thrust past her helmet, jabbing a finger in the direction of the large building with the giant gear on it.

Naris sprinted again, too soon after running herself to the point of exhaustion. Every five or six steps, she swung around to fire at the nearest beast. Fortunately, her laser rifle worked as well on these creatures as it did on humans, and they went down easily. However, killing one or two did little to slow the onrushing horde. The imagined voice of Ein came to mind, saying 'I told you so' over and over.

This has to be a dream, right?

Tiny legs squeezed her sides, and the child screamed, "Help!"

One of the creatures had gotten close enough to grab the girl's trailing hair. Naris stuck the rifle back over her shoulder, liquefying the beast's skull with a point-blank blast. Eden's head snapped forward as its grip failed. Whimpering, the child clung tighter.

Naris pulled her sidearm off her belt, holding it up past her helmet. "Here, shoot them."

"I'm not allowed to use guns. I'm only seven."

"I'm giving you permission to use guns."

"I'm sorry, Naris. Guns are too dangerous for children."

What the hell is wrong with this kid? Aside from still being alive in this shithole. Maybe she's in all in my head? Naris pivoted to jog backward, rifle in one hand and pistol in the other. Eden squeezed on tight, clasping her wrist at Naris's chest and wrapping her legs around. *No. Too heavy for a hallucination.*

Naris unloaded on the approaching beasts, taking out more than a dozen before it struck her as futile. She stuffed the energy pistol back on her belt and sprinted forward with a two-handed grip on the rifle.

Seventy-two seconds of running later, Naris emerged into a bubble of clear air. The fog saturating the city stopped at a neat line, forming a curved wall in front of the enormous Volunrad building. A sculpture of gears-in-gears dominated the center of a large, round area by the entrance. Naris advanced in a slow spin, dumbstruck by the standing wall of mist that refused to breach the courtyard. A chime in her helmet brought her attention to the external sensors reporting the air here as Earth-Normal. "What the…?"

"That is most peculiar," said Ein from the speakers. "There is an overpressure atmosphere here keeping out the contamination. The sensors are reading clean, normal air inside the high-pressure region."

"Go!" wailed the girl. "They're coming! In there. This is it."

Naris ran around the statue, leaping a bench encircling the standing artwork. As expected, the front doors of the building were locked—but a well-placed shot opened them. The Volunrad office tower lobby was predictably empty, like everything else in this place. Unlike the rest of this planet, the facility appeared new and unused, a display model of expensive corporate construction. No trash or silt defiled the interior. The plain dull green walls looked immaculate, as did an inlaid set of bronze gears in the floor.

"That way." Eden pointed left.

Naris shot a brief glance at the sea of black swarming the courtyard, then followed the girl's directions without a second thought. A long hallway led to a right turn, and then another. At what must have been the opposite point of the building from where they entered, they stopped at a heavy armored door. She looked it up and down, no confidence at all her laser rifle could bother it. At a tremendous *crash* behind her, she whirled about, raising her rifle to aim at shadows growing on the wall from around the corner.

"I'm sorry, Eden."

The girl let go and slid down her back. She moved to the side, dusting herself off, and pressed her tiny hand against the wall. A concealed panel popped open, revealing a keypad into which she entered a code. Overhead lights flickered to life, and the distant whirr of an approaching elevator grew louder.

Beasts spilled into the corridor. Naris flicked the mode selector switch and held the trigger down. A continuous beam of red light scythed apart the scrambling monsters like a hot wire on marshmallow figures. Jet-black blood and body parts spilled into a miasma with each sweep back and forth. The energy cell ran out in nine seconds. She swapped it and repeated the process, lasering down creature after creature—though the horde kept pushing closer.

Eden folded her hands behind her back, watching the display with a look of calm interest. When the wall of ravening beasts reached within twenty yards, she bit her lower lip.

Oh, now *the kid's nervous.*

The second energy cell ran dry. Naris had no more; she slung the rifle on her back and picked off another twenty or so with the pistol before it ran out, too. The mounting dead seemed to slow the onrush, but they'd be on her anyway in seconds.

"Get behind me." Naris pulled a long knife from a sheath on her left thigh and held it at the ready, tip wavering in the air.

Eden glanced at the door. "Don't be scared."

Yeah, right. "Uhh."

"The elevator's here."

Ping.

Naris turned, sweeping the girl into a hug as she rushed past the parting doors. She moved to the rear wall of the large chamber, shielding the child in the corner with her body. Steam obscured her visor, increasing the sense of claustrophobic fear.

"It's not closing."

Eden wriggled out of her grip and smacked a panel on the wall. "You have to push the button."

One of the beasts lunged forward, its snapping jaws entering the elevator as the doors slammed closed with a pneumatic hiss and a squishing *whump*, crushing its skull. Black ichor sprayed everywhere; dark jelly blobs slid down the mirror-like doors.

Two seconds later, scratching and pounding rattled the elevator. An entire army of those beasts couldn't harm the massive door. The room vibrated and her stomach lurched. *Down?* Naris shivered. *Down can't be worse than staying in that hallway, can it? How the hell are we getting out?*

Eden looked up at her with an innocent expression. "What I have to show you is downstairs."

As soon as the veil of fog coating the inside of her helmet faded, she locked stares with the child, who waved and smiled. Calm as a leisurely stroll in the park, Eden folded her hands behind her while shifting her weight from heel to toes and back again. Naris fell to her knees, staring at the grimy urchin. An increasing sense of something being wrong dueled with her knowing she had to protect this girl. *This kid is creepy as hell. Why do I feel so sorry for her? I'm risking my life for this kid like she's my own daughter and I've never seen her before. Is... something affecting my mind?*

"We're almost there," said Eden. "Oh, Naris?"

"Yeah?" She tried to get her breathing under control. A patch of fog appeared and faded in front of her mouth.

"You called them aliens before." Eden bit her lip, twisting her big toe into the metal floor. "They're not the aliens here. We are."

"Uhh, right. Just a figure of speech." Naris sighed at her belt, and the lack of another charged energy cell. *If there's anything nasty in there, I'm screwed.* She clenched a fist around the handle of her knife.

Bands of white light emerged from the floor and ran up the walls. A moment passed in silence. The ascending stripes slowed in time with the whirring elevator, then stopped. Eden turned as the doors opened. The hallway ahead held silence and midnight dark; light from the elevator highlighted walls lined with dozens of ridged plastic tubes that ranged in size from a foot in diameter to finger-width. Thick bulkheads every twenty meters made it resemble the central thoroughfare of a starfreighter, running at least ninety meters down to another heavy door.

Eden took her hand, leading her out over the glossy floor. Naris stared at the tiny, dusty footprints the child left on the polished surface, letting the girl pull her forward. Thick plastic hoses on the walls twitched and pulsed from the weight of whatever fluid they carried. Odd buzzing scrapes rushed back and forth inside them every so often, the eeriness of the sound unsettling her. A strong sense of foreboding crept into her mind, making her doubt she would ever leave this place alive.

The cleanliness of everything here screamed a warning.

After easily more than a hundred meters, they reached the end of the corridor where a giant reinforced door blocked the way. This one, thicker than the last, looked as if it could take a hit from her ship's main guns and laugh at them.

Eden released her grip and shifted to face her, hands folded in front. "Naris?"

Every time she asks me a question, something bad happens. "Yes?"

Buzzing in the tubes grew louder. She whirled around as a *bang* from the elevator end rang out. One of the larger hoses had split open, spewing an inky cloud of fog. What at first appeared to be mist took on the appearance of sand, fine particles spraying into piles on the floor.

"Daddy did something very bad." The child looked down. "You're not going to take SP-92 off the planet, are you?"

The pile moved, swelling upward and taking on the form of a human figure of black smoke. It advanced, reaching toward them.

"N-no, Eden. No. I heard you calling me. I knew you were here and needed help. I..." She backed into the door. "This is messed up crap. It can stay here."

"Promise?"

Another figure, then two more, climbed out of the sand. A second tube ruptured, spewing even more. Seven, then eight, then nine shadow people crept down the hallway toward her.

"Yes."

The nearest figure floated as a blurry mass, a human body made of a thousand-thousand gnats flying in formation. It drew closer, arms spreading.

Eden looked up. "Say, 'I promise.'"

"Not funny, kid. I swear I'll get you out of here and leave this freaky shit behind. Come on, if you can open the door, open it."

She swayed back and forth, biting her lip.

Naris looked from the innocent face to the approaching mass of death.

"Project SP-92 is Silicon Piranha. Weaponized autonomous nanobot clouds capable of deconstructing a living body in under four seconds. They can be programmed to seek specific targets and spare others. Your e-suit protects you from breathing them, so they are learning to take on shapes that can attack you."

No wonder she's so calm. They won't go after her. Naris wanted to scream. "Yes, please. I promise I won't take it with us." She looked back and forth once more. "Are you really a little girl?"

"Yes." Eden stuck her hand into a small cubby containing a silver electronic panel. A line of cyan light swept up and down over it.

Every seam in the door, including the engraved Volunrad gear logo, filled in with bright white light. A rumble vibrated in the ground. Eden ran to the enlarging seam, slipping through while it remained too narrow for an adult. Naris hovered at the opening, looking back over her shoulder every few seconds at the approaching, thrumming figures. As soon as the foot-thick doors parted wide enough, she squeezed between them into a pitch-dark room. To her left, Eden's face and chest glowed in the castoff light from a small access panel. The child poked a button, and the massive gate reversed direction. Naris froze, paralyzed in horrified awe as she stared into the non-eyes of the man-shaped clouds in the hallway outside. When the door closed with a heavy slam, she slouched in relief and started breathing again.

Lights came on. A slow turn revealed a chamber resembling the surgery complex of a large space station hospital. White walls, rows upon rows of workstations with large display screens, and several floor-to-ceiling tanks surrounded her.

"Is this some kind of test lab?" Naris trembled, staring at the body-sized tanks.

"I'm not sure," said Eden, looking around. Once she spotted her target, she grabbed Naris's hand and tried to pull her. Her feet skidded, squeaking on the polished floor, leaving grimy smears. "Come on, we're here."

Naris locked eyes with her. Eden's eerie calm remained. She tilted her head, still looking innocent.

"Please? I have to show you."

"I got a bad feeling." Naris swallowed.

Eden's expression became desperate. "Please. I need you. You have to see this. I promise it won't hurt you. Daddy said I had to show you this machine before we can go away."

The tone of the girl's voice crawled up her spine and filled her with an overwhelming feeling of protectiveness. Naris nodded and followed the girl around a bank of machinery in the center of the chamber. Great clusters of silver-wrapped hoses wiggled about in the ceiling, coursing with some mysterious substance. In the center of the immense apparatus, a small chamber flooded with blue liquid contained the inert nude figure of a little girl who could have been Eden's twin sister. A metal orb-shaped helmet surrounded her head, with dozens of wires connecting into a bundled cord running up into the roof of the tank. Stationary bubbles trapped near the child's mouth made the gel appear solid. *Frozen.*

Naris put a hand on the glass, disturbing a layer of iced condensation.

Eden gawked. After a moment, her shock turned to mirth. She giggled, jumping up and down. "I'm not a ghost! I didn't die!"

Systems in the floor and ceiling around the blue tank came to life with a loud thrumming that faded to a noticeable but unobtrusive background noise in short order. Eden clapped and jumped into Naris, hugging her.

"What?" Naris asked. "Ein? You got anything?"

Nothing came over the speakers.

Shit. Must be too far underground.

"I'm not really dead! I thought I was a ghost like the fireflies, but I'm sleeping. That's me in there!" Eden grinned and promptly fainted.

Naris held the limp girl upright, shaking her, but got no response. *What the hell?* A horizontal line of lighter hue crept down the blue stuff in the tank from top to bottom, freeing bubbles to rise as it passed. Strands of the girl's thigh-length black hair wavered about. A moment after the color shift vanished into the base of the tank, the floating child's eyes snapped open.

Naris covered her mouth and gasped.

The girl in the tank smiled wearily. She reached up and pressed a small hand against the clear wall.

You came.

Eden's timid voice flooded her mind, loud, consuming, overflowing with joy and gratitude. Naris whirled around, searching. The girl in her arms remained inert.

Will you please help me get out of here?

"What the hell is this?" Naris eyed the wires, wondering if a seven-year-old had a cybernetic interface connecting her brain to loudspeakers.

You came from far away because I called for help. I don't have much time left. This place is almost out of power and I will die for real. The girl you are holding is an android Daddy made to look like me so I could wait for someone nice. She tapped the helmet. *It was so long ago I forgot. I thought I had died and was a ghost. All I wanted was not to be lonely.*

Naris found herself crying as the terror of being chased by murderous nanobots and bloodthirsty beasts collided with the sense of loneliness wafting from the child. *I can't even imagine... the only one alive on an entire planet.* "Okay. I thought this was some kind of trap."

A little girl's giggle echoed in her mind before the child again spoke telepathically. *I am sorry I didn't tell you. I did not remember. I have been sleeping a long time. Before you open this, you must clean the air or I will get very sick.*

"How am I going to get you back to my ship? I can't clean the planet's air."

There are spare suits in the storage compartments. Go to that console. The girl raised her arm to point past Naris into the room. A faint blue glow appeared in her eyes.

Thoughts flooded Naris's mind. Images of the suits, the lockers, even the access codes to the computer terminal felt like things she'd known for years. She wandered across the room, awash with sorrow, joy, and numbness all at the same time. The tiny voice continued in her mind, making her feel somewhat tired, but walking her through the procedure to vent the air out of the underground facility. She somehow knew all four passwords required to get into the system, passwords that would more than likely also give access to the research data on SP-96. Naris shook her head. *No, I want no part of bringing that evil off this place.*

She *felt* a smile in her mind and shivered. *That poor girl... is she one of their weapons too? Such a potent telepath.*

Naris paced, waiting for the vent system to work. A chime rang out after a few minutes and she glanced back at the tank expecting it to drain. Instead, the primary door opened. Two men in black enviro-suits entered. The one on the right hit the door control, closing the exit behind them.

"Greetings, Naris," said the other. "We appreciate your assistance finding this place. We never thought the little android was anything but a curiosity."

"She always made me kind of sad, actually," added the man on the right. "I thought the old man cracked before he died."

"Volunrad?" Naris took a step back.

"Yep. I'm Davin, and that's Xonn." The man on the right approached, holding his hand out to shake. "Great work."

"I said I'd think about it. I never agreed to get your data. I"—she glanced over her shoulder at the now-unlocked terminal—"I don't think this thing should get off the planet. You lost control of it once."

"A small oversight," said Xonn. "That happened forty years ago. We've completed work on the programming that drives them; however, without Dr. Piet's data, we have been unable to replicate anything even close to the same level of power in such small nanotech devices."

"How the hell did you get past those aliens?" Naris found herself doubting her eyes again.

"Ahh that." Davin chuckled. "Simple. We landed on the roof. Those creatures were an earlier weapons program we'd deemed too dangerous to deploy. Apparently, the computer decided you were worth the risk and set them loose."

They lie, said Eden's telepathic voice. *The monsters were always on this planet.*

"And that black shit outside?" A chill spread down Naris's back at memory of the skull-faced shadow man.

"The Silicon Piranha system does not attack individuals designated as friendly. It is a tool for targeted elimination." Xonn walked over, arms out as if they were long-lost buddies.

Daddy didn't want the company to hurt me. He made the nanobots eat everyone. He tried to stop them.

Machinery whirred in the floor.

"Only a complete idiot would risk using a weapon this horrible." Naris pulled her sidearm, pointing it at the terminal. "I can't let you do that."

Shit. It's empty.

Xonn smiled. "It's not horrible; the targets don't feel a damn thing."

Davin raised his left hand. An orb of energy flew from his forearm guard, catching Naris in the chest. The HUD on her visor scrambled to static as paralytic pain scorched every nerve fiber within her body, knocking her to the ground in a convulsing heap. Agony like falling into boiling water came on in waves. Her jaw refused to move, denying her even the ability to scream.

"Stay down and stay out of our way," said Davin. "It is none of your concern. Despite this little attack of idealism, we're still willing to express our gratitude financially for your part of the job. We've been trying to get into this chamber for the past thirty years."

"Never realized the kid was a key." Xonn laughed.

They stepped over her and went up to the terminal. Naris roared with clenched teeth, trying to force her body to move. She grabbed the leg of a worktable and pulled herself sitting. Davin shook his head and punted her in the helmet. Naris went facedown, and he shot another orb into her back. That one transcended simple pain and dragged her straight to unconsciousness.

FRIGIDITY SURROUNDED EDEN. HER WEIGHT HUNG ON THE CHIN STRAP FOR A second before it slipped away and flicked her nose. Seconds later, her toes touched the smooth steel of the tank bottom, but her legs refused to hold her weight. She rode the draining fluid to the floor and curled up in a shivering ball. Thick, azure gel smeared the walls, gliding downward in clumps and glops. One landed on the side of her foot, making her draw a sharp hiss of breath at the cold.

Bad men hurt Naris. Eden struggled to move, but her muscles wouldn't listen. *I have to help.*

She managed to lift her head and brace a hand on the clear tank wall, glaring through a blurry haze of blue goop at two men on either side of Daddy's terminal.

Xonn patted his associate on the arm before pointing at her. "What about that?"

"Hmm?" Davin swiveled. "What the hell? Another robot?"

The men approached, their figures growing huge and ominous over her. Eden shivered and curled her little body tighter. Overhead, the ponderous metal helmet, the link to her robotic doppelganger, dangled on its wire. Eden struggled to wipe gel from her face. Her hair, thick with slime, clung to her skin like a gooey blanket made of gelatinous ice.

Xonn exhaled. "Nah, man. Kid's got a thermal signature. She's alive."

Eden narrowed her eyes at them. She strained with all the strength she could find, but couldn't sit up.

"She doesn't seem too happy to see us." Davin tapped his fingers in midair, navigating a virtual holographic terminal in his suit computer. "Looks like Dr. Piet's daughter, Eden. Wow, they'll have a field day with her back on Verdantis."

Go away before you get hurt. Daddy doesn't want SP-96 to leave this world.

Eden projected her voice into their minds as loud as a scream, while her long-frozen lungs produced only a feeble wheeze that echoed in her clear-walled prison.

The men took a step back, woozy.

Davin shrugged. "I love getting threatened by little kids. What are you gonna do about it, girl? You can't even lift your arms."

"She's been in that tank for over forty years. I'm astounded she's even alive." Xonn rubbed the side of his helmet. "Come on, man. Let's get the data first. We can unpack the kid in a few minutes." He patted the tank. "Relax, honey. We won't hurt you."

I won't warn you again. Go away. They won't let you take the bad. Already, the whispers of angry fireflies nattered at the back of her mind. She called out to them.

"What about that merc?" Xonn pointed at Naris.

Davin shrugged. "I'll give her another stun on the way out. By the time she can move again, we'll be long gone. Gotta leave her alive so the boss can send credits. Any heat for violating the quarantine falls right on her head, not the company."

Xonn chuckled. "Nice and neat."

They approached the terminal. Eden grunted, struggling to push herself up into a seated position. A clump of icy gel slid down the middle of her back. She slapped both hands against the plastic barrier, emitting a feeble snarl in reality and deafening telepathic shout in their minds.

Don't do it!

Both men grabbed their helmets at the loud scream.

Davin pushed past the pain and reached for the console.

Eden let her anger go free, beckoning the fireflies, telling them what this man was about to do.

NARIS GASPED, ROLLING ONTO HER BACK. TWO MEN STOOD A SHORT DISTANCE away at the console. Tingles like an army of electric spiders walking on needles rippled up and down her limbs. Her body refused to move, still paralyzed from the stunner. She stared at Davin's arm, hating that her mind instinctively recoiled in terror from a device that could cause such excruciating pain.

She looked at the tank, at the pathetic little girl crawling to the glass. Sick to her stomach, she could barely move, but her need to protect that child gave her the willpower to sit up. Her breaths came in ragged gasps as she struggled to overcome the agony of imaginary flames burning her arms. *I've come too far for her. I can't give up now.* Naris screamed mentally and eased herself upright.

Eden flattened her palms on the tank wall and pressed her forehead against it. Anger wafted off the child like heat from a naked flame, a palpable presence forced into the mind. The little girl stared at the men, the dark blue glow from her eyes glinting from spots of slime on the cylinder glass in front of her face.

The men twitched, swatting at their arms as if covered in stinging insects. Davin grabbed his helmet and screamed. Xonn staggered drunkenly to the side. A point of green light appeared on Davin's chest. His suit melted away from the spot and a tiny orb of emerald luminescence fluttered out into the room. Screaming in agony, Xonn whirled around, raising raised a sidearm at Eden.

The child screamed in rage. Naris roared and surged to her feet, but her weapons had run dry. Growling, she flung herself into Xonn, making his shot go high. The laser passed through the clear walls of the chamber without harm, leaving two clean spots where it incinerated the gel. Naris dragged him to the ground, wrestling for control of his gun.

Davin howled, flailing. Point after point of green light appeared on the outer surface of his suit. Dozens of fireflies burned out from within, flying into an orbit around him. His agonizing screams grew louder and higher, tinged with utter panic. Wild-eyed, he raised his sidearm under his chin and fired. His body fell flat on his chest.

Fury consumed Naris out of nowhere. This man tried to shoot Eden. She bashed his hand repeatedly into the floor until the gun went flying. Xonn shuddered and screamed. Blood sprayed up out of his throat, spattering the inside of his visor. A lone firefly emerged from his mouth and melted a hole in his facemask. Naris leaned up and away, scooting back as an uncountable number of the little creatures burrowed out of Davis, melting holes in his suit, and swarmed onto Xonn.

Both men caught fire under a mass of jade fireflies. Their bodies melted into piles of smoking, bloody goop. The cloud of light spots lifted away from the smoking remains, rising into an emerald cyclone circling the room, beautiful and deadly. As they passed over her head, the whispers of thousands of voices teased at the outskirts of her consciousness.

A single firefly settled on the tip of her finger, an orb about an inch across. Within the glowing nimbus, a tiny core of darker green seemed to look at her. Naris tensed, waiting for the pain—none came. An odd sense this same firefly checked her out back at the residence tower came from nowhere. It radiated gratitude.

Overwhelmed by the emotion it gave off and her screaming muscles, she passed out.

EDEN LAY AT THE BOTTOM OF THE TANK IN A PUDDLE OF COLD SLIME. SHE hadn't wanted to watch what the fireflies would do to the bad men. The echo of her breaths in the chamber made her somehow feel colder. She huddled there until the screaming stopped. Once the mood of the fireflies changed from vengeful to content, she sat up and stared in awe at the glimmering creatures swirling about. When one settled on Naris's finger, she grinned until the woman lapsed into unconsciousness.

As if sensing the dire look the child gave the terminal, the fleck of light floated into the air. It orbited the workstation for a few seconds before plunging straight into the screen, destroying it in a shower of sparks. It came around again, circling the tank. Eden waved at it, as much as her arm would move. The firefly zoomed off, circled the room once, and disappeared into a ventilation duct near the ceiling. Sympathetic overloads spread among the electronics in the room. Soon, the lights failed and died with a blast of sparks, leaving the area to the mercy of red emergency lamps.

She winced, squishing into frigid ooze to sit in the center of the tank. Shivering, Eden wrapped her arms around her legs and stared at her half-submerged feet. Naris remained asleep. She tried to shout in the woman's mind, but it didn't wake her. After a few minutes of that, she gave up and crawled around the bottom of the tank, pushing at the wall. Traces of cryonic gel turned violet in the glow of the backup lights. Whatever medicine her Daddy had given her to protect from the freeze had started to wear off. Her toes went numb, as did her fingers.

Help me.

A moment later, a lone firefly emerged from the vent and glided in a slow, shimmering trajectory to the front of the tank. It burned a hole in the plastic cylinder and landed on her bent knee, filling her with warmth. Could it be the same one that lingered before, the one who'd said hello to Naris? Eden smiled at it and gathered the light orb in her hands.

As soon as she cradled it, she knew they all stayed here because of her. She called them back. Now, they wanted to go somewhere else. She held the glimmering creature up to her face and radiated gratitude.

Eden turned her head, pulling a thick mass of slimy hair across her back. She glanced at Naris, noting the woman still breathing. *I'm not lonely anymore.*

Something peeled away from her consciousness. A burden lifted. The firefly leapt from her hand and orbited her in an emphatic spiral, vibrating with joy. It plunged into the base of the chamber, passing into the metal without damaging it. Seconds later, a heavy *clank* vibrated the base and an electric motor whirred.

The plastic tube separated from the ceiling with a soft sucking sound and sank into the pedestal upon which she sat. She pulled herself to the edge, limp legs dragging after her, and bent forward to reach her hands to the floor, slithering forward. Soon after her chest touched the metal tiles outside the tank, the firefly emerged, floated up to her cheek as if to kiss it, then raced off, vanishing into the ceiling like a ghost.

She waved at the spot where it had last been, smiling. "Bye, Daddy."

Too weak to stand, she dragged herself across the room, the coating of slime making it easy. Upon reaching Naris, she propped herself up on her knees and placed a hand on the woman's helmet.

Time to wake up.

NARIS MOANED AND OPENED HER EYES TO FIND A SMALL GIRL SPRAWLED IN front of her, wearing only a layer of transparent blue gel. Her pain had stopped. Her limbs felt like dense metal, but she could move. Eden stared at her as she sat upright, smiling. The child shivered and clung.

A glance left at the puddled remains of two Volunrad men reminded Naris of the glowing eyes and the swarm of devouring... things. She gasped, scooting backward. Eden gave her a confused look and crawled after her. The child attempted to speak, but produced only a hoarse whisper and coughed up trickles of dark blue slime. Naris hesitated, strange motherly concern dueling with abject terror at what she had seen the child do. The coughing ended. Eden's gaze rose to meet hers.

I'm sorry I scared you. She pulled herself closer. The eerie calm lasted only until Naris continued to scoot away, then Eden looked hurt. *Please don't be afraid of me. I had to call them. I couldn't let anyone have the bad. You didn't want them to take it. They hurt you.*

"Y-you didn't kill them?" Naris gasped as her back hit a wall. *I'm cornered. Her voice in my head.* Nowhere to go, she went rigid as the little girl crawled up over her legs. A cute button nose touched the outside of her helmet. Eden smiled.

No. The fireflies were angry with the bad men. I would never hurt my new mommy.

Naris pondered the statement, and her fear ebbed. This girl had come out of a giant metal and plastic womb, was naked, all but helpless, unable to walk, and covered in slime. *How like an infant she is the first time their mother lays eyes upon them.* Naris swallowed hard and put an arm around the child. *What am I doing? I dunno if I want a kid yet. Shit, I didn't even get to have fun making her.* Eden obligingly curled up in a fetal position in her lap. Her small body trembled, teeth chattering. Naris cradled her; worry gave way to concern as she wiped the slime out of the child's hair and off her back.

I called you, and you came to save me. Thank you.

Earth-Normal still showed in the lower right part of her visor. Naris disengaged the helmet interlock and pulled the heavy thing off, gulping down clean, fresh air laced with spearmint, likely from the cryo-gel. The chilly temperature didn't bother her too much, though it did explain why her goo-covered foundling had blue lips. She pressed a slimy kiss into the top of the girl's head, squishing in her hair. The gel indeed tasted minty. Eden giggled, then started coughing.

"How am I going to get you out of here?"

Eden looked up, trying to talk past clicking teeth. "There is—" She wheezed and choked more. *There is a spare suit in the lockers.*

The telepathic voice should have startled her, but somehow Naris expected it. "What of the fireflies?"

The child snuggled tighter to Naris's suit. *They died a long time ago, but stayed to protect me. They're gone now.*

Her question triggered a dozen more. Naris thought of the myriad voices and wondered if she had seen the souls of the dead descend upon the city they once called home. She stood and rushed to the locker before the shivering girl froze to death. Inside, she found an adult-sized black enviro-suit. She laid it flat out on the floor and opened it before setting the child inside it like a sleeping bag. Eden tried to stick her head into the helmet while Naris sealed the suit around a body way too small for it. After re-securing her own helmet, Naris sighed at the door. The weaponized nanobots would likely still be outside.

Eden struggled to point at a small door with the big, floppy suit arm. For no reason Naris could understand, she knew it led to a one-use rocket-powered elevator intended as an emergency evacuation device from the top-secret development lab. Naris gathered Eden in her arms and carried her to the hatch, pausing to offer an apologetic glance at the inert child android, feeling guilty for leaving it behind.

Don't be sad, said Eden's telepathic voice. *It's only a remote-controlled shell.*

NARIS GAZED OUT OF THE VIEWPORT AT THE SICKLY GREEN CURVE OF ACHERON-18, surrounded by deadly silver-white defense satellites. Fortunately, they hadn't fired at her on the way out. She put one foot up on the console and leaned back, crossing her ankles. Her thigh-length shirt still smelled of fabric softener. Ein busied itself scanning job boards for a cargo run their ship could handle and risky enough to be worth the effort without being too illegal. The AI muttered complaints to itself every so often at a contract paying far above average, even for the risk of hauling contraband... because it knew Naris would pass.

"What?" asked Naris.

"You would have passed on these hops *before* you had baggage."

Naris frowned. "Don't call her baggage. She's part of the team now. No one is ever going to lie to us again."

A tiny foot appeared on the console to her left, soon joined by another as Eden crossed her ankles in a mimic of Naris's pose. Her borrowed white sweatshirt with a dark blue Nascent Technologies logo fit her like a shift dress to mid-thigh. Naris laughed at how far forward the girl had to slide in the chair for her legs to reach. Eden sniffed at her drink, then gave Naris an expectant look without sipping from it.

A holo-panel opened at the middle of the console, tinting the cockpit in pale blue light. It displayed a roster of nine cargo contracts Ein picked out as being the best ratio of money to effort/risk. Each line contained a planet of origin, planet of destination, cargo type, and payout.

Naris read it over before glancing at her little co-pilot. "So, where do you think we should go?" She took a sip from the warm cup cradled in both her hands.

Hot chocolate.

She coughed on it, not prepared for so much *sweet*. Eden waited for Naris to get control of herself and extended one arm with the untouched drink. They traded. The girl slurped at the cocoa. Naris took a long, beautiful sip of black coffee.

Eden tapped her little foot on nothing, smirking at the viewport filled with stars and a hint of Acheron-18's sickly pea-green glow. "Anywhere but here."

ACKNOWLEDGMENTS

Thank you for reading The Far Side of Promise!
Additional thanks to Lee Sheridan for editing.
Cover by www.damonza.com

ABOUT THE AUTHOR

Originally from South Amboy NJ, Matthew has been creating science fiction and fantasy worlds for most of his reasoning life. Since 1996, he has developed the "Divergent Fates" world, in which *Division Zero, Virtual Immortality, The Awakened Series, The Harmony Paradox, and the Daughter of Mars series* take place. Along with being an editor at Curiosity Quills press, he has worked in IT and technical support.

Matthew is an avid gamer, a recovered WoW addict, Gamemaster for two custom RPG systems, and a fan of anime, British humour, and intellectual science fiction that questions the nature of reality, life, and what happens after it.

He is also fond of cats.

Visit me online at:

    Facebook: https://www.facebook.com/MatthewSCoxAuthor
    Pinterest: https://www.pinterest.com/matthewcox10420/
    Goodreads: https://www.goodreads.com/author/show/7712730.Matthew_S_Cox
    Email: mcox2112@gmail.com

OTHER BOOKS BY MATTHEW S. COX

Divergent Fates Universe Novels

Division Zero series

- Division Zero
- Lex De Mortuis
- Thrall
- Guardian
- Harbinger
- The Shadow Fixer

The Awakened series

- Prophet of the Badlands
- Archon's Queen
- Grey Ronin
- Daughter of Ash
- Zero Rogue
- Angel Descended

Daughter of Mars series

- The Hand of Raziel
- Araphel
- Ghost Black

Virtual Immortality series

- Virtual Immortality
- The Harmony Paradox

Prophet of the Badlands Series

- Prophet's Journey

Divergent Fates Anthology

(Fiction Novels - Adult)

The Roadhouse Chronicles Series

- One More Run
- The Redeemed
- Dead Man's Number

Faded Skies series

- Heir Ascendant
- Ascendant Unrest
- Ascendant Revolution

Temporal Armistice Series

- Nascent Shadow
- The Shadow Collector
- The Gate to Oblivion
- The Queen of Discord

Vampire Innocent series

- A Nighttime of Forever
- A Beginner's Guide to Fangs
- The Artist of Ruin
- The Last Family Road Trip
- The Phantom Oracle
- How Not to Summon Demons
- Ordinary Problems of a College Vampire
- A Vampire's Guide to Surviving Holidays
- An Introduction to Paranormal Diplomacy
- A Vampire's Guide to Adulting
- How to Stop a Vampire War in Six Easy Steps
- Ancient Vampire Death Cults and Other Annoyances

Standalones

- Wayfarer: AV494
- Axillon99
- Chiaroscuro: The Mouse and the Candle
- The Spirits of Six Minstrel Run
- Sophie's Light
- The Far Side of Promise anthology
- Operation: Chimera (with Tony Healey)
- The Dysfunctional Conspiracy (with Christopher Veltmann)
- Of Myth and Shadow
- The Girl Who Found the Sun

Winter Solstice series (with J.R. Rain)

- Convergence
- Containment
- Catalyst
- Catacombs

Alexis Silver series (with J.R. Rain)

- Silver Light
- Deep Silver
- Silver Quarrel
- Silver Crucible

Samantha Moon Origins series (with J.R. Rain)

- New Moon Rising
- Moon Mourning
- Haunted Moon

Vampire For Hire series (with J.R. Rain)

- Moon Master
- Dead Moon
- Lost Moon
- Vampire Destiny

- Infinite Moon
- Vampire Empress

Maddy Wimsey series (with J.R. Rain)

- The Devil's Eye
- The Drifting Gloom
- Dark Mercy

Samantha Moon Case Files series (with J.R. Rain)

- Blood Moon

Immortal Operative (with J.R. Rain)

- Broken Ice

Four Elements series (with J.R. Rain)

- The Elementalist
- The Black Rose
- The Wakefield Curse

Young Adult Novels

The Eldritch Heart Series

- The Eldritch Heart
- The Cursed Crown
- The Sapphire Soul

Evergreen Series

- Evergreen
- The World That Remains
- The Lucky Ones
- Nuclear Summer
- The Nuclear Frontier

Progenitor Series

- Out of Sight
- Out of Mind

Diary of a Teenage Fey

(Short story series)

- Elder Horror
- The Hag of Barrow Falls
- Babysitter's Nightmare
- Lharakki
- Bauble for a Soul
- Simulacrum
- Amorphous
- Manticore

Standalones

- Caller 107
- The Summer the World Ended
- Nine Candles of Deepest Black
- The Forest Beyond the Earth

Middle Grade Novels

The Adventures of Ubergirl series

- My Dad is a Mad Scientist
- Aliens Ate My Homework
- The End of all Halloweens
- Dr. Infinity and the Soul Smasher

Tales of Widowswood series

- Emma and the Banderwigh
- Emma and the Silk Thieves

- Emma and the Silverbell Faeries
- Emma and the Elixir of Madness
- Emma and the Weeping Spirit

Standalones

- Citadel: The Concordant Sequence
- The Cursed Codex
- The Menagerie of Jenkins Bailey